Liam pulled her close. They fit perfectly.

He tasted wine and Dolley, all in one spicy kiss.

Someone moaned. Maybe it was him.

The past month had been leading up to this one perfect moment.

Her head tipped back in surrender. Her fingers gripped his hair.

How had they waited this long?

"Wait." Her word was muffled against his mouth. "Stop."

He pulled away, gasping. "Incredible."

"No." She shook her head. "No. That shouldn't have happened. It can't happen."

"But..." His fingers tightened on her arms.

She stepped away, her hand covering her mouth. "If we keep going, everything will be ruined. Ruined."

Dear Reader,

Welcome back to Fitzgerald House. If you haven't visited before, Fitzgerald House is a bed-and-breakfast set in Savannah's wonderful historic district. The three Fitzgerald sisters, Abigail, Bess and Dolley, own and operate the expanding B and B.

In *A Savannah Christmas Wish*, Fitzgerald House book two, you briefly met Liam Delaney, an Irish photographer and documentary maker. Liam stays at the B and B and shares Christmas with the Fitzgeralds. *Through a Magnolia Filter*, Fitzgerald House book three, overlaps with book two. Don't let that worry you. The books can be read as stand-alones! In the beginning of this book, Bess and Daniel aren't together. I had a blast writing the Christmas scene from Liam's and Dolley's perspectives. I'd love to know what you think about seeing the scene through a different set of eyes. You can contact me through my website, www.nandixon.com.

Dolley wants what Liam has: to travel the world for a career in photography. Liam longs for roots, family and a home—everything Dolley has but wants to give up.

This couple is one of my favorites (don't tell the others!). Liam has a swoon-worthy Irish accent and needs love and family. And spunky, brilliant Dolley deserves love and to have her talent recognized.

If you'd like to see some of the incredible Bonaventure Cemetery statuary, check out my Pinterest page. I create a board for each of my books: www.pinterest.com/nandixonauthor.

Enjoy Savannah!

Nan Dixon

NAN DIXON

Through a Magnolia Filter

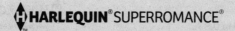
HARLEQUIN® SUPERROMANCE®

Recycling programs
for this product may
not exist in your area.

ISBN-13: 978-0-373-61000-6

Through a Magnolia Filter

Copyright © 2016 by Nan Dixon

This is a work of fiction. Names, characters, places and incidents are
either the product of the author's imagination or are used fictitiously,
and any resemblance to actual persons, living or dead, business
establishments, events or locales is entirely coincidental.

This edition published by arrangement with Harlequin Books S.A.

For questions and comments about the quality of this book,
please contact us at CustomerService@Harlequin.com.

® and TM are trademarks of Harlequin Enterprises Limited or its
corporate affiliates. Trademarks indicated with ® are registered in the
United States Patent and Trademark Office, the Canadian Intellectual
Property Office and in other countries.

Printed in U.S.A.

www.Harlequin.com

Nan Dixon spent her formative years as an actress, singer, dancer and competitive golfer. But the need to eat had her studying accounting in college. Unfortunately, being a successful financial executive didn't feed her passion to perform. When the pharmaceutical company she worked for was purchased, Nan got the chance of a lifetime—the opportunity to pursue a writing career. She's a five-time Golden Heart® finalist, lives in the Midwest and is active in her local RWA chapter and on the board of a dance company. She has five children, three sons-in-law, one grandchild, one grandchild on the way and one neurotic cat.

Books by Nan Dixon

HARLEQUIN SUPERROMANCE

Fitzgerald House

Southern Comforts
A Savannah Christmas Wish

Visit the Author Profile page at
Harlequin.com for more titles.

To Mom and Dad always.

Just like Dolley, I never shared my dream of becoming a writer. I hope you would be proud.

Mom, you took a chance and left everything and everyone you loved in England and followed your heart to America. You were amazing. To my wonderful, fabulous family, thank you for supporting my writing. Lily—you are a bright light and I can't wait to meet Harper!

Thank you to my Harlequin team for believing in this series and guiding me through the publication process: Piya Campana, Megan Long, Victoria Curran, Deirdre McCluskey and all the others whom I don't even know.

I couldn't have envisioned this book without my critique group challenging me to dig deeper. Thank you, Ann Hinnenkamp, Leanne Farella, Neroli Lacey and Kathryn Kohorst. And my Golden Heart sisters keep me sane— Dreamcatchers, Lucky 13s, Starcatchers and the Unsinkables. And my writing community— MFW, you're the best.

And last, this book is for the group that started it all—my sisters. Mo, Sue and Trish.

CHAPTER ONE

Use a picture. It's worth a thousand words.

Arthur Brisbane

LIAM DELANEY WAS an orphan. Again. He laced his hands together and waited for the priest to bury his godfather. A sigh whistled between his lips. At thirty, being alone shouldn't matter. But it did. Was it wrong to want a home, a family? To belong?

The wind caught the priest's deep voice and swirled it round the cemetery. Latin. English. The languages blended in the breeze.

Ignoring the words, Liam listened to the priest's tone for any hint of sorrow at the passing of the man in the coffin. He heard none. No surprise that. He'd lived with the man for eleven long years.

This day couldn't end soon enough. He was ready to escape Kilkee for the final time. Leave this reminder of his childhood and catch a plane— anywhere. Just so he wasn't in Clare, Ireland.

As a distraction, he plotted how he would film Seamus FitzGerald's funeral. With a wide angle, he'd pan from the crumbling dark stone wall through the gray-and-white crosses and sinking headstones. While the priest droned, he'd linger on the yellow warbler perched on a cherub statue and let its sweet, clear song play. The camera would swing to the Celtic cross marking his godparents' graves. The towering cross lorded over the monuments of the other FitzGeralds buried near.

Seamus's wife had died twenty-five years ago. Liam had only known her through pictures he'd found in the manor. Photographic evidence Seamus had once been happy.

When Seamus buried his wife, he'd buried his smile.

After pausing the camera on the cross, he'd pan to the eight mourners gathered round the open grave. The priest. The housekeeper. The mortuary man. The groundskeeper. Three strangers, one young and two who must be Seamus's chums. And him, the unloved godchild. Standing alone.

Compared to memories of his parents' funeral, this service was stark. For his da and mum there had been flowers, music, tears and hordes of people. Liam had stood next to his scowling godfather, grieving. He hadn't realized he would never be hugged again. A lad of eight needed hugs.

He'd learned to expect no affection from the man in the coffin.

A gust of wind fluttered the flower petals in the arrangement straddling the yawning hole. A bee flitted from the single funereal wreath. His camera would follow the bee as it left the daisy to circle Father Patrick's head.

The priest intoned, "Because God has chosen to call our brother, Seamus James FitzGerald, from this life to himself, we commit his body to the earth, for we are dust and unto dust we shall return."

Liam would shift the camera frame to the housekeeper's face. Wind tugged strands of gray hair free from her bun and ruffled her black skirt. He'd track the tear slipping down her lined cheek in a harsh unforgiving close-up.

Why would anyone shed a tear for Seamus?

Cut.

This day was such an un-Irish, un-Seamus fall day. It was a chilly ten degrees for October, but sunlight lit the Kilkee countryside.

The man he'd lived with from the time he was eight until he'd escaped with his cameras at nineteen had just been laid to rest. Instead of sorrow, he felt—empty.

Here lies an unhappy man. Liam wanted to engrave the words on the cross.

The graveside service concluded. The small group waited, the silence broken by the warbler's joy-filled tune.

Liam refused to add any bitter words to the priest's platitudes, and the mourners eventually shuffled away from the yawning hole.

A young stranger placed a meaty hand on Liam's sleeve. He was large enough to play American football. How had he known his godfather?

Squinting against the sun, the man said, "Mr. Delaney, I'm sorry for your loss."

"Thank you." Liam turned to leave.

The man's hand tightened on his arm. "I'm Seamus's solicitor, Ian Lachlan."

Liam shook Ian's outstretched hand.

"When you can make the time, I'd like to speak with you," Ian said.

Behind Ian, the housekeeper, Mrs. Needles, waited. Liam nodded in her direction.

"Are you staying at the manor?" Ian asked.

Absolutely not. He rolled his shoulders. "I'm at the inn."

Ian tugged out a card. "Please, call me at your earliest convenience."

Liam tucked the card in his pocket. "I planned to motor back to Galway today." And find somewhere else to go. Somewhere he felt welcome.

"But Seamus's will?" The solicitor frowned. "Your godfather has specific requests for you. You must stay."

Requests? Why should he do anything for that curmudgeon?

Ian glanced back at Mrs. Needles. The priest joined the housekeeper. "Could we meet this afternoon?"

Reluctantly, Liam said, "Aye."

He accepted condolences and words of sorrow. He listened to a recounting of Seamus's last days from Mrs. Needles. Apparently, he made the right noises because neither the priest nor the housekeeper looked appalled.

What could his godfather want now?

He wanted to be anywhere but Kilkee.

"I DON'T WANT IT." Liam leaned forward in his chair and set his bitter coffee on Ian's desk. "I don't want anything from my godfather."

"But Seamus loved the house." Mr. Lachlan's chair squeaked as he leaned forward. "The will stipulates the manor passes to you."

"My life is no longer here in Clare. I've a flat in Galway." He hadn't set foot in Kilkee for almost five years.

"But the house was built in 1785. It's a treasure."

"The house is drafty and dismal. Unless Seamus loosened his pocketbook, it needs repairs that will cost more than I'll earn in the next ten years. Sell the bloody place."

"Oh, no." Ian's thumb tapped the papers on the desk. "Why don't you wait to make that decision? Recover from your grief."

Liam wasn't grieving. The only grief remaining was the lingering wisps of sorrow for his parents.

"Mrs. Needles has committed to stay through year end. My office handles Seamus's financial affairs. We could continue that plan," Ian added. "And there's some money that goes along with the manor house."

"I'll wait a while." He didn't want to deal with decisions on the manor. "But I doubt I'll change my mind. Keep up his arrangements."

He could sell the mausoleum next year. Seamus couldn't have left him enough money to keep him here. There wasn't enough money in all of Kilkee to tie him to his childhood nightmares. "The only thing I'd like is my godfather's cameras."

As a child he'd never been allowed to touch the Hasselblad or Rolleiflex.

Ian shifted in his seat. "About the cameras."

Liam's shoulders sank. Were they gone? Had Seamus been that spiteful? "What did he do?"

"It's not what Seamus did." Ian rocked forward, and the chair let out a long screech that clawed up Liam's spine. "He wants *you* to do something."

"What?" Liam spit the word out.

"A few years ago, your godfather started working on his family tree." Ian leaned back and the darn chair squealed again. "I helped him with the software and some research. He traced a branch of the FitzGerald family to Savannah."

"Savannah?" Where was that?

"Savannah. It's in Georgia," Ian said. "The family runs a B and B there."

"Georgia? By the Black Sea?"

"No. America."

America? "Did Seamus leave the cameras to these relatives?"

"No. No." The chair squeaked again.

Liam was bringing an oil can if he met with Ian again.

"He had letters he wanted to give to his American relatives, the Fitzgeralds," Ian said.

"American relations?" Ian wasn't making any sense. He'd never heard of any relatives.

"Seamus found letters from his great-great-great-uncle James in America to James's brother, Michael, who stayed in Ireland. James was the second son and decided to make his fortune somewhere other than at the Irish quarries. Michael stayed here."

Liam's head reeled from all the relationships. "I need a road map."

Ian pulled out a family tree and spread it on the table.

"James moved to America before the famine, around 1830. His brother, Michael, stayed in Clare."

"Why was Seamus so interested in these… Americans?" He took a sip of his now-cold coffee.

"It seems James did well for himself, first with shipping, then banking and real estate. The family was able to hang on and prosper after their civil war."

Liam waited. "And?"

"Seamus talked about visiting the family. Showing them the letters, but his doctor said *no*."

"My godfather wanted to meet them? He hated people." Liam couldn't believe Seamus would pursue something this crazy. "Did he lose his marbles in the last few years?"

Ian shook his head. "He was of sound mind."

Liam paced to the window and stared at the pub across the street. A pint might help him swallow this strange tale.

"His faculties weren't impaired." Ian was being kind.

Liam bet the solicitor had felt the sting of Seamus's tongue more than once in their working relationship. "This doesn't affect me. I'm not related."

Ian frowned. "Seamus wants you to take James's letters from America back to his relatives."

"Why bother?"

"Because it was a dying man's wish." Ian handed him a file. "I've copied the pertinent facts for you and included the material Seamus put together on the family.

"The will is specific." Ian took a deep breath. "If you don't take the letters to the Savannah Fitzgeralds, you don't get the cameras."

"You're kidding." This was Seamus's final payback for Liam refusing to run the quarries. The bastard knew all Liam wanted was the cameras. "Can't you just mail the letters?"

"They have to be delivered. By you."

Liam swore. "And if I refuse?"

Ian held up his hands. "I can't authorize Mrs. Needles to release the cameras."

Liam pushed away from the desk, pacing the small office. Bugger Seamus. He didn't need more cameras. He had plenty.

But the cameras were his childhood's forbidden fruit. The golden apple just out of reach.

"When do I have to bring these letters to my uncle's relatives?"

Ian smiled. "You have six months."

Six months. He crossed the pond a couple times a year to meet with his producers in New York.

Maybe Savannah was close enough to swing over for a day.

Ian pushed the file across his desk. "Take a look at the information. I certainly wouldn't mind visiting the family."

Liam flipped open the file. In front was a printout of an article with the title *Fitzgerald Family Expands B and B to Include Carleton House.* Four smiling women stood, arm in arm.

Family. He swallowed back his longing. "This is the only way?"

Ian nodded. "Yes."

He looked at the Fitzgeralds. "Bollocks. I'll do it."

"Good." Ian pushed a piece of paper toward Liam. "We'll make it nice and tidy. Then Mrs. Needles can release the cameras and anything else you want."

"I just want his cameras." Liam dashed his signature on the line.

He didn't want to stay in Kilkee any longer than required. "I'll go up there now."

"I'll notify Mrs. Needles." Ian loaded Liam down with a box of papers and folders. "The Fitzgeralds' copies are in this envelope. I've had copies made for you, too. There's also a copy of Seamus's will."

Ian held the door and walked Liam to his car. "Let me know if you need anything."

"Sure." Not if he could help it. He wanted to be free of this place. And he definitely didn't want to head to the manor. But he turned the car up the cliff road.

The house overlooking Kilkee Bay hadn't changed. The blue-gray stone manor had dark, tiny inset windows framed with tan limestone. The faded red door wasn't inviting. The roof was a sorrowful gray slate. Seamus had boasted all the stone had come from FitzGerald quarries.

Liam's chest tightened as he parked in the drive. The loneliness of his childhood weighed down his shoulders.

The house could have been quaint or even elegant. It was neither. It was his worst horror. A place where he'd grieved his parents and no one had cared.

The flagstone drive, also from the quarries, muffled the strike of his shoes. He stopped in the courtyard, glaring at the house.

The door pulled open with a dull pop.

"Come in, come in." Mrs. Needles waved him inside. "I'm sorry for your loss, Master Liam."

"It's just Liam." No one had called him Master Liam since boarding school. "Thank you for your sympathy, but you worked for my godfather. You know we weren't close."

"Oh, how proud he was whenever one of your books came out." She eased off his leather jacket and hung it on the tree before he could protest. "Mr. FitzGerald bragged on how he'd taught you everything you knew about photography."

"He followed my career?" Liam blurted out.

"Oh, he did. Loved to boast about you down at the

pub." She patted his arm. "He wasn't as keen on the documentaries, but he watched them all the same."

This didn't make any sense. When he hadn't stayed in Kilkee, he and Seamus rarely talked.

"Seamus did love photography," Liam said. The only thing he'd loved. And his godfather had made him slave long hours in the darkroom.

"He was proud of you. Come on back to the kitchen." She tugged on his elbow. "I've just brewed a pot of tea."

"I hadn't planned on staying. I'm only here for the cameras."

She ignored his reluctance, leading him down the dim, narrow hall. The lemon polish on the shining wood didn't mask the musty smell of the old house.

"I've everything packed in a box and a few of your school things Mr. FitzGerald saved." Her eyes twinkled. "You must have been a terror in school. There's a number of notes from headmasters."

She pushed open the kitchen door. Bright yellow curtains graced the windows.

"I can't believe Seamus sprang for something new in this mausoleum," he spat out.

She winked. "My mince pies got me those curtains."

A peat fire burned on the grate, the pungent scent warming the room. Mrs. Needles poured two mugs as he settled in a chair in front of the hearth. Then she piled a plate with raspberry tarts and shortbread cookies.

This wasn't the house he remembered. For once he felt...welcomed.

He took a bite of a crisp cookie. Buttery sugar melted in his mouth. Then he popped a tart in his mouth, the crust flaky and the jam sweet. "These are tops. If you'd been housekeeper when I was a child, I don't think I'd have gotten in so much trouble at school."

"If I'd been housekeeper, you would have behaved. I raised three boys from lads to men. I'm a grandmother three times."

He let her ramble on about her children and sipped his strong black tea, feeling strangely at ease in a house he hated.

She walked into the breakfast room and came back with a box. "Are you sure you don't want to look around the place? Identify things you'd like packed up? Maybe stay the night?"

"Thanks, no. I'm at the inn." But for once, he was tempted to linger.

She pointed at the empty plate. "How about another cup of tea and a few more biscuits?"

"I'd like that."

"ONCE MORE WITH FEELING," Dolley called, reducing the f-stop on her camera.

Damian, the bar owner, rolled his eyes, but picked up a martini glass and pretended to hand the bright blue drink to Dolley's coworker, Anne. On the dark wood bar sat two more cocktails, one electric pink and the other neon green.

Dolley made sure Anne, Damian, the drinks and the wall of gleaming bottles behind the bar were in focus. She snapped away. "Smile."

Anne's and Damian's smiles were forced.

"Come on, think of something fun," she suggested. "Like vacations or…sex."

They both grinned. Exactly what she wanted. She captured a few more photos and then pulled the camera away. "Perfect."

"Finally." Damian dropped his elbows to the counter and heaved a sigh. "I've got thirsty customers to serve."

Dolley caught a few more shots of Damian as he worked. He was so darn cute. And married. Oh, well. "You'll have more customers once I update your website."

She hoped the last pictures of Damian turned out. His dimpled grin would pull in tons of female customers.

"I can't wait to see it." Damian put the martinis he'd made for the photos on a tray, adding a clear martini. "Here. For your trouble."

Anne grinned. "Thanks."

Dolley grabbed her jacket. "I'll send the website link in a couple of days."

She and Anne took the tray out to the patio. It was a perfect October night in Savannah.

"I'm jealous you get to design websites *and* take

pictures for them." Anne sipped the bright blue drink. "Oh, this is delicious."

"You could, too."

"Have you seen my client list? Georgia Gravel Company. Chatham Reclamation." Anne shook her head. "I'll let them take their own pictures, thank you."

"You have no sense of adventure. You could climb the gravel piles, wade through garbage."

"Not happening." Anne shook her head hard.

Dolley tasted the neon-green drink. "This one's apple."

"Let me try." Anne took a sip. "That's good."

"Anything new at the office today?" Dolley asked.

"Be glad you worked from home." Anne twirled her glass. "Jackson was on a rampage. We weren't meeting deadlines. Clients were mad." Anne shoved her gorgeous blond hair over her shoulder.

What Dolley wouldn't give to have straight hair like her friend. Instead, her curls looked like she was auditioning for the lead role in *Annie*. "Glad I wasn't there."

"There has to be somewhere else to work." Anne slumped in her chair.

"If you want to leave Savannah."

Dolley sure did. She wanted to quit her job as website designer at Jackson Promotions and travel the world.

But she couldn't. Her family's bed-and-breakfast

was a golden shackle around her ankle, chaining her, the invisible sister, to Savannah.

Dolley let Anne complain, nodding and humming in the right spots, but not really listening. Anne had at least spent a semester studying abroad. The farthest Dolley had gotten was a long weekend in New York City to visit her older sister.

The server hustled over with chips and salsa. "Boss says whatever you want is on the house."

Dolley rubbed her hands together and looked at Anne. "Appetizers?"

"Most excellent idea." Anne nodded.

They ordered wings, fried zucchini and mozzarella sticks. That ought to cover dinner.

"No more work talk." Dolley held up her drink.

Anne sighed. "I'm in the mood to bitch."

"Nope. How was your date last weekend?" Dolley asked.

Anne pouted. "I thought you didn't want me bitching."

Dolley laughed. "I told you he wasn't right for you."

"You were right." Anne waved her hand around the patio. "Pick someone."

Dolley scanned the tables, lingering on a group of men gathered near the patio bar. "Nothing yet. I'll keep my eyes open."

"How was your date with Robert?" Anne asked.

Dolley grinned. "Apparently a lot better than yours."

Anne grabbed her hand. "You slept with him? Tell all."

"This was only date three." Dolley shook her head. She'd learned to wait, hoping any man who made it to date four saw her as more than just a computer help desk or a friend with benefits.

"What did you do?"

Dolley tapped her fingers on the tabletop. "I helped him with some computer stuff."

"That's not a date." Anne wrinkled her nose. "That's work."

"We were supposed to go to a movie, but he was having trouble loading his students' artwork to the school's website."

"Right." Anne's eyebrows shot up to her hairline. "How do these guys find you?"

"Robert's not like the others."

Anne pointed her finger. "You did his work for him."

"So we could have more time together. Besides, he bought dinner."

"Let me guess—pizza?"

"I picked the toppings," Dolley protested.

Anne shook her head. "Didn't you learn anything from that guy who had you clear the viruses from his computer?"

"John." Dolley rolled her shoulder. "Never date a guy who spends that much time on porn sites."

"And there was that other idiot. You built his website—for free."

"He wasn't an idiot." Dolley had been the idiot. "He was an attorney. Gordon."

"A cheap one—who didn't pay for the work you did."

"They all wanted to stay friends," Dolley said.

"So they could use you again." Anne snorted.

"Robert's not like that. I volunteered to help him."

Anne leaned forward. "Has he called you since you helped him?"

"No." Dolley chewed her lip. "But he had tests to grade."

"Right. He teaches at SCAD." Anne sipped her drink. "Too bad we didn't have teachers that cute when we went to school."

She and Anne had met while attending Savannah College of Art and Design. "You might have studied harder."

Their food arrived, and they dug in, keeping the conversation light.

"Dolley?" a male voice called.

She turned and spotted a familiar face. "Connor?"

Connor's arms wrapped around her, pulling her out of her chair. "I haven't seen you in years."

She hugged him back. "How are you?"

"Good. Great." Connor pulled away and tugged on her hair. "You look the same. I would have known your mop of red curls anywhere."

She brushed an offending hank of hair off her face. "Was that a compliment?"

"Absolutely." He slung an arm around her shoulder and turned to face their table.

"I haven't seen you before." Anne set down her drink and smiled. "Are you an old friend of Dolley's?"

Connor rubbed his knuckles on the top of her head. "We endured high school Advanced Chemistry together. If she hadn't helped me with my homework, I might have blown my scholarship chances."

"We got each other through the course." She elbowed him so he'd stop rubbing her head. "We were the only juniors in the class. The seniors refused to talk to us."

"The guys always talked to you. You had the textbook memorized."

Dolley winced. She had a great memory. "What are you doing back in town?" she asked.

"Home for my mom's birthday weekend. I'm meeting my brother for a beer." He glanced around. "As usual, he's late."

"Do you want to join us until he comes?" Anne smiled.

"Sure." Connor gave Dolley's shoulders a squeeze.

Anne kicked Dolley under the table and tilted her head toward Connor.

Dolley shook her head. Connor wasn't right for Anne. Besides, she'd had a massive crush on him in high school.

All he'd wanted was help in chemistry.

Connor talked about his job while Anne hung on every word.

"You really stayed with chemistry?" Dolley asked.

"Biochemistry. I work up in the triangle."

Anne frowned. "The Bermuda triangle?"

Connor leaned in to Anne, laughing. "The Research Triangle Park in North Carolina. I live in Raleigh."

Anne still looked puzzled, so he explained, leaning even closer.

Her friend wasn't stupid. Dolley expected Anne had heard about the biotech park. Maybe she should leave them alone. "I'll be right back."

Heading to the bathroom, she greeted a couple of the locals, waving and smiling.

She spotted a blond at the indoor bar. Her heart picked up a couple of beats. Robert was here.

Hurrying over, she wrapped a hand around his waist. "Hey, handsome."

Robert whipped around. His eyes widened. "Dolley?"

"I had fun last weekend." She gave his belly a little poke. "You must have gotten all the tests graded by now."

His face went blank. "What tests?"

Her shoulders tightened. "You said you had tests to grade."

"Right. Yes. Lots of tests." His gaze darted around the room. "I'm taking a break."

"So you had time to stop in for a drink—" she let out a deep breath "—but didn't call me?"

"Like I said before—it's the tests." His eyes avoided her gaze. "I needed to get grades in."

Dread settled like a weight on her shoulders. "Did you even give a test this week?"

He finally looked her in the eye. He held up his hands and then let them fall to his thighs with a slap. "A short quiz."

"A quiz." The appetizers she'd eaten churned in her stomach.

Based on the way Robert shifted back and forth, she wasn't dating him again. "Got it." She turned to go. "I…"

"Dolley." He grabbed her arm. "We had fun. I appreciate your help last weekend."

She glared at his hand on her arm until he let her go.

"Were you even interested in me?" she asked. "Or did you endure two dates just to get computer help?"

"Dolley, no." He caught her hand. "Can we still be…friends?"

She had to get away. "I don't think so."

"I'm sorry." Robert, the jerk, looked relieved.

She stepped backward, then hurried into the hallway.

Why did this always happen to her?

That's it. She was taking a dating break.

Her phone rang as she exited the bathroom. *Unknown number.* What now? She answered.

"Is this Dolley Fitzgerald?"

"Yes."

"Congratulations. This is *Bridal Party Today*. Your photograph won first place in the amateur division of our contest."

Her heart pounded. "It won?"

"It sure did."

"My photograph." She'd entered a picture she'd taken at Mamma's wedding. She shook her head. "Me?"

"If you're Dolley Fitzgerald." The woman on the other end of the call chuckled. "Your picture will be included in our January magazine. I'll send you interview questions for the article."

"Sure. Sure." After confirming her email address, Dolley hung up.

A photograph she'd taken had won. The first contest she'd ever entered. And it was a picture of Mamma dancing with Martin, her groom, at their wedding. Dolley couldn't stop the grin filling her face. She'd won. Punching the air, she spun in the hallway. *Who cared about Robert now?*

She rushed out to tell Anne.

Connor and Anne had their heads tucked together. Connor's younger brother occupied the empty chair at the table.

Her enthusiasm vanished. They wouldn't understand her excitement. They weren't the youngest sister of two exceptional siblings. They wouldn't understand her need to prove herself.

Dolley straightened her shoulders. Spotting an empty chair, she dragged it over to the table. "Hey, Jason. Haven't seen you in ages."

"Hi, Dolley. Connor said you were here." Jason grinned. "How's my favorite babysitter?"

Lord, she'd babysat Jason. "Apparently old. Are you sure you can drink?"

He flipped out his license. "Legal and everything."

She forced a smile on her face. This wasn't the time or place to tell people about her silly contest win. She'd get a copy of the magazine, leave it at the B and B and see if anyone read the article. No one would guess a photography career was her secret dream.

LIAM CLOSED THE folder on the Fitzgeralds and pushed away from the small desk in his room at the inn. He still hadn't escaped Kilkee.

Seamus's long-lost relatives and their location sounded too good to be true. A mother who had started the business and three daughters who ran it now. His godfather had collected enough Savannah travel information that Liam wanted to book a flight tomorrow. Did families like this really exist?

All this reading about family had his muscles tightening. He should walk around town to work off this…anxiousness. Maybe grab one of his godfather's cameras and head to the bay. He never tired of taking pictures of the sunset on the sea.

Instead, he sat, rolled his shoulders and scrolled through the Fitzgerald and Carleton House bed-and-breakfast website. Someone had a nice hand with the photographs. *Dolley Fitzgerald.*

He flipped open the file to the picture of the Fitzgeralds and wondered which one she was. Their Irish heritage was evident in their fair skin and red hair. Would they care about letters written years ago?

He checked out pictures of Savannah's St. Patrick's Day parade. Clicked on a few links. Savannahians celebrated their Irish roots. And this small city had the second largest St. Patrick's Day parade in America. Why?

He kept clicking. Found a documentary on the Irish building railroads in Georgia, found other sites touting the Irish regiments in their civil war. Well, his country, too. His father had been an American. Seamus had scorned his dual citizenship. Which made this mission to deliver letters even more puzzling.

But the idea of researching Savannah's Irish roots...took hold. Dug in. He could stay at the Fitzgerald's B and B and work in Savannah. Pretend he was part of their family for a time.

Once he finished the voice-overs for his Irish Travellers documentary, he needed a new project. Americans were fascinated with their Irish heritage. Why not create a story around the Irish in Savannah?

He kept searching and didn't come up for air for an hour. "This might work."

He could deliver the letters, but he would also get a new project out of the task.

He checked the time. His producer should be in her sleek New York office. When her brisk voice came over his mobile, he leaned back.

"Hallo, Barbara."

"Liam," she said. "I'm so sorry about your god-father. How was the funeral?"

"Small." He cut off any additional sympathy.

"It would still hurt to lose the man who brought you up." She took a breath. "I'm not pushing, but when do you think you'll be back in the studio?"

He was done here. "I'll complete the voice-overs next week."

"Great."

Liam stared out at Kilkee Bay. The waves were gentle this evening. So different from the racket in his head. He smiled. "I have a proposal for my next project."

CHAPTER TWO

The single most important component of a camera is the twelve inches behind it.

Ansel Adams

"FITZGERALD HOUSE," DOLLEY SAID.

"I'm hoping to book a long term stay." The man on the phone had a delicious Irish accent. "I tried to book online, but wasn't successful."

"I can certainly help you." Dolley closed her eyes. Yum. She could listen to this man's voice for hours. Her fingers flew over the keyboard as she logged in to the reservation system. "When will you arrive?"

"December fifteenth through…the twenty-fifth of March."

A three-and-a-half month stay? Dolley bit her lip, afraid she'd blurt out *hot damn*. She loved being the sister who caught these calls. She searched for available rooms, then it hit her. "Oh, dear. We close the week between Christmas and New Year's."

"You're closed?" Papers rustled on the line. "Is there any way I could…incentivize you to let me stay?"

A three-and-a-half month reservation was a pretty big incentive, especially since Carleton House was opening next year. "How many people in your party?" she asked, trying to stall while she figured out what to do.

"Just me until mid-February. Then I'll bring in my film crew."

"Film crew?" This guy was in the movies? "How many rooms would you need?"

"Three more, beginning, let's say, February 20 through March 25."

If she was a swooning woman, she'd be dropping to the floor. What a perfect way to open Carleton House.

But they weren't open over Christmas.

After Mamma opened the B and B, she'd always insisted they celebrate Christmas as a family. Dolley drummed her fingers on the desktop. Just last week, she and her sisters had agreed to stick with Mamma's tradition.

But this was a *three-and-a-half month reservation*. With more rooms starting in February. Dolley shook her head. This booking was *not* going to a competitor.

Maybe Abby would make an exception. Bess, their other sister, would agree with Abby.

"I'll talk with my partners, but I think we can work something out. It might not include breakfast, afternoon tea or wine tasting during the week we're closed. Would that be a problem?"

"Hmm. Would I be able to eat elsewhere?"

"Absolutely." She'd personally create a list of open restaurants for him. "I'd be happy to set up reservations for you and your party during the holidays."

The grandfather clock at the end of the foyer ticked like a slow metronome, filling the long silence.

"I'll be alone." His tone was soulful, like he didn't have anyone in the world.

No family during Christmas? Now she definitely had to convince Abby to make an exception.

"Let me get your information."

She wrote everything down. Liam Delaney. Even his name was drool-worthy. "After I check with my partners, I'll call you back."

Dolley danced down the hallway to the kitchen, pushing through the swinging door. Abby handled all the breakfasts, teas and appetizers offered by the B and B. Eighty percent of the time she could find her sister baking or cooking.

She was in luck. Abby stood next to the counter on her phone.

"Dolley walked in." Abby waved her closer. "She'll know."

Dolley moved to the counter.

Her sister pushed the speaker button and set the phone down. "Mamma wants to know how many more beds we need for Carleton House."

"Hey, Mamma." Dolley rested her head on her hand.

"Hi, sweetie. Aunt CeCe and I have been having fun hitting antique stores and estate sales. We found some great Victorian bed frames and one tester, but I couldn't remember how many more beds we need. Also, are we still looking for lamps?"

The smile in Mamma's voice had Dolley grinning. Her newlywed mother sounded so excited. "Great-Aunt CeCe is shopping with you?"

"Her arthritis is better in the morning. We've gotten in the habit of hitting the stores early." Mamma lowered her voice. "She loves feeling useful and spending money. If she could, she'd shop all day."

"Let me think." Dolley closed her eyes and pictured the inventory spreadsheet on her computer. She'd updated it last week. "Six more beds. Bess added a request for four small bookcases for the upstairs parlors. Two pairs."

"We did find bookcases." Mamma's voice brimmed with energy. "Aunt CeCe, were those bookcases in pairs?"

There was a quiet conversation between Mamma and Cece.

"We'll go back to that store and put the bookcases on hold. We think there was at least one matching pair. And lamps?"

Dolley scrolled down the spreadsheet in her mind. "We need a dozen table lamps and we'd take floor lamps, too."

"Good. There was an estate sale today that had wonderful lamps. We put holds on the nice ones. I'll take pictures and send them to you. Love to all."

Abby ended the call. She and Dolley looked at each other and laughed.

"I'm glad Mamma volunteered, or we'd be running all over Georgia and the Carolinas looking for furniture," Abby said.

"It sounds like Aunt CeCe's having a great time, too." Dolley spotted a tray of sweets. "Anything to eat in here?"

Abby waved at the counter. "Leftovers from tea."

Dolley snapped up a sandwich and grabbed a plate off the stack. Deviled ham? Worked for her. Anything her sister made was delicious. She could chew and mull over how to approach Abby.

Abby stood in front of an open fridge with the inventory list Dolley had designed for her. "Did you need something?"

"I stopped in to say hello to the Scrapbooking Sister group I booked." Dolley dusted the crumbs off her fingers and took a deep breath. "What do you think about another long-term stay?"

Abby wiggled her fingers, engagement ring sparkling. "I sure liked the last one."

"Yeah, yeah. You got a fiancé out of it." Dolley moved to the coffeepot and poured a mug. "He's not asking for dinner, so I don't think Gray has to worry you'll fall for another man."

Abby bumped her shoulder and took a sip of Dolley's coffee. Her sister's gaze softened. "Gray never has to worry about that."

Dolley rolled her eyes. Her sister and Gray were *in love*. Sickeningly so. She was happy for her sister, but why couldn't she find her own guy?

"Back to business." Dolley snapped her fingers

in front of Abby's silly smile. "Three-and-a-half months. He hasn't asked for a discount. And he'll need three more rooms starting February 20 until March 25."

"Four rooms." Abby straightened. "I say *yes*. Absolutely."

"So do I." Dolley took back her coffee. "It would include the week of Christmas."

"Christmas?" Abby's shoulders sank. "We're closed."

"I told him. He's willing to work something out and just wants to make sure he can get meals someplace."

Abby paced to the sitting area. "One person, or is he bringing someone else?"

"Just him." Dolley sighed. "The poor man says he'll be alone during the holidays."

"Alone during Christmas?" Abby jerked around to look at her.

Dolley nodded.

Her sister twisted her ring. "We agreed to keep our Christmas break just last week."

"I know."

"Is there something unusual about him?" Abby pointed a finger at her. "Did you Google him?"

"No." But she would. She wanted to know about Mr. Liam Delaney of the sexy voice. "He just said he'd be alone."

She sighed again, trying to tug on Abby's tender heart. "How sad not to have a place to go during the holidays. I'm so lucky to work with my sisters and have Mamma within spitting distance."

"Of course we'll take him." Abby took Dolley's hand. "And he'll have his breakfast, too. For the week we're closed, he can eat in the kitchen like Gray did."

"You're so good-hearted." Dolley brushed a kiss on Abby's cheek. "I'll call him back."

Abby frowned. "Did you just play me?"

Dolley snagged one more sandwich. "Never."

Abby's eyes narrowed. "Just for that, you tell Bess."

"Will do." Dolley grinned. She wasn't looking forward to shoehorning a massive reservation into their clunky booking system. But at least she could listen to Liam Delaney's gorgeous accent again.

LIAM TAPPED THE floor with his foot. He knew he would get the go ahead. He had to.

But he'd had project ideas shot down before.

So here he was…waiting…and worrying. The idea of this Savannah documentary had grabbed hold and wouldn't let go.

During the week Barbara was taking his idea for final approval, he'd stopped in New York. Something he'd never done before.

Liam stared out at the silver forest of buildings flanked by turbulent skies. December snowflakes floated through the air, waiting to drop and join the gray slush blanketing New York City. Even standing in his producer's office, he couldn't clear the petrol smell from his nose. In Kilkee, at least he'd been able to smell the bay.

He paced from the window to the door. And back again. His anxiousness wasn't normal.

The office door burst open. Barbara called out, "I've got your approval."

He let out a sigh, sinking into a chair. "I knew you could do it."

Barbara tossed a red cardigan on her desk. Big red flowers covered her black dress.

"I might have promised them my firstborn." Her black hair swung around her chin. "I didn't tell them he was turning thirteen."

He shook his head in mock horror. She doted on her son, David.

"Can I pick my crew?" he asked.

"You've got Jerry. I'm working on the rest." She leaned against her desk. "Legal revised the consent form we want you to use."

Liam rolled his eyes. "Again?"

"Yes." Barbara slipped around her desk and slid into her chair. "Make sure to grab copies from Samantha."

"Lovely." He hated explaining that people were signing away their rights—forever. "I'd like to take a portable video camera with me."

"Talk to Samantha." Barbara fingered the stack of pink phone slips. "Are we still on for lunch with Toni and Mark?"

"Yes, they confirmed." His agent and manager had both approved the contracts, pending project approval.

He paced in front of the window. This was happening. He had his excuse to head to Savannah.

"You're pushing hard on this one." Barbara tipped her head. "Why?"

"The place I'll stay in Savannah is run by the Fitzgerald family."

"FitzGerald. Like your godfather?"

"Yes." Returning to her guest chair, he tapped his fingers on the wooden back. "The only way I could get my hands on Seamus's cameras was to agree to take some letters to them."

She frowned, leaning back in her chair. "Is this why you suggested this documentary?"

"Not originally." Liam stuck his hands in his pockets. "But when I checked the sisters and Savannah out, I was intrigued."

"Sisters?" His producer raised her eyebrows. "How pretty are they?"

"Not in that way." Although Dolley's face was… engaging. He'd toyed with the idea of including her family in the documentary, but didn't know how the story would unfold or if they would fit his premise. "What did you think of the title, *Savannah's Irish Roots*?"

She smiled and nodded. "We'll test it."

That was the best he could ask for. "Good."

"Since you're this side of the pond, why don't you spend Christmas with us?" Barbara asked.

"I'd rather be in Savannah than up here in the cold." He shivered.

Barbara shook her head. "You shouldn't spend Christmas alone."

"Holidays don't mean much to me." He couldn't let them. "Even when I was in boarding school, Seamus usually left me there."

"The old scrooge." Her tone was incensed. "You deserved better."

"I survived." He crossed his legs. He'd learned how to fit in and ingratiate himself with the other students. "School chums invited me home for the holidays."

"That's just wrong." Barbara sighed. "Come to my house. You should be around people who care about you."

"I'll think on it." Now that he had his approval, he wanted to immerse himself in the Irish stories of Savannah and dig into the research.

And he wanted to meet his shirttail relatives, the Fitzgeralds. How should he play this?

It was boarding school all over again.

DOLLEY PULLED THE cork on another bottle of wine, and it opened with a pop. The tart aroma mingled with the pine of the Christmas tree in the corner. Evergreen boughs on the mantel and the spicy appetizers added to the incredible smells filling the library.

It wasn't Dolley's night to host the wine tasting, but since Abby's fiancé was back in town, she'd volunteered. Abby had jumped at the chance to spend time with Gray. Her sister hadn't even noticed Dolley's new dress.

Dolley had planned to volunteer anyway. Mr. Liam Delaney was checking in tonight. *The voice.* She tugged on her hem. The black dress hugged her curves but kept creeping up. It was probably better for clubbing than for the B and B, but—Liam Delaney. Enough said.

Online, she'd found a wealth of information on their guest. When she grew up, she wanted to be Liam Delaney. He was a documentary filmmaker *and* a photographer. Envy shot through her. His body of work was amazing. He'd traveled the world, linking his photography to his films. She planned to pick his brain about his career, without being creepy.

She checked the flames under the chafing dish and opened the last bottle of wine.

Her one claim to photography fame was the picture of her mother. And she hadn't even told her sisters she'd won the contest. Somehow the words just wouldn't leave her mouth.

Abby and Bess were so talented. One picture was nothing compared to what her sisters had accomplished in their careers, Abby in the kitchen and Bess with her landscaping.

A honeymoon couple walked into the library, arm

in arm. The newlyweds had stayed at Fitzgerald House for the last few days.

"How was your day?" Dolley asked.

"We kayaked off Tybee Island." The bride massaged her upper arm.

"Did you get to the salt marshes?" Dolley asked.

The groom nodded. "Almost had to pull Gretchen across the bay. There was a little chop, but we got there."

Now she remembered their names. Gretchen and Denny.

The couple headed to the wines and food. Tonight's offerings were from Germany: a Riesling, a pinot gris and pinot noir. She sampled the red. Not bad. She checked the cards Abby created for the appetizers. Then she took a plate and added pork turnovers, pretzels, warm German potato salad and barbequed kielbasa. She skipped the sauerkraut crepes.

Checking the food layout one more time, she headed to the foyer. Her heels echoed on the marble floor. She would let the guests enjoy their wine and keep an eye out for Liam, the last guest checking in tonight.

She skirted the foyer table. Her sister, Bess, had designed a tower of poinsettias shaped like a Christmas tree. The red-and-pink leaves sparkled with glitter. Another Christmas tree twinkled in the front window. They'd decorated seventeen trees in the House this year, a new record.

She took a seat at the Queen Anne secretary they used as a reception desk.

The front door opened, and she started to stand.

It was another honeymoon couple. They waved and headed toward the library.

Dolley sank back into her chair. What if Mr. Delaney didn't show? That would hurt. He'd eventually asked for a discount, but they were still going to clear a tidy profit from his stay. She'd held firm that they couldn't discount rooms during the St. Patrick's Day festivities. They had to maintain their prices during high season.

Finishing her dinner, she returned the plate to the packed library. Cheryl, a B and B employee, restocked the food. They smiled at each other. Dolley bussed a tray of dirty dishes to the kitchen.

Might as well check the reservation line messages. She put a hold on a room and returned the call, entering the credit card information. Then she pulled this year's reservation data down into a spreadsheet. For fun, she created a comparison graph with the prior year's reservations. These cool facts would be nice to show at their next sister meeting.

She pushed back a curl that kept falling in her eye. What next? Pulling out her bag, she settled behind the desk. She would work on photo cards, her creative contribution to the gift shop scheduled to open in January.

She glued pictures on a pale blue fold-over card

stock, hoping the result was classy and contemporary. They would sell the cards as six-packs. Each pack included a picture of Fitzgerald House and the rooms the guests saw most: the formal dining room, library and sunroom. All photos she'd shot. The rest of the packet varied, with shots of the gardens or guest rooms. By the time she'd glued all the pictures, she'd made ten packs.

She checked her watch. Almost eight o'clock. Mr. Delaney was supposed to have been here by six. This was getting ridiculous. She'd never waited at the reception desk for a guest.

The front door opened, and there was a swoosh of nylon rubbing nylon. A lean man with dark wavy hair lugged two large suitcases across the foyer. Mr. Delaney?

"Let me help." She grabbed a roller bag.

"Thank you." He turned, his gaze catching hers, his eyes a brilliant blue that almost looked purple. "I'm checking in."

Hurrying around the desk, she asked, "Liam Delaney?"

"Absolutely." He raised a dark eyebrow. "And would you be Dolley Fitzgerald?"

"Guilty."

"After all our conversations, it's lovely to finally meet you." He reached out a hand, his expression way too serious.

"Oh. Thank you. You, too. Or me, too." Flustered, she shook his hand, hanging on a little too long.

He dropped her hand and reached into his back pocket, pulling out a wallet.

Shoot, she was supposed to be checking him in. Her fingers danced over the keyboard. "How was your trip?"

She glanced up long enough to see him grimace.

"I raced through the Atlanta airport to catch my flight, then there was some broken widget on our plane, so we all trooped off." He pushed back his black hair with long artistic fingers. "They sent us to another gate where we sat and sat. When I got to the car rental, they'd let all the cars, so I waited for one to be turned in."

"I'm so sorry." She had his reservation in front of her.

"I'm looking forward to sitting someplace where I can stretch my legs."

Dolley peeked. He had a lot of leg.

Taking his credit card, she said, "We'll charge your card each week in advance."

"That works." He signed the slip.

Handing him a key card, she explained breakfast, tea and wine tastings. "I'm afraid you've missed tonight's wine tasting."

"Damn." He huffed out a breath. "I guess I could use a recommendation for a restaurant."

"I can throw something together in the kitchen."

Relief filled his deep blue eyes. "I'd be ever so grateful."

"Sure." Moving around the desk, she grabbed his bag.

"That's my cameras," he said. "I can get it."

"I'll be careful. You're juggling two suitcases."

She led the way to the elevator. "There's always coffee, tea and soda in the dining room." She pointed to the library. "Our evening wine tastings are held there. Feel free to borrow the books and movies."

He kept glancing at his camera bag. Or was he checking her out?

She tightened her glutes.

"The house is lovely," he said as they wedged into the elevator.

"It is." She inhaled, catching a whiff of his scent. Nice. "We just finished the full renovations in August."

"Your website said you were under construction."

"That's Carleton House." She stepped out of the elevator and stopped at the window overlooking the adjacent mansion. "We're in the process of restoring the house next door. I've booked your crew into Carleton House. It opens in February. If you prefer, we can move you there when they arrive."

"I'll think on it." He stopped in front of his room. "This it?"

"Yes. You're in the Martha Jefferson room." Instead of setting the bag down, she handed the strap to him so he wouldn't worry. "If you use the front stairs and head down the hallway by the reception desk, you'll find a swinging door. That's the kitchen."

He touched her shoulder. His scent wrapped around her. Mint, apples, lemons. Not a fragrance she would associate with a man—but he made it work. She leaned in and took another sniff. Delicious.

His gaze caught hers. "I appreciate the help with my bags. It was a long day."

She stepped back. Her objective was to learn more about photography, not drool over him or his cologne. She headed to the back stairs. "Let me see what food I can scrounge up."

She would ply him with food and if there was an opportunity—questions. Find out if she could use her photography for more than selling cards.

LIAM ROLLED HIS suitcases next to the bedroom door, settling the camera bag on the bed. It was foolish, but he unzipped the bag. The Hasselblad, Rolleiflex, his Canon, Nikon and all his lenses and filters looked undamaged. Barbara had come through with a portable, and it was fine.

Dolley had been careful. And watching the bag had given him the opportunity to admire a really lovely bum.

He stretched, working a kink out of his lower back. Ms. Dolley Fitzgerald was more interesting in person than in her website photograph. She had…

energy. A camera couldn't capture her gleaming green eyes or the life in that mass of red curls.

He unpacked a few things, plugged in his phone to recharge and set the stack of releases on the desk with his computer.

His stomach rumbled. He pocketed his key card and headed downstairs.

The curved railing was silky smooth under his palm. What a difference between the uncared-for Kilkee manor house and this well-preserved Savannah mansion.

He would get something to eat, take the lay of the land with the first Fitzgerald sister and then fall into bed.

Tomorrow he planned to wander Savannah, get a sense of the city and the historic district. He loved exploring and listening to the natives. It didn't matter that this wasn't an aboriginal community in Australia or a small tribe forced out of their hunting grounds in Africa.

Skirting a tower of poinsettias, he found the right hallway and pushed on the swinging door.

Dolley stood in front of a stainless steel counter, containers covering the surface. The worktops, grills and a wall of fridges made this look like a restaurant. But in the back was a small sitting area with a glowing fire and a Christmas tree.

"You found me." Dolley pointed to the back area. "Grab a chair by the fire. I'll bring everything over."

He snatched a chunk of cheese as he passed by the counter. "Thanks ever so much."

"What would you like to drink? Beer, wine, soda? We have Jameson if you'd prefer."

He sank into an armchair. "A Jameson, neat, would be appreciated."

She dropped off a tray of cheese, sausage, crackers and fruit. "I'll grab your drink."

She pushed through the swinging door. Her short black dress flirted with her tidy bottom. Nice.

He piled a cracker with cheese and meat and took a bite. Followed up with some cool green grapes. He kept going as if he hadn't eaten in days.

Ever since Seamus's funeral, his appetite had been—off. His meals had been haphazard at best. He'd do better. He'd comply with the schedule Dolley had rattled off. She'd said the hours were in the pamphlet she'd handed him. He'd make sure he didn't miss meals like he'd been doing in Ireland.

"Sorry it took so long. Jameson is in the library." Dolley pushed through the doorway. "It's always there for guests, FYI."

The room brightened. Why? He turned his photographic instincts to the question. Dolley? It wasn't just her hair, it was her—her smile—her sparkle. Being in Kilkee had drained him. Maybe in Savannah he could absorb some of her vitality.

"This is great." He waved his hand over the half-decimated spread of food.

"I could make you a sandwich," she offered.

He took the tumbler from her hand and their fingers bumped. Awareness surged through him. "This will hit the spot."

"Would you like company?" she asked.

"Please."

She took the armchair across from him, curling her feet underneath her trim bottom. She tipped her wineglass. "Welcome to Savannah. *Sláinte.*"

Her pronunciation was spot-on. *"Sláinte."*

They both stared into the fire. He popped grapes in his mouth, enjoying the silence, so different from the cacophony of airports and planes.

"Did you fly straight from Ireland today?"

He shook his head. "I was in New York for a week. Meetings."

"My sister, our chef, trained in New York." Her smile dimmed. "I visited when I was seventeen. Not sure I could live there. I enjoy fresh air too much. But the city—everything moved and breathed. It was alive."

Weird that she mentioned the one thing that bothered him about the city—the smell. "I can never get the stench of petrol out of my nose. I hate the crowds."

"I love crowds." Her grin made her green eyes twinkle. "Savannah smells like life to me. Green and growing. And when you get closer to Tybee, the ocean." Her shoulders lifted and dropped. "I love it here, but I'd like to see…the world."

The world? Been there. Done that. "Tybee sounds like Kilkee, but warmer."

"Kilkee? Is that where you live in Ireland?"

"Only for part of my childhood. Before that I lived in county Kerry."

"It sounds so—glamorous."

He shook his head. "It's a small coastal village."

"I checked out your website." She leaned forward. "It's amazing. I love your Irish landscapes—well, all your landscapes. But the Irish ones made me feel like I was walking a path home to a cottage. Or I'd just stepped into a pub and someone built me a Guinness."

Her compliment sounded genuine. "Have you been, then?"

"To Ireland? No. Closest I've come is Kevin Barry's pub here in Savannah." She laughed. "Sad when we're Irish-Americans, isn't it?"

"No." He popped one last cracker in his mouth. "You take the photos for the website, right?"

She nodded, chewing on her lower lip.

"You've an excellent hand with the camera." He tried not to stare at her mouth. He was supposed to be scoping out the territory. But the sight of her lower lip, now wet and slightly pink from her teeth, was…entrancing.

"Me?" Her eyes widened. Her fair skin turned a beautiful peach color with her blush.

"Your photographs are well composed. You use light like an artist."

"Coming from you, I'm awestruck." Her hand pressed against her chest. A rather lovely chest, at that.

He forced his gaze up to her face. "Did you study under someone?"

"I took classes in college, but nothing serious." She shook her head, and her curls danced. "Nothing like what you must have done."

"I never went to university."

She leaned forward. "But you're so good."

Her frock gapped, and he got a small peek of the valley between her breasts. *Devil take his soul*, he was having trouble keeping his eyes where they belonged.

"I apprenticed with some wonderful photographers," he said. "That sounds grander than it really is. I hauled equipment and spent hours in the darkroom, or scrolling and deleting blurred photos, but I watched them work. They critiqued and explained and made me the photographer I am."

"You were an apprentice." Her fingernail tapped the cutie-pie curve of her top lip. "I don't suppose you need one while you're in Savannah? I really want to learn more."

"I've only had one apprentice." He exhaled. "It's a commitment to bring out the artist in a photographer."

And that hadn't ended well. Kieran had used him to get ahead. That was expected. But his apprentice had had little patience. He'd falsified a recommendation by using Liam's own email.

Since Kieran, he'd been reluctant to take on anyone else. His focus in Savannah was his documentary, not training a novice.

But working with Dolley might be another way to absorb the Fitzgerald experience.

"Let me get some sleep." He stood. "I'll think on your request."

CHAPTER THREE

Diligence is the mother of good luck.

Proverb

DOLLEY'S FINGERS BEAT a rhythm on her keyboard. Three o'clock. What was Liam doing? Maybe tea at Fitzgerald House?

She could accidentally run into him there. He might have an answer about taking her on as an apprentice. She rolled her head, easing the tight muscles in her neck.

What would it be like to apprentice with Liam Delaney? Could he be her ticket to showing her family she had creativity, too? She wouldn't be the youngest Fitzgerald sister anymore. She'd *be* someone.

Anne poked her head over the cubicle wall. "I'm heading across the street for coffee. Do you want anything?"

"No, but I'll walk out with you. I need to run over to Fitzgerald House." She shut down and tucked her laptop in her bag.

Time to stalk Liam Delaney. God, she was sad.

"I heard from Connor," Anne said, pushing open the door. "He asked me to drive up to North Carolina to visit."

"You kept in touch?" Dolley would never have put them together.

"We saw each other a couple of times the weekend we met." Anne started across the street. "Then got together during Thanksgiving."

"And you didn't tell me?" She and Anne were friends, close friends.

Anne chewed her thumbnail. "When we met, you didn't approve of us as a couple."

"That's because Connor's self-absorbed." Or had been during high school.

"He's not." Anne stopped in front of the coffee shop, hands on her hips. "Sure, he likes to talk about his job, but it's interesting. You should hear what they're researching. Ways to deliver chemotherapy in fat cells, nanotechnology and injecting tumors with viruses." Anne shot Dolley a stern look. "What he's doing could change the world."

Dolley sighed. "I...I didn't realize."

"He's amazing," Anne said.

"You don't need my approval to date Connor." What did she know about successful relationships?

Anne's shoulders relaxed. "But he was your friend first. I don't want this to be between us."

"Never." Dolley caught her hand. "I think you'll be great together."

Anne squeezed her fingers. "Really?"

"Really." Dolley hated that her friend had hesitated to tell her about a relationship. Maybe letting her in on her secret might soothe her feathers. "The reason I'm heading to Fitzgerald House is because our long-term guest, the Irishman, is considering whether he'll take me on as a photography apprentice."

Anne's eyes were as big as saucers. "An apprentice?"

"Yes." She took a deep breath. "Maybe he can jump-start my photography career. He must know all the right people. It would be the perfect leg up."

"You want to change careers?"

"I hope so," Dolley said. "And Liam could help me hit the fast track."

"I don't want to be alone at Jackson." Anne pouted.

"You won't be alone. And who knows if I'm any good." Dolley winced. "Don't tell anyone."

Anne turned a key on her mouth. "Is the Irishman as hot as his accent?"

"Hotter." And Dolley wasn't kidding. "Total eye candy."

Anne fanned herself. "Go, girl."

"It won't be a hardship to befriend the man." Dolley grinned. And maybe she could get him to smile.

Dolley cut across Columbia Square and skirted the fountain. Everyone around her was pairing up. Anne and Connor. That was a shock. Abby was engaged. Bess and Daniel had been hot and heavy for a while, but that had ended. Even so, Bess didn't want to stop for drinks anymore.

Soon there wouldn't be anyone to go clubbing with her, and she'd sit at home, become a recluse and take in stray cats.

Across the street from the B and B, she stopped and stared at Fitzgerald House. At three full stories plus the attic, it towered above Carleton House. The black wrought iron balconies gave it a feminine look.

Dolley didn't remember Fitzgerald House ever being her home. She'd been five when Mamma had opened the B and B.

She only remembered Papa through pictures. He'd died when she was four. But whenever she smelled Old Spice, she got a warm, happy feeling. Abby was the one who'd told her it had been Papa's aftershave.

Sunshine sparkled on the windows. A cascade of red poinsettias flowed across the porch and down the steps. Dolley had wrapped fairy lights around the green garland draped along the low wall running the length of both Fitzgerald and Carleton House. Her fingers clenched, wishing she had her camera.

The day they'd decorated, she'd taken tons of pictures. That B and B blog had gotten the most hits ever. The blog was her small contribution to finding new guests.

She took the Fitzgerald House porch stairs two at a time and pulled open the bright blue door. She sniffed. Ginger molasses cookies? Abby was baking her favorite treat.

She wanted to see if Liam was attending afternoon tea, but she also wanted to grab a warm cookie. She inhaled. Darn it. A career she was passionate about was more important than her sister's cookies, right? She forced her feet to move down the hall, away from the kitchen.

In the sunroom, guests gathered in groups of two or four, drinking and eating the offerings. She leaned against the door frame.

Liam sat next to the bay window. A group of local women who came to tea each month formed a ring around him. Wouldn't they love his accent?

His knuckles were white around his plate. His teeth clenched. Poor man.

She entered the room.

His head jerked up. Relief filled his deep blue eyes and he scrambled to his feet. "Excuse me, ladies."

Pressing her lips together, she held back a laugh.

"Ms. Fitzgerald." He almost lunged toward her. "Just the person I was hoping to see."

She smiled. "Good to see you, too."

"Is there someplace we can talk? Someplace other than—" he looked back at the ladies "—here?"

She took pity on him. "Follow me."

"Goodbye, Liam," a woman called.

"Goodbye, Mr. Delaney," another said.

"Let me know if you need more information on my family," a woman called as he left.

As soon as they turned the hallway corner, she burst out laughing.

He slumped against the wall. "Devil take me, those women were talking my ears off."

"I know just what will help, my sister's molasses and ginger cookies." She linked their arms. His was firm and muscular. "They're the best."

She would be able to talk to Liam *and* have her favorite cookie. Score.

"As soon as I told the group what I was doing in Savannah, they…they attacked." He was a little breathless. "And they all looked alike. What are you doing down here, cloning crones?"

She glanced behind her, but they were far enough away from the sunroom that no one could have heard him. "They all went to school together, and they're wonderful."

"I'm sure they are, but they're overwhelming." His words ran together, a lovely Irish slur of sounds.

She slipped her arm out if his. If she wanted an apprenticeship, she wouldn't complicate things by acting too familiar.

Photography was her focus.

She pushed open the kitchen door.

Abby slid cookies onto racks. She glanced up, her ponytail bouncing. "Hey, Dolley."

Liam stepped in next to her. Even through the magnificent smell of molasses, sugar and ginger, his scent came through.

"Abby, have you met Liam Delaney?"

"Not yet." Abby grabbed a towel and dusted her hands. Moving across the kitchen, she shook his hand. "So glad you chose Fitzgerald House for your stay."

"Thank you for making an exception during the holiday."

"You are very welcome."

"I rescued him. He was corralled by the Saint Peter School ladies." Dolley raised an eyebrow. "They were overwhelming him."

"They offered to help with my research." Liam winced. "Even the women who weren't Irish."

"What are you researching?" Abby asked.

"Savannah's Irish roots. For a combination book and documentary."

"That sounds like fun," Abby said.

"It will be."

"Since your tea was interrupted, would you like a cup in here?" Abby offered.

"Yes, please." His words rushed out. "I'd kill for one."

Dolley snatched up a couple of the warm cookies.

Abby smacked her hand. "I'll serve. Go light the fire."

"They're best right out of the oven." Dolley moved back to the sitting area. Passing Liam a cookie, she whispered, "I filched one for you, too."

He grinned, a wicked pirate grin that promised adventures and fun. It was the first smile she'd noticed crossing his face.

She frowned. He hadn't smiled at all last night.

"I won't rat on you." He leaned close, his dark,

wavy hair brushing next to her ear. "But I'd best get rid of the evidence."

She couldn't help inhaling his scent. Could cologne be addictive?

Liam took a bite. His eyes closed. "Oh, my," he mumbled, his mouth full.

"I know." Dolley devoured her cookie and then pushed the buttons on the gas fire. It lit with a whoosh.

"I saw that," Abby scolded, although she was smiling. She set cookies and bars on the coffee table.

"These are incredible." Liam plucked another cookie from the platter.

It was a sacrifice, but she nudged the cookies closer to him. A sugar high might lull him into agreeing to the apprenticeship.

Abby set a teapot with cream, sugar and mugs on the table. "I'd love to chat, but I need to refresh the tea."

"Go." Dolley waved her off. Besides, she didn't want Abby finding out about her request for a mentorship. Especially if Liam said *no*.

He poured cream in his mug and added tea. "It's nice to get a real pot of tea. Some places I stay, I can hardly find a tea bag."

He prepped a cup for her. She couldn't think of any man ever making her a cup of tea, or much of anything.

"How was your morning?" She slipped deeper into her chair.

"I took a long ramble around the squares, getting my bearings." He took another cookie. "Savannah is beautiful."

"Wait until the azaleas bloom."

"And when will that be?"

"Early March," she said. "They peak around the St Patrick's Day invasion."

"I can't wait." Liam took another cookie. "I want to film the festivities."

She sipped her tea. How could she steer the conversation to the apprenticeship? "Did you take any pictures?"

"Thought I would scope things out first." He downed his tea. "But I took a couple."

"When you're doing a documentary, do you think in photographs or film?" she asked, not sure how to blurt out her request.

"No one's ever asked me that question." He refilled his mug and slid back in his chair. "Both, I guess. I see moments that unfurl into scenes, into movement or a story." He shook his head. "That sounds thick."

"I see that." Her pictures tended to be of the B and B, but it was pictures like the ones of Mamma's wedding, where Martin was twirling her in a circle, that she loved. It was a story of joy. "I get it."

"I did do one other thing today." Liam pushed back his black hair. It was thick and long enough to curl around his shirt collar. What would his hair feel like?

She refocused on his face, although that was distracting, too. "What?"

"Called my producer. I've got room in the budget to put you on the payroll."

Dolley's feet hit the floor. "You do?"

"You can be my—Savannah guide." He held up a hand. "I'm not promising an apprenticeship. I'd want to assess your skills before I commit. Are you still interested?"

She juggled her mug, setting it down before she spilled. This didn't sound like an apprenticeship. "I'd be on trial?"

"Probation. It won't be much money." He named an hourly rate that was barely over minimum wage.

Her stomach dropped. She still had to live. "How many hours a week?"

"Let's say—ten to fifteen to start. If I need more hours, we'd reassess the money." Liam leaned close enough for her to catch a heady whiff of his cologne. "Is the money a problem?"

Money was *always* a problem for the Fitzgerald family, but she wouldn't tell Liam that. She wanted a chance to improve her skills. This might be her big break or it could be a lowly gopher job. How would she pay her bills?

"I'll see if I can cut back my hours at work." She kept her tone calm, when inside, everything started to shake.

He frowned. "I thought you and your sisters ran the B and B?"

"We do. I also work for a website design company." Jackson had always let her flex her hours.

His dark eyebrows almost formed a straight line. "I don't want to mess up your job."

"You won't." She picked at the pleat in her pants. "I'd planned to cut my hours when Carleton House was up and running." Not quite this many hours. "It's no problem. Really. I'll just do this a little earlier. Really." Now she was babbling like her sister's fountain.

"You're sure?" A puzzled look crossed his face.

"Really." Had she really said *really* again? "When do you want me to start?"

"Can you give me a half day tomorrow? Say, in the afternoon."

"Perfect." She'd get to the office early, finish the website she was working on and then talk to Jackson. With an early delivery on her current project, she'd soften him up. Then she'd tell him about cutting her hours.

If she survived her probation, this might be the start of a new career and the end of an old one. Her hands shook, and she tucked them under her legs. "Why don't I meet you here at one thirty? I'll drive."

"THE DUNES' WEBSITE just went live." Dolley leaned against Jackson's doorway.

He glanced up from his array of screens. "When was it due?"

"Next week."

He smiled. "Wonderful."

"Hold that thought." She moved into his office and settled into a guest chair.

"What's up?"

She cleared her throat. "I need to cut my hours a little earlier than I thought."

"You and your sisters having problems at the B and B?"

"No." She took a deep breath. "I have an opportunity to apprentice with a world-class photographer."

"And that affects your work—how?"

She swallowed. "I need to cut back to ten to fifteen hours a week."

If Liam took her on, she'd end up working long hours for a while. Somehow she would juggle her job, working with Liam and the B and B. Her stomach churned. Who needed sleep?

"Ten hours?" Jackson was shaking his head. "You're my best designer. People ask for you."

"They do?" He'd never told her that.

"Yeah, they do. What's with the photography bug anyway?"

"I...I like taking pictures."

"Then you can take more shots like you did for—" he snapped his fingers "—that...that pub last fall."

"I want more than having my pictures on other people's websites." She was tired of fading into the background just like in her family.

Jackson shoved his fingers through his short curly hair. *Bad sign.* "I've given you a lot of leeway."

She nodded, a chill running down her back.

He aimed his dark brown gaze at her. "When you wanted to flex your hours, I didn't complain."

Her hands clasped together in her lap. "I hope you know I appreciate that."

He waved her statement away. "You have more latitude than any other designer."

Was there a *but* in his tone?

"I don't know if I can let you drop below thirty hours a week. I definitely can't grant any benefits at the levels you're talking about."

"What are you saying?" her voice squeaked.

"You'll have to become an independent contractor." He froze her with his stare. "No benefits. And you'd bid each project."

Bid. Not get a salary. Not even get an hourly wage. If she had problems with a site, she could end up working for pennies. She'd assumed she would be paid hourly from now on.

If Liam didn't take her on, she'd just burned a major bridge. She wouldn't have steady income. She wouldn't have money being set aside for her retirement. She'd have to go on the B and B's health plan. Sweat trickled down her back.

She let out a shaky breath. "When do you want me to start bidding?"

LIAM GLANCED AT his watch. The day was crawling. He had another half hour before he saw Dolley again.

She'd accepted his offer, even though he hadn't committed to mentoring her. He wasn't sure he wanted to take on the responsibility that came with an apprenticeship. Bonds formed if he worked that close with someone. Kieran, his only apprentice, had betrayed their friendship.

Would Dolley be as ambitious as Kieran? He didn't have to decide right away, but he couldn't keep her dangling, either.

He slipped the Savannah history book back on the shelf of the Fitzgerald House library. He hadn't found anything new in it. Then he checked the grandfather clock in the hall to make sure his watch was correct. 1:10 p.m.

This was odd. He'd never been bored on a project. And he wasn't bored. He just wanted to see Dolley and soak up some of her sparkling energy.

Guilt had him rolling his shoulders. He'd agreed to work with her because he was toying with the idea of using the Fitzgeralds as the core of his film. The documentary could highlight the difference between James's journey to America and the poor Irishmen who built canals and railroads and oversaw plantations.

James's letters might be the carrot to get what he wanted—an exposé on the difference between the Fitzgeralds' ancestors and the countrymen who fled Ireland during the potato famine. The age-old conflict of rich versus poor. Haves versus have-nots.

Hopefully, spending time with Dolley would determine the perfect approach to integrate their family into his film. He didn't want the sisters tossing him out on his arse.

The clock read 1:15 p.m. He headed to the dining room to grab one last cup of coffee.

"Hi, Liam." The newlyweds he'd met at last night's wine tasting were pouring mugs of coffee.

"Hey, Becca, Hale. Did you have a good time at the fort?"

"We did. Now Becca wants to shop." Hale rolled his eyes, but was grinning.

"Oh, stop." She added cream and sugar to a mug and handed it to her husband.

The couple shared an intimate smile that had Liam shifting on his feet.

"Thanks." Hale touched Becca's cheek as he took the mug.

What was it like to have someone know how you took your coffee?

"See you at the wine tasting tonight?" Hale asked, taking his bride's hand and heading out the door.

"I'll be there."

Maybe coming to a B and B that catered to newlyweds was not the place for him. Why have what was missing from his life shoved in his face every day?

Quick footsteps echoed out in the foyer. Dolley entered the room and filled it with light.

"Hi." She took a mug, poured coffee and took a deep drink. Her eyes closed. "I needed that."

"Tough morning?" he asked.

"Just issues I have to work through." She smiled, but it wasn't the joy-filled smile he'd seen before.

"Anything you want to talk about?" His knowledge on website design could fit in a teacup, but he could listen.

"No." She sipped her coffee and hummed.

He couldn't tear his gaze away from her face. He'd never watched someone who was that into the moment. Her peach-colored lips wrapped around the edge of the cup. Her pale throat moved up and down as she swallowed.

If he took her picture, would it translate onto film?

Her green eyes blinked open. "Where would you like to start?"

He shook his head. What she was talking on about?

One corner of her mouth turned up. "Where do you want to go this afternoon?"

"Oh." He finished his coffee, dredging up his plan. "I'd like to check out cemeteries."

"Good." She shifted her bag higher on her shoulder. "Which one?"

"The one with all the statues."

"Bonaventure. I love going out there."

"And the Catholic Cemetery." He set his empty mug on the tray set up for dirty dishes.

"Here's a little-known fact." She raised an eyebrow. "The colony of Georgia forbade the practice of Catholicism."

"Really?"

"It didn't change until after the Revolutionary War." Her smile was coming back.

"Fascinating." Having Dolley around was going to help focus his research.

"We can't do both cemeteries justice in an afternoon." She set her mug next to his. "You'll need to choose—statues or Irish?"

"Statues."

"Grab your cameras. I can't go there without taking tons of pictures."

He pointed to his camera bag. "Ready."

"Okay, then." Dolley led him to a small Volkswagen.

"I pushed the passenger seat back as far as it could go." Dolley glanced over at him. "You have a lot of leg."

He tucked himself into her car. "Next time we take my rental."

"What are you driving?"

"Audi sedan."

Her grin was full and happy. "Will you let me drive?"

He shook his head. "I don't think I can."

"Drat." She drove with one hand on the wheel and the other on the stick shift. "We'll circle a lot of the squares. This is Columbia Square. That's Wormsloe Fountain. It came from the Wormsloe plantation, which was down on the Isle of Hope. It was owned by—" she tapped her nose "—Noble Jones. In the mid-1700s."

She continued to give him background as they passed through the historic district.

"How do you remember it all?" he asked. "I wouldn't be this good a guide if you came to Ireland."

"Oh, I wish I could see Ireland." Her fingers drummed on the stick shift. "I do the historical write-ups for the B and B's blog."

"I'm impressed."

As Dolley drove, she spouted off information like she was a fountain. She intrigued him. Easy on the eyes, and she smiled—all the time.

He wanted what she had. She and her sisters worked together. Their family owned a mansion their ancestors had built. He wanted to be part of something that—deep. Have roots sunk into bedrock, so no one could yank them free.

What would his life have been like if his parents had survived their car accident? Would he have smiled more? Been happier?

He would never know. He'd been torn away from everything and everyone he loved and forced to live with Seamus.

"Liam?" Dolley jostled his elbow. "Where'd you go? You're frowning."

"Sorry." He forced himself back to the car. "I hope I didn't miss anything."

"Maybe I should tape my tour guide talks."

"Would you?"

She shook her head. "I was kidding."

"I'm serious." He turned toward her, their knees bumping. "Do you know much of how your ancestors got here?"

"Us? Our immigration was generations back. I don't even know how many." She shook her head.

"Well, I do. My four-time great grandfather James Fitzgerald left Ireland in 1830. Came with some money and invested it in warehouses and shipping. Eventually, he was a part owner in the bank."

"Facts just roll off your tongue. You're some kind of walking computer, right?"

Her jaw clenched. "Something like that."

They left the historic district. Squares no longer appeared every few blocks, but Spanish moss still swung from the massive oak trees, sheltering the streets. She pulled under a stone archway and into a small parking lot.

"We'll walk from here." She pulled her bag crossways across her chest. The strap molded her sweater to her breasts.

He shouldn't admire the effect. She was essentially an employee.

He unfolded his legs. Grabbing his bag, he waved. "Lead the way."

They walked between two weathered rock posts. Roads angled away from a building labeled Information. Avenues of oaks dressed with moss shaded the drives.

The cemetery stretched far as he could see. What a difference from the small graveyard set on a Kilkee hill where he'd buried his godfather.

He should find Michael FitzGerald's grave in Ireland and see if he could find James Fitzgerald's grave here in Savannah. He could use the two graves in the documentary.

Dolley led him deep into the cemetery.

Small stone borders, wrought iron fences or rounded tiles separated most of the family plots. There were headstones and markers. Some monuments had piles of stones on the memorials.

"Do they still bury people here?" His voice lowered in respect.

She nodded.

Their tree-lined road narrowed, changing to dirt, shells and sand. Birds serenaded them from the trees. In every direction, statues of angels, people and obelisks had blackened with soot or lichens. Some plots had signs that said *Do Not Maintain.* In those sections, headstones were tipped and weeds were knee-deep. Others were trimmed and looked like good spots for a garden party with their conveniently placed stone benches.

"When my great-grandmamma was young, they would picnic here. It was a social event."

"They'd eat lunch in a cemetery?" On second thought, it sounded morbid.

"Over on the banks of the river." Her smile crinkled her eyes. "We like eccentricities in Savannah."

At a crossroads, signs pointed to different graves. Dolley stopped in front of a black iron picket fence. "This is Little Gracie Watson, probably the most photographed statue of Bonaventure."

He knelt to peer through the pickets. The statue of the little girl was beautiful. Gracie sat wearing a dress that looked as if it would ruffle in the breeze. Her hair curled around her shoulders, and her eyes were magnetic.

"She was six when she died from pneumonia. A beloved fixture at Pulaski House Hotel, near Johnson Square." Dolley's smile was pensive. "The statue was made from a photograph."

"It's lovely." The little girl's face was sweet.

"There are rumors her ghost haunted the last people to live on the cemetery property. Of course that story could be made up for visitors." Her smile was just this side of cheeky. In a deep voice she said, "They say her statue stays warm at night, as though it's alive."

Liam had a healthy respect for the spirits. "So you've been here at night?"

"Kids in high school would sneak over the fences."

"Did you?"

"I was pretty studious, and we all needed to help Mamma with the B and B." She shook her head. "I wish we could get inside the fence, but with so many people visiting her grave, they needed to protect Gracie."

She pulled out her camera, squatting next to him. Her shutter clicked several times.

"Let me see," he said.

She handed him a good quality Nikon. Her photos were nicely composed, clear.

"What emotion were you trying to evoke?" he asked.

She winced. "I wasn't thinking about emotions."

He tapped her nose, and she blinked. "Always think about what you want a viewer to feel. Even when shooting pictures of inanimate objects."

"No one ever said that in any of my classes."

He raised his eyebrows. "Do you see that branch?"

She nodded.

He pulled out his camera, squatted, angling his body, and waited. The branch swung in the slight breeze and dropped into the frame. Click.

In the next picture he refocused on the bars, giving the photo an ominous feel.

"Depending on whether you're going for eerie or happy, I'd suggest using black and white or color." He handed Dolley his camera. "Especially if the branches behind Gracie flower."

She scrolled through the ones he'd taken. "Your pictures are—sad. Bleak."

"Good. I was thinking desolate. It would come across better in black and white."

Her auburn eyebrows snapped together, shadowing her lovely green eyes. "Yes."

"All great photographs evoke emotions, even when you're looking at a landscape or cityscape."

She looked up at him and sighed. "I have a lot to learn."

"You just have to put your soul into your photos."

"That's all." Her eyes twinkled as she handed back his camera. Their fingers brushed. He pulled away, but he'd felt—something.

"Come on." She replaced her lens cap and slung the camera over her shoulder. "There's more to see."

Dolley kept up a stream of interesting facts, talking about the cemetery and graves they passed and the statues created for the interred Savannahians.

When she talked about bodies that had been moved from another cemetery, he finally asked, "How do you retain all this information?"

"I...just remember things." She wouldn't look him in the eye.

He pulled her to a stop and made her face him, holding her hand so she didn't escape. "You have a photographic memory."

She stared at their dusty shoes. "Not quite."

"This is fantastic." He thought of all the notes he had to take to retain everything she stored easily in her brain. "Do you remember my credit card number?"

"No!" She tried to pull her hand away. "I make sure I don't."

"What do you remember of my particulars?" He was really curious.

She bit her lower lip, changing the color from pink to red. "Your phone number." She rattled it off. And then added his address and the date he'd first called. "It's kind of a pain."

"I wish I had your memory." He slung an arm around her shoulder. "Maybe I need to change your job title to fact checker."

"I don't think so." She nudged his arm away. "I'm hoping you'll teach me how to be a better photographer."

Either she didn't like to be touched or didn't like *him* touching her. He forced a professorial tone into his voice. "And your first lesson was emotions."

"You want emotions? Let me show you Corrine." She led him toward a river.

"Where are we?" he asked.

"The Wilmington River. This is where my great-grandmamma would picnic."

She stopped in front of a large plot. *Lawton.* The statue was a beautiful woman sitting in front of her headstone. "Corrine was in love with a man who was not of her class. Her family insisted she marry a man she did not love."

He checked the date of her death, 1877. There would have been class issues at that time.

"The day of her wedding she rode to the Savannah River and drowned herself." She raised a graceful hand, pointing to the statue of Jesus at the back of the plot. "Her family was so upset, they buried her with her back to Jesus."

"How sad."

She grinned. "It's a ghost teller's story. Corrine wasn't engaged. Her parents weren't forcing her to marry. Based on letters and her obituary, she was ill, possibly yellow fever since Savannah had an epidemic that started in 1876 and continued into 1877. The statue was carved in Sicily."

She bumped her shoulder into his chest. "I told you the fake story because I want you to be aware that the tales told in our fine city are not always the truth."

Dolley pulled the lens cap off her camera. "She's my favorite statue."

Liam moved next to her, trying to see what she was framing. In the distance, faint streams of lavender and pink threaded through the clouds. He pulled his camera up to his eye. Would the sunset be too far away?

Dolley waited. And waited. Finally, the sky flooded with color. Her camera clicked away. It was a joy to watch her concentration.

He knelt behind her, wanting to see what she'd done.

Pulling the camera away from her eye, she replayed her photos, tipping it so he could look over her shoulder.

The statue was swathed by the soft sunset as if Corrine were an angel caught in the clouds.

"Peace," he whispered. "I feel it."

"Yes." She stared into his eyes. "That's what I wanted."

Dolley was talented *and* took direction.

But Kieran had been talented, too. Kieran's problem had been insatiable ambition.

A fiery curl blew across Dolley's eyes. He brushed it away, but his fingers lingered, fingering the silky texture.

Her green eyes grew as big as saucers.

A cart drove up next to them. "Cemetery's closing, folks."

He yanked his hand away as she jumped up.

"I lost track of the time." Dolley stuffed her camera in her bag, her actions clumsy with haste. "I'm sorry. It's after five? Really?"

"Well past," the guard said. "Hop in."

Shoving her hair off her face, she took the passenger seat, leaving him the backseat. She stared straight ahead.

Fingering Dolley's silky hair had been feckin' stupid.

"I'll be your mentor," he blurted out. He wanted to spend more time with her.

She turned, a frown plowing a furrow in her forehead. "You will?"

He nodded.

A grin ignited her face. "Thank you."

His motives for helping Dolley mixed with a

budding awareness of her as an interesting, exciting woman.

Of course, they might be working together for months.

He would button up this…attraction and concentrate on improving her skills. For now.

CHAPTER FOUR

It is more important to click with people than
to click the shutter.

Alfred Eisenstaedt

DOLLEY HANDED THE clean porcelain wall sconce to
Bess. "This one has a chip."

Bess turned the sconce, found the chip and
dabbed enamel on the spot. "Not anymore."

"I hate cleaning lights." Dolley picked up a rusty
sconce and plopped it on the worktable she and Bess
had set up in the carriage house.

This mindless work wasn't enough to keep her
from reliving the moment two days ago when Liam
had brushed back her hair at Bonaventure. His fingers had rubbed the strands like they were...precious.
Was the pull she'd felt between them the reason he'd
agreed to mentor her?

She'd almost reached out and touched *his* hair.
Thank goodness the cemetery guard had arrived.

There was too much at stake. She was sticking
to her dating hiatus. She'd given up her day job to
work with Liam. Just spending an afternoon together had improved her pictures. He could take
it away as easily as he'd agreed to work with her.
Nothing was going to screw up her apprenticeship.

Dolley shot a glance at Bess. She needed to break

the news to her sisters. Not only was she working for Liam, Jackson had changed her employment status. She blew out a big breath. Already this morning, she'd bid on a project for one of her old clients. That sucked.

With a toothbrush, she loosened the dirt around the base and metalwork. "How many more do we have to clean?"

Bess glanced at the boxes. "I don't want to depress you."

"Great." Dolley dipped her cloth in the soapy water and rubbed gently on the bronze fixture. "Should we take off the patina?"

They both stared at the sconce.

"Mamma had us strip all the Fitzgerald House's lamps." Bess chewed on her thumbnail.

Dolley touched her hand. "Let's find out if we have more metal or porcelain."

They spread everything on the floor, organizing the lamps by type.

Crossing her arms, Dolley said, "Holy cow, that's a lot of work."

"Abby's just finishing up breakfast. She'll be here soon." Bess walked around the lamps and sconces laid out on the canvas. "I would like to have everything bright and shiny."

Dolley sighed. "Okay, we remove the patina just like Fitzgerald House."

"How come you're not working today?" Bess settled back into her folding chair.

"I've cut back my hours." She opened the bronze cleaner, the smell sharp and unpleasant. Pouring a small amount on a clean cloth, she gently rubbed the metal.

Bess frowned. "I thought you planned to wait until January."

Dolley's finger tapped the edge of the table. "I'm helping out Liam. Delaney," she added in a rush. Just saying his name had her remembering the stroke of his fingers in her hair.

"Delaney?" Bess's reddish-blond eyebrows popped up. "Is he the long-term guest? The Irishman?"

"Yup."

"How are you helping him out?"

She focused on bringing the lamp back to its original gleam. "Research. And he agreed to take me on as an apprentice." The words spilled out in a stream.

"Wait." Bess laid her hand on Dolley's arm. "Apprentice?"

Abby walked in. "You're taking on an apprentice, Bess?"

Dolley rolled her eyes. Of course an apprenticeship wouldn't be about her, right? She was void of creativity.

"It's Dolley," Bess explained.

Abby pulled out a chair next to Dolley. "I didn't know they used apprentices in website design. Is that a new thing?"

"It's not for website design." Dolley huffed out

a breath. "Liam Delaney is mentoring me in photography."

Both sisters' heads twisted, and they stared at her. Their eyes, variations of green and hazel, were wide with surprise.

Their shock hurt.

Abby placed a hand on her back. "You want to be his apprentice?"

"I want to improve my photography," she said.

Bess rubbed Dolley's arm. "Is this just for the website?"

Her sisters, the two people she was closest to in the world, didn't know she wanted to be a photographer. She swallowed. "I want to be…better." *I want to make it my career.*

"Then it's good Liam is here." Abby bumped her with her shoulder. "And he's not bad on the eyes. Does he ever smile?"

Dolley frowned. "Not often. Once? That I caught." And she'd never heard him laugh.

Did that make him romantically tragic, or just tragic?

She took a deep breath. "And I added myself to the B and B's health plan."

Abby grabbed a sconce. "Why?"

Dolley shrugged. "Jackson made me an independent contractor."

"Oh." Abby's eyebrow went up. Censure filled that single syllable.

"Cheryl raves about Liam's accent." Bess winked.

Dolley pressed her chest. "I could listen to him for hours."

"Oh. Ooooh." Bess drew out the last word, pain twisting her face. "Be careful."

"It's not like that." Dolley hated the sorrow in her sister's eyes. Daniel Forester had done that. He and Bess had dated, but Daniel had pulled the plug and broken Bess's heart.

"This is purely professional," Dolley added. "Besides, I'm on a dating hiatus."

She should tell her sisters she wanted a new career. Dolley bit her lip. A career change that involved travel would affect the B and B and her family.

Staying in Savannah wasn't in her future, but she wasn't ready to break that news to her sisters. "Liam's helping me improve my pictures."

"If you're his apprentice, why aren't you with him today?" Abby asked.

"It's part-time. He's in Statesboro. Georgia Southern has an Irish Studies program, and he's interviewing the department head."

"I do have homework." She pushed away from the desk and dug out her camera. Her assignment was to take pictures of people, inanimate objects and scenery. "I feel like I'm back in school."

"You always loved school," Abby said.

"I can also use the shots for the B and B's blog." Standing on the opposite side of the table, she said, "Work, slaves."

Her sisters laughed.

Dolley snapped a series, hoping to capture camaraderie and joy. Then she arranged the sconce she'd polished behind all the dirty lamps. Hope was what she wanted to capture, shining through the tarnished wasteland.

"Our last long-term guest was pretty fantastic." Abby flashed her ring. "Liam is here through next year. I wonder what will develop."

"And if it will be in black and white or Technicolor," Bess said.

"I *shutter* to think," Abby replied.

"Good one!" Bess fist-bumped Abby.

"You two should take this act on the road." Dolley rolled her eyes, but she smiled as she cleaned tarnish. She'd told her sisters about the apprenticeship. Her loss of income could wait until she had a plan to replace the income or reduce her expenses.

THE SUN WAS setting as Liam parked at the B and B. He pulled his equipment out of the car, tugging on his overcoat. He'd made it back in time to catch the wine tasting. Then he planned to head to his room and review the tapes.

"Hi." Dolley came out of a carriage house. "How was the interview?"

Her smile warmed him more than his jacket.

"The professor was great." Professor Aiden had highlighted how different the FitzGerald immigration to America was compared to others. James

had come with money. The men who had built canals and railroads had come with little more than
the clothes on their backs. His breath caught in his
chest. This was the core of his story. The difference
between Dolley's family and the poor immigrants
Aiden had described.

Dolley hopped up on an iron table, her legs
swinging. "Good info?"

"Fantastic stuff, but the poor man was nervous."

Her eyes glittered like polished emeralds as if she
had joy bubbling inside her. Something fluttered
in his chest. What would that feel like? He knew
peace when a photo turned out exactly the way he'd
planned, but joy? His had died with his parents.

"So, did you have techniques to help him?" she
asked.

"Some." She smelled of—silver polish? "What
have *you* been up to?"

"Cleaning old lamps." She rolled her eyes. "My
least favorite job of a restoration."

"Ahh." He sniffed. "You smell of metal cleaner."

"It's gross." Even in the dimming light, he could
see her blush. "I'm heading home to scrub off the
stench."

An image of her in the shower, soap lather
streaming down her naked body, had him taking
in a sharp breath.

"The smell isn't so bad," he choked out. "Actually
reminds me of helping clean my mum's tea trolley."

"That's a nice memory." She hopped off the table. "Do you have plans tonight?"

"Trying to catch some of your sister's offerings, and then I'll review today's film."

"You need to see Savannah." She touched his shoulder, the heat seeping through his coat. "I'm meeting friends at a pub. Do you want to tag along?"

He should say *no*. But sitting in his empty room sounded lonely.

"It's just friends getting together." When she grinned, her curls danced. "I'll tell them they can't mob you."

"Oh, well—" He should work.

"It'll be fun."

Fun? He couldn't remember the last time his name and *fun* were mentioned together. "What time?"

THE WALL OF noise enveloped Dolley as she and Liam entered O'Gara's pub. The yeasty scent of beer and fried food hit her along with the heat. Lights twinkled above the bar, and glittering snowflakes hung at intervals from the ceiling.

"Fantastic." She bounced onto her toes. "I didn't think it would be this busy."

Liam's eyes had glazed over, his face frozen in a resigned grimace.

"Smile," she insisted.

He didn't.

Tonight she wanted to see him smile at least five times. A happier man would be a better teacher.

"Do you want people to know what you're doing in Savannah?" She leaned close so he could hear her. Close enough to catch his crazy scent that made her insides melt.

"Yes, that's all right." He rubbed his chin, and his seven o'clock shadow rasped under his hand. "Is the pub always so loud?"

"It's a holiday." She tugged his arm. "This way to the fun."

He followed, dragging behind her a little. What was up with that?

"Dolley!" Zach picked her up by the waist and spun her in a circle.

She pounded his shoulders. "Put me down."

He dropped her to her feet and gave her a smacking kiss. "Merry Christmas."

She patted his cheek. They'd dated years ago when Zach had needed help on a paper, but Zach had been right. They were better as friends. "Merry Christmas to you."

Liam hung behind, a frown pushing his sharp black eyebrows together. She towed him to a table filled with people. *The more the merrier, right?*

"Gang, this is Liam. He's staying at Fitzgerald House through March." She introduced the people she knew; others filled in their names. "He's making a documentary."

If that didn't get people talking to him, she didn't know what would.

Chairs were dragged to the table. Liam slipped along the wall, sitting next to a pretty blonde. He wasn't frowning, but he wasn't smiling, either.

Dolley took a spot closer to the middle of the table. She could watch his face but couldn't hear what he and the blonde were saying. Her chest squeezed a little, but she pushed it away. He was her teacher, and she was on a hiatus.

"How are things?" she asked Zach.

"Pretty damn good." He wrapped an arm around the brunette sitting next to him. "Meet Erica."

Erica smiled. "Hi, Dolley."

After chatting with Erica for a while, she leaned in to Zach. "She's perfect for you."

"I know." He grinned and pressed a kiss to his girlfriend's cheek.

Zach's grin reminded her of tonight's objective. Get Liam to smile.

She looked down the table, and Liam was staring—at Zach and Erica.

When the server came over, she ordered a martini called Santa's Jollies. Might as well get in the Christmas mood.

Her drink arrived, and she held it up, giving Liam a silent toast. He saluted her with his beer. And smiled. Number one. She wracked it up on her mental spreadsheet.

The blonde leaned in and pointed at his beer. Liam nodded as he responded to her.

"Zach," she asked. "Who's the girl at the end of the table?"

He looked over. "Shana?"

"Right."

"You should worry about your friend." Zach leaned closer. "She just jettisoned her last boyfriend and is looking for a new conquest."

Shana pointed to the dance floor, tugging on Liam's arm.

Dolley's throat constricted. Would he dance?

He shook his head, and the blonde pouted.

Dolley was stupidly relieved.

Liam tipped his chair back, resting against the wall. Mamma would scold him for balancing on two legs, but it gave her an opportunity to admire his lean form. The man made black jeans look like a work of art. With his black hair and bright blue eyes, he was striking.

She sighed. Not for her. But he sure was easy on the eyes. She stared for a minute, frowning. He wasn't—engaged. He talked to people next to him, but he didn't lean in like he was part of the conversation. It was like he was a spectator.

The band changed to playing fifties music, happy songs. The walking bass had her toes tapping.

A friend she hadn't seen in a couple of years touched her shoulder. "Dolley, how are you?"

"Brad?" She gave him a hug. "I'm great. And you?"

They yelled over the sound, trying to catch up. Finally Brad rolled his eyes. "It's impossible to talk. Let's dance."

"Sure."

She checked on Liam. He was frowning again. She tried to give him head signals, suggesting he ask someone to dance, but he apparently couldn't read Savannah sign language.

Maybe she'd have to ask him to dance. A little jolt went through her. What would his arms feel like holding her?

Nope. Being held by Liam wasn't her objective. She wanted to ease the solemn look off his face and have him participate in the evening. Was that too much to ask when she threw strangers together? He needed to smile four more times. Maybe if he asked Shana to dance, she could accomplish that.

And maybe he would go home with Shana.

She stumbled.

Brad tugged her into the familiar steps of the Lindy. She let the music and Brad spin her into a happy place.

She and Brad had learned how to Lindy from his parents. They'd dated once, but as usual, they'd decided they were better off as friends. Her dating history was pathetic.

Brad pushed her out so their arms extended, then

he tugged and she spun back to him. They rocked back and forth to "Rock Around the Clock."

They settled into the setup of their signature move. Brad grabbed her by the waist, and she swung her legs from one of his hips to the other.

"Do the flip?" he mouthed.

She shook her head. "No!"

They were laughing as the music ended, and he spun her into his arms once more.

"That was great," Brad gasped.

Dolley twirled around. "I loved it."

"Thanks." He walked her back to the table. "Nothing like reliving our youth, but I'll be stiff tomorrow."

They talked for a few more minutes, then the people at Brad's table waved him back.

"You looked good out there," Zach said.

"You should dance with your girl."

"I'm holding out for a slow song." The band finished a song to applause and then broke into a ballad. Zach grabbed his date's hand. "That's my cue."

Dolley grinned as they moved to the dance floor. They looked good together. She took a swig of her drink. Damn. It was gone. She caught the server's eye, and the woman gave her a nod.

"I'm going to have to call you twinkle toes." Liam's deep voice above her head rumbled through her core. He sank into the chair next to her, smiling. There was number two. Only three more to go.

"Abby has the twinkle toes in the family." Dolley bopped her head to the music. "She used to dance."

"You could have fooled me." He set his half-drunk beer next to her empty glass. "Can I get you another?"

"I just gave the server the high sign." She twirled the empty martini glass, not looking at him. "You should ask Shana to dance."

"What? No." He was shaking his head when she looked up.

"You should." She bumped his shoulder. "Have a little fun."

One elegant black eyebrow arched over his amazing blue eyes. "I'm here to work."

"You can't work 24/7."

He blinked, then frowned.

"You work every waking hour, don't you?" she asked, appalled.

"I…" he rubbed his head. "Sometimes it's easier. I'm more comfortable working."

"That has to change." She spun in the chair, her knees touching his thigh. "Since you're teaching me about photography, I'm going to teach you how to lighten up. You're now *my* apprentice in the world of having fun."

"What?"

"I'll teach you how to have fun." She nodded. "You might even get assignments."

"You wouldn't."

"Oh, yes, I would." She grinned.

"You're having fun." He waved a hand around the room. "How do you know all these people?"

Who had she talked to? "Brad and I went to high school together."

"To dance the way you did, you must have dated." His eyes held hers.

"One date." She picked up her glass, but it was still empty. "We discovered we're better as friends."

"And this man?" He pointed to the chair he was sitting in.

"We went to college together. That lasted two dates." Two dates. One paper. And then he'd avoided her for almost a year.

"What's wrong with men in this country?"

She shrugged. It wasn't the men. It was her.

She didn't let Liam ask any more questions. Just grabbed his hand, tugged him out of the chair and onto the dance floor. "First homework…dancing."

"I'm not very good," he warned, his breath warming her neck as he made himself heard above the noise. "I can't do what you were doing with that other man."

"Doesn't matter." The band now played "Blue Suede Shoes." "Just let your body feel the music."

He moved his shoulders and wiggled his lean hips.

She nodded and rocked away.

And he smiled. Number three. Only two to go.

He moved closer. She could teach him some steps, but the goal was to get him to ask other women to dance, help him break out of his shell. He had nice rhythm and great hip action. Unwanted heat zipped through her body.

The music changed to a ballad. She turned to leave.

This time, Liam caught her hand and reeled her in. "Not so fast."

His arms settled on her lower back. Hers slid up and rested on his shoulders. *Too close.* But she didn't ease away. It was his darn cologne. It had her getting closer, sniffing his neck.

"What are you doing?" he asked.

"You smell so good."

He chuckled. She hated the heat filling her face.

He looked down at her. And smiled. Number four.

She grinned up at him. "Let's talk about your homework."

LIAM ALLOWED HIMSELF one slow dance with Dolley. It was like holding lightning in his arms.

He finished off his pint and watched as she flitted around the pub. She must have known half the people in the room. And each encounter left her more animated. Even if he were in Galway, he wouldn't know as many people as she'd talked to this night. And he wouldn't want to talk to all of them in one evening.

He and Dolley were opposites. He thrived in solitude, she flourished in crowds. Just one more reason to keep his hands off his apprentice.

And anyway, he should be in his room taking notes on the professor's interview. Alone.

He liked being alone. He liked listening to people talk. But sometimes he was tired of always feeling like he was looking through the window at other people's happiness.

Her offer to let him be *her* apprentice in learning how to have fun could be viewed as a gift. She might teach him something after all. But she'd told him to mingle. He wasn't a mingler.

He would never have what she had. Never know the wonder of having a family to hold him up, to help him through the pains and joys of life. He was better off staying on his own. No one could disappoint him. No one could ignore him.

He checked his watch. Time to head back to the B and B.

Dolley hurried over, her curls bouncing as she stopped next to his chair. "You're doing it again."

"Doing what?"

"Being an island." She leaned closer. "You need to do your homework."

"I mingled." For a while.

"You let other people talk." She shook her head. "You listened."

"Being a good listener is part of my profession." He stood. "I'm heading back to Fitzgerald House."

Her smile crumpled. "Let me say a few good-byes."

"Stay. You're having fun."

"And you're not." She sighed. "I'll be right back."

He nodded and waved at the people he'd spent the night listening to. Dolley was right on that point.

"Hope to see you again, Liam," Shana called out.

"Me, too," he lied.

Tugging on his jacket, he headed outside. The cool air scented by the nearby river was lovely. He inhaled, letting his body relax.

The cobblestone street reflected the streetlights and neon spilling from the bars and buildings. A mist softly diffused the light. His fingers flexed, wishing he'd brought a camera. He was afraid of the emotion he'd want to evoke. Solitude? Isolation?

Laughter echoed from a nearby street.

The door jingled, and Dolley walked out, looking around. She spotted him, and her frown disappeared. "There you are."

He nodded.

"Did you at least have fun?" She wrapped her multicolored scarf around her neck. The heels of her boots clacked on the sidewalk as she approached.

"Watching you was fun."

She shook her head. "That's not the same as *you* having fun."

"It worked for me." They turned toward the B and B.

She wobbled on the uneven pavement, and he cupped her elbow.

"Thanks."

"My pleasure." He smiled.

"Ahh, number five. Goal accomplished."

He stopped. "Number five?"

"I should not have said that. Too many drinks." She slapped a hand on her mouth.

"Now I'm curious." He pulled her hand away from her mouth. He shouldn't touch her, but he couldn't stop himself.

"You smiled five times tonight." Her eyebrows popped up. "That I caught. I'm sure you smiled more than that."

"You counted my smiles?"

"You frown a lot." She winced. "I wanted to help you smile."

"No wonder they've been aching." He rubbed his cheeks. "Five times in a night. Must be a new record."

"Sorry." She bumped against him as they started walking again. "I shouldn't have said anything."

"No." What an odd creature she was. And she was holding a mirror up to his moods. He'd only smiled five times. What did that say about him?

She looked sideways, mischief creasing her face. "Smiling is good for a person. Healthy. You'll live longer."

"Then you'll live well into your hundreds."

"Oh. That's nice."

He wasn't sure he'd meant it as a compliment. "How can one person have so much to smile about?"

Her shoulders straightened. "You can go through life moaning about the cards you've been dealt, or you can make lemonade with the lemons that have been piled on you."

He shook his head. "Mixed metaphors explain why you're always so happy?"

She crossed her arms around her waist. "Maybe."

"I wasn't making fun of you." He touched her shoulder, and she faced him. "I envy you."

They were standing too close, but he didn't want to step away. Her energy was like a magnet. He caught that warm scent that was all Dolley. His hand cupped her face. Despite them being polar opposites, he wanted to press his lips to that pink, sweet mouth.

Dolley swayed, her eyes half-closed. Then her eyes jerked open. She stumbled back. "No."

"Sorry." He took a step back, his hands in the air. "I thought…" She'd invited him to meet her chums, not to kiss her.

"No. No problem." Her voice was clipped.

He swallowed back another apology.

"This is where I leave you," Dolley said, her tone brisk. "Can you find the B and B from here?"

"Aye." The answer croaked out.

"What time shall we get together tomorrow?"

"Let's say one." He needed time to settle, time to tuck away any attraction he mistakenly thought they were both feeling. Pity.

CHAPTER FIVE

If I could tell the story in words, I wouldn't need to lug around a camera.

Lewis Wickes Hine

"LET ME HELP with that." Liam moved into the library and picked up a chafing dish from the trolley, setting it on the base.

"Thanks." Bess placed another dish on an empty holder and slipped a platter of smoked salmon and crackers on the large table. "The way you keep helping out, we might have to put you on the payroll."

"So long as I don't have to clean the loos." He placed another big server on a waiting base. "Do you want me to light the flames?"

"I'll get that." Bess glanced at the line forming behind him. "Yikes. Would you mind opening wine?"

"No problem." He liked being useful. Liked feeling as though he was part of the flow of Fitzgerald House. Liked pretending he *was* a Fitzgerald.

"What's tonight's theme?" He hadn't checked the cards Abby always prepared.

"The United Kingdoms."

Liam caught the scent of mulled wine from the tureen on the wine table. Then he read the label on the bottle. "I didn't know they had enough wineries to ship overseas."

"Abby's distributor loves to find wines for her."

Bess whisked off the covers and displayed sausage rolls, stuffed mushrooms and shepherd's pie.

"This is a feast." He pulled the cork on a sparkling wine from Cornwall. Then one of a Sangiovese from Ireland. "This seems—bigger than normal."

"It's the last meal before our break." Bess opened more bottles.

"I forgot everyone will be leaving." As much as he liked his solitude, he would miss the camaraderie of his mornings and evenings with the Fitzgerald House guests, listening to their stories.

"You'll have the place to yourself tomorrow." Bess poured a few glasses of sparkling wine and took one for herself. "This is pretty good."

"I remember my mum making mulled wine for Da." Liam took a mug and filled it, inhaling the spicy scent, and sipped. "This is lovely."

"So why aren't you celebrating the holidays with them?" Bess asked.

His back stiffened. "They died when I was little."

"I'm sorry." She rubbed her hand on his shoulder. "You must miss them."

"I do." He nodded, his eyes welling up a little. "I ended up with my godfather, who knew nothing about kids."

"That must have been hard."

He didn't want to talk about his childhood. "Abby says your mum is coming in today."

"She's here." Bess's eyes glowed. "She'll be down for the tasting soon."

"I can't wait to meet her." The sisters spoke with such affection about their mum. He'd decided the letters would go to the head of the Fitzgerald family.

"Can you keep your eye on things?" Bess asked. "I'll take the trolley back to the kitchen. Then I have to check on a problem in my greenhouse."

"Of course."

He gathered some goodies and stood next to a couple celebrating their fortieth anniversary. "How was your day?"

"We went to the cemetery like you suggested," said the wife.

"Our guide was great," the man said.

Probably not as good as Dolley. The couple talked about the statuary and family plots.

And he thought about Dolley. They worked together every other day, very businesslike on both sides. But sometimes he swore sparks arced between their bodies. A magnetism that wanted satisfaction.

He didn't feel the same thing from Bess. She was—fragile. For some reason, he wanted to protect her from harm.

Dolley was the Fitzgerald who made him sit up and take notice.

"Did the guide take you to Gracie's statue?" he asked when there was a lull in the conversation.

The wife shivered. "Our guide made me believe her ghost actually played with children."

The flame under a chafing dish sputtered out.

"Let me just check that," Liam said. He replaced the Sterno container and relit the flame.

Straightening, he nodded to the woman standing across the buffet from him. Her hair was sunset bright like her daughters, and her eyes were a paler green. "You must be Mrs. Fitzgerald."

"Mrs. Robbins." She raised her eyebrows. "You're our Irishman?"

"Aye." He held out his hand. "Liam Delaney."

"Mamie Fitzgerald Robbins." Her hand was soft but strong. Like Dolley's.

He moved away from the back of the buffet. "I've looked forward to meeting you."

"Let me taste Abby's food, and we can get to know each other."

"I'll get you something to drink. What do you fancy?" he asked.

She tapped her lip. "The mulled wine. Abby adds something to it that she won't share with her own mother."

He laughed, poured her a mug and topped his off. Shifting two armchairs so they had some privacy, he took a seat and waited.

Mamie glided to the chair he'd set up. She and Abby moved the same way.

He stood as she seated herself, feeling oddly formal.

"Oh, sit." Mamie waved him down. "Tell me about your documentary."

"Let me first say, you are as lovely as your daughters."

Her smile brightened. "Thank you."

He took in a deep breath. "My godfather was a descendant of Michael Fitzgerald, your ancestor James's brother."

Mamie tipped her head. "That's an interesting coincidence."

"No coincidence. After Seamus, my godfather, died, his solicitor showed me the family-tree information Seamus had been working on."

Mamie leaned forward. "Are there cousins still living in Ireland?"

He shook his head. "Not that Seamus found."

"How did you come to live with…?"

"Seamus FitzGerald." He swallowed. "My parents had named him and his wife godparents. When my parents died in a car accident, Seamus's wife was already dead. Seamus took me in."

Mamie touched his knee. "How old were you?"

"Eight." He spit the word out like it was bitter.

"I'm sorry." She patted his arm. "My girls were young when they lost their father."

He'd never thought about Dolley losing her father. She seemed so grounded in her family. "You must have done a wonderful job raising your daughters. I can't see any ill effects from you being their only parent."

"You say the sweetest things." Her drawl drew out the vowels as if they were separate syllables.

He wanted to tape her with her daughters. Wanted that soft, strong voice recorded.

"Tell me how you go from looking at a family tree to spending months in Savannah?" she asked.

"Seamus's research intrigued me. I was looking for a new project. The more I dug, the more I thought there was a story in all the Irish in Savannah." He talked more about the project, how it would include a book of his photographs.

She asked questions, and he relaxed into his answers. "Give me a minute. I promised Bess I would keep an eye out, and it looks like I should open more wine."

She nodded like she was a queen.

And she was. Queen of her family. The B and B literature all described how she'd turned the house into a B and B.

"You fit in nicely." Mamie rose. "I think I'll check in with the other guests. Do you have dinner plans?"

"Oh." Grabbing a plate of whatever remained on the buffet and taking it to his room to work. "Not really."

"Abby's making Beef Wellington. Since you're practically family in a roundabout southern way, you'll join us." She gave a sharp nod.

Before he could disagree, she'd gone to a group of guests standing near the fire.

He grinned so large, Dolley would need to count it as two smiles.

What a grand expression—*practically family.*

DOLLEY PUSHED THROUGH the courtyard door into the kitchen. "Hey, Abby, where's Mamma?"

Abby pointed to the sitting area.

Mamma was already moving toward her. "Right here, dear."

Dolley threw herself into her mother's embrace, Mamma's perfume filling her nose. "I'm so glad you're back."

"I missed you, too." Mamma took her face in her hands and kissed her. "I've caught up with Abby and Bess. Tell me what you've been up to."

"Busy. Very busy." Had her sisters mentioned she worked with Liam? After talking about the blog and the B and B, she said, "I cut back my hours with Jackson."

"Did I hear you're working with Liam?" Mamma asked.

"I've been helping him with his research and touring Savannah with him. Between that and Carleton House coming online, I'm almost staying out of trouble."

"He's a nice young man." Mamma took a sip of her wine.

Nice was not the adjective Dolley would use. Hot. Sexy. Tantalizing, maybe. Not that she would suggest those to Mamma.

It was warm near the fire. She wished she had a glass of something to cool her down. "Do you want me to top that off?" she asked, pointing to Mamma's flute.

"I'm good."

"I'll be right back." She peeked over Abby's shoulder. "Something smells great in here."

"Beef Wellington."

"Awesome. Want anything to drink from the tasting?"

"I'll try the Brut. Bring back a bottle, would you?"

Dolley nodded. She grabbed two flutes and an unopened bottle, barely stopping. Then she kept a smile on her face for the guests as she headed back to the kitchen.

Liam came down the hallway.

She was always surprised to find guests in the area she thought of as *family territory.*

"Need help?" he asked.

"I've got it." She backed into the swinging door, but Liam pushed it open. She ducked under his arm, catching that delicious scent of his. *Num.* "Thanks."

And Liam followed her in.

She frowned. "Umm—"

"—There you are, Liam," Mamma interrupted. "Dolley, make sure he has something to drink."

"It smells wonderful in here." Liam moved to the sitting area like he belonged.

Dolley jerked to a stop, her mouth dropping open.

Abby laughed at her.

Setting down the bottle and glasses, Dolley asked, "Liam, what would you like?"

"Whatever the rest of you are having." He smiled at her and held up two fingers.

Two? What was that about?

She went to the butler's pantry and brought back another flute. Then she pulled the cork, watching Liam and her mother talk.

"What's going on?" she whispered to Abby.

"Mamma invited him to dinner."

"With us?"

Abby nodded.

Dolley was trying to maintain a professional relationship with Liam, and Mamma was inviting him to a family dinner? She huffed out a sigh. Enjoying Abby's great food and wine together wasn't exactly businesslike.

"What?" Abby asked.

"Thinking about work," she lied.

"Maybe you need to cut back." Abby rubbed Dolley's neck. "You're holding down three jobs."

"I'll survive." Dolley leaned into her sister. "Luckily, the B and B's holiday break starts tomorrow."

"That just means you'll work on Carleton House setup." Abby frowned. "Let me know if you need help with anything."

"Thanks." She couldn't add to Abby's burdens. Her sister had a wedding to plan. "What can I help with here?"

"After you bring Liam his glass, set the table."

Shoot. She'd forgotten about Liam's drink. Had he really wanted the Brut? Usually he had Jameson, neat. Not that she paid attention to what he drank during wine tastings.

She poured three glasses and took one to the sitting area along with the bottle.

"Thank you." He took the glass, brushing her fingers and sending unwanted shivers up her arm.

Bess walked in from the courtyard. "Hey, Liam, thanks for helping out tonight."

Helping out?

Liam shook his head. "I just opened bottles and kept things flowing."

"But I appreciate it. There was a problem with the greenhouse heating. I wanted to make sure it was fixed before this cold snap swings in tonight."

"No problem." Liam shook his head. "I got dinner out of it."

Mamma held up her glass, and Dolley topped it off.

"You're at dinner because you're a shirttail relative," Mamma said.

Dolley almost dropped the bottle. "We're related?"

"No." Liam held up his hands. "My godfather was a FitzGerald."

"The godfather who brought you up?" Bess asked.

Liam nodded.

How did everyone know this stuff but her?

Apparently Liam *was* keeping things professional. He'd probably had second thoughts after their near kiss. Normally guys waited until *after* they'd kissed her to have second thoughts.

Abby turned. "Once the table is set, we can eat."

Dolley headed to the pantry to grab dishes.

Liam followed her. "I can help."

"Sounds like you're helping everyone." She gathered plates and handed them to him, and then picked out the silverware. "Why didn't you tell me you were brought up by a FitzGerald?"

"It was not a happy time in my life." He didn't add any more.

She wanted to ask questions, but that would be merging their personal lives with the business. She wouldn't be the one muddying the waters.

They set the table. Bess and Abby brought the food, and somehow she ended up sitting across from Liam. She angled sideways so she wasn't staring into his eyes every time she looked up.

"Liam, thank you for the Irish whiskey cookie recipe," Abby said, passing the meat. "They got rave reviews at afternoon tea."

"I might have snatched a few," Liam said. "They were as good as I remembered."

"A recipe you didn't have?" Dolley asked, astounded.

"We were talking the other morning, and Abby had never heard of the cookie." He smiled. "My mum made them at Christmas."

Then he held up three fingers where only she could see. What was he doing?

She shook her head.

He pointed to his face, smiled and then held up four fingers.

He was counting his smiles. She swallowed.

That had been such foolishness at the pub. And he'd remembered.

"There's a few cookies left, but I'm saving them for Christmas." Abby shook her finger at him. "I heard you snatched more than a few this afternoon."

It was like Dolley was an outsider with her own family.

"You'll be celebrating Christmas with us, Liam," Mamma said. "And there won't be any arguments."

The biggest smile she'd ever witnessed rolled across Liam's face.

Dolley pressed her hand to her stomach. She'd focused on making sure her apprenticeship worked and forgotten Liam was alone for the holiday. Shame heated her face.

"I would be honored to join you." He swallowed. "You're so kind."

"As I said earlier, you're almost family." Mamma held up her glass. *"Sláinte."*

They dug into Abby's fantastic dinner.

And Dolley plotted. Liam had a childhood he wouldn't talk about, he was alone during a holiday when families should be together and Mamma had apparently adopted him.

Maybe she should get on the bandwagon and make this a Christmas for Liam to remember.

She smiled.

Liam looked over at her and held up one finger.

She shook her head. He was counting her smiles, too.

CHAPTER SIX

I hate cameras. They are so much more sure
than I am about everything.

John Steinbeck

DOLLEY JUGGLED THE presents in her arms and
headed down the back stairs. Without guests,
Fitzgerald House was eerily quiet.

A step creaked behind her. Her arms tightened
around the gifts, and paper crinkled.

"Father Christmas is female and a redhead." Liam's
musical voice filled the stairway, his accent as seductive as his cologne. "Who knew?"

All she'd wanted to do was run down and make
Christmas morning tea for her sisters. Instead,
Liam caught her in her pj's and robe. She took a
deep breath before turning. "I'm not applying for
Santa's job."

"It might be fun. Happy Christmas."

"Merry Christmas," she mumbled, wishing she
could tug the belt of her robe tighter. Sure, it covered most of her body, but, damnation, she was in
her robe in front of a guest, in front of her mentor,
with bed head and no makeup. Her face had to be
the same color as her curls.

Over the last few days Liam had been excruciat-
ingly…proper. No reaching out to touch her cheek,

no dancing with her. Exactly what she wanted, so why did she miss the few brief touches?

What made his behavior so strange was Mamma had included him in every meal, treating him like family.

Even at Christmas Eve dinner last night, he'd barely smiled. Okay, four times. Counting his smiles had become habit. Maybe today she could top his five-smile record. Her sisters had loved the idea of giving Liam a Christmas to remember.

"Can I carry something?" he asked, pointing at the pile of packages.

"Nope. I'm just making a pot of tea for my sisters."

"May I join you?"

She nodded.

He let her lead the way to the kitchen.

"Teapot?" Liam asked.

She pointed to the cupboard. After tucking the presents under the tree, she tightened her belt.

He leaned against the counter as she went through the ritual of warming the pot, adding the tea and then the water. He was so…appealing. Her mouth watered a little. Black jeans hugged his long legs. He wore a blue sweater that shouldn't make her want to stroke his chest.

Hiatus.

"What?" he asked.

"Nothing." No more mumbling or mooning over

him. As the tea steeped, she grabbed a tray. "You're up early."

"Thought I would take a ramble before breakfast." He clasped his hands behind his back. "I don't have to impose on your family on Christmas."

Dolley thought about the presents she'd just set under the tree. "Oh, but you do. I mean—you're not imposing. We expect you to spend the day with us."

Could she sound more stupid? She tugged on her belt again, hoping he wouldn't see the T-shirt and ratty candy-cane flannel pants she'd worn to bed.

"You're sure?" he asked.

She nodded, grabbing the half-and-half out of the fridge. By the time she'd loaded mugs onto the tray, the pot had steeped. She added cream, and Liam strained tea into the mugs. Their shoulders bumped every now and then. And once when the robe gapped open, he stared at her chest.

Her face went hot.

"Can I carry something?" he asked, taking a sip of his own mug.

"I've got it." She flexed her muscles, but it was lost in her oversize robe.

He held the door. "I'll see you at nine."

"We'll eat in the kitchen."

He gave her a smile. Number one for the day. She climbed the stairs, hoping her blush would fade before her sisters noticed.

Dolley bumped open the door to the Lady Bird Johnson room. "Merry Christmas, sleepyheads."

Abby and Bess rolled over and sat up.

"It's too early," Bess mumbled.

"It's Christmas." Dolley set the tray down and handed out mugs. "Time to wake up."

Poor Bess sighed and wiggled upright. She was still heartbroken over that jerk, Daniel.

Dolley and Abby would get Bess through the holiday, but Dolley wanted to hurt Daniel for making her sister unhappy.

She settled at the foot of the bed with her own mug.

Abby pulled her hair back into a ponytail. "Merry Christmas!"

"Yeah. What you said." Bess took a big gulp of her tea.

Dolley rubbed Bess's foot. "It's okay if I punch Daniel, right?"

"No." Bess took in a shaky breath. "Just…keep him away from me."

"We will." Abby patted Bess's shoulder. "If I'd known Daniel had broken your heart, I wouldn't have invited the Foresters over for Christmas dinner."

Bess dropped her head on Abby's shoulder. "I wouldn't want Deb worrying over Samuel and a holiday meal. He's so weak from his chemo. Deb says all the right things, but she's exhausted. Having them here is what I want. But…"

Dolley filled in the blank. It was going to hurt to see Daniel. "He won't get near you."

Now she had two goals. Keep Daniel away from

her sister and give Liam a Christmas that would have him smiling more than five times.

After talking and making one more run to the kitchen to refill their mugs, Dolley called out, "Dibs on the first shower."

"I'm next." Abby raised her hand. "Unless someone else plans to make breakfast."

"Go before me." Dolley wasn't a bad cook, but Abby was a star.

After they'd dressed, Dolley played sous-chef to Abby as they prepped breakfast.

Liam came in the courtyard door, his cheeks rosy from the cold.

"How was your walk?" she asked.

Abby shot her a *how did you know* look. Dolley ignored it.

"Lovely and quiet. Just a few pet owners out and a couple of runners."

Martin and Mamma pushed through the swinging door. Martin started the fire, and Mamma set the table. Gray came through the door, rushed over and dipped Abby into a dramatic smacking kiss.

Applause broke out in the group.

Liam stared—stunned.

When Gray let Abby up, her sister's eyes were sparkling. An ache spread through Dolley's chest at the love in their eyes.

The family and Liam filled the kitchen for breakfast.

Liam's blue sweater made his bright blue eyes

pop. She wanted to take pictures of just his eyes. He watched everyone, always observing. How could she pull him out of his shell?

As they moved dirty dishes to the counter and headed to the tree to open presents, he said, "I'll leave your family to your celebrations."

Dolley caught his arm as he moved around her. "Stay."

"But you'll be opening gifts," he said. "I don't want to impose."

"I saw a package or two with your name on it."

"My name?" His eyes went wide and filled with raw longing.

Making the effort to surprise Liam had been the right thing to do. No one should be as alone as he was. "You have to come to the sitting area."

Chairs were tugged near the fire, and presents were handed out.

"Oh, this is lovely," Mamma said, opening the gift of a vase Dolley had found at an estate sale.

"It's as elegant as you," Dolley said.

Martin teared up when he opened the present of the photograph Dolley had taken at their wedding. Her award-winning photo.

"Thank you, Dolley. This is beautiful." To Mamma, Martin said, "I didn't realize all three of your daughters were so talented."

As nice as his compliment was, his assumption that she had no creativity made her blink, afraid her eyes would water. Yeah, she was the non-talented baby sister.

"May I see?" Liam asked.

She bit her lower lip. If he critiqued her work in front of her family, the tears would drop.

"This is wonderful. The lighting is perfect." He looked up at her. "Joy?"

"Joy." Not that she'd been thinking about emotions when she'd taken it. "It won an award."

"What?" Abby asked. "You won an award and didn't tell anyone?"

"It was an amateur contest sponsored by *Bridal Party Today*." Heat filled her cheeks. "The picture and an interview will be in their January issue."

There was a flurry of hugs and congratulations.

"Next time you tell us." Mamma hugged her.

Dolley's laugh was tight. "I don't know that I'll enter any more contests."

"You have a gift. You don't need contests to tell you that," Liam declared. He handed the picture back to Martin. "You should get it signed. She has real talent."

Dolley's body shook. "Thanks."

Her sisters grinned at Liam and her.

The rest of the gift opening was a blur. She'd given Abby and Gray a picture of them dancing at Mamma's wedding that everyone said they loved.

Finally Dolley pointed at Liam's packages. "You need to start unwrapping."

He blinked. "I…"

"Open something," Bess called.

He pried the tape off the first package as if he were at a bridal shower and planned to save the wrapping paper. Opening the box, he grinned, his blue eyes shining with delight. "A book on Savannah!"

Dolley handed him another.

This time he wasn't as careful. He tore into the rest of his presents. "This is fantastic."

His smile made her insides puddle a little. Why was she so mushy today?

"Thank you, all of you." He stared at Dolley.

"You're welcome," she said. The gifts had been simple books on Savannah, but it was like they'd given him Hemmingway first editions.

"I'd like to do something for you and your family." Liam scrubbed his hands over his face. "Could I at least take a...a family portrait?"

"A Liam Delaney picture?" Dolley exclaimed. "Absolutely."

He folded a small piece of the wrapping paper and stuck it in a book, then gathered everything into his arms. "I'll be right back."

Paper was thrown. Bags and bows were saved.

"I've something for your family," Liam said as he walked back into the kitchen. He stopped in front of Mamma. "My godfather found these. Before he died, he wanted to connect with your family, but he was too ill. He thought you might enjoy having these copies."

Mamma's forehead wrinkled as she opened the clasp on the manila envelope. She slid out papers, her eyes scanning the pages. "Oh, my."

"What is it?" Dolley asked.

"Letters. From James to Michael FitzGerald." Mamma read—

Greetings my family,

I have settled in Savannah. It is an amazing town and bustling port. I am hopeful my shipping interests will thrive here. The colonies, I mean America, rely on water transportation. This should be good for my interests.

I have started to build warehouse space and once that is complete, will begin the search to build a home for you, dear Fiona, for I miss you madly.

Dolley and her sisters sat at Mamma's feet as she read the letters and passed them around.

Mamma wrapped Liam in a hug. "Thank you so much."

His mouth dropped open for a moment, then he closed his eyes and hugged Mamma back.

She cupped his face. "Young man, wherever you travel, you are welcome to spend the holidays with us."

Mamma kissed first one and then the next cheek. "I mean that."

Liam's eyes sparkled, and he pulled Mamma into another hug.

Dolley's jaw dropped, too. *Liam here for holidays for the rest of their lives?* What was Mamma thinking?

But this might work to her benefit. Liam being indebted to her family wasn't a bad thing. She bit her nail. But it could backfire. What if he stopped mentoring her?

"I just might take you up on that offer." He wore a massive smile. "There's something about Savannah—or maybe it's just Fitzgerald House—that feels like home. Let's take that family portrait." He lined them up, all business.

No one had makeup on, but Dolley thought they looked pretty good for a Christmas morning.

After he'd taken several, Abby asked, "Does that camera have a timer?"

He nodded.

"Then set it and join us," Bess said.

"Me?" Liam's expression held so much yearning, Dolley wanted to give him a hug.

"Come on," she called. It was like he'd never been included in a group picture.

He fiddled with the timer, his head down. "Okay?"

Everyone called out, "Yes."

He scurried back, his eyes bright, and knelt on the floor next to Dolley. "Happy Christmas, everyone."

The prelim flash went off. She held her smile for the second flash.

"Once more," he called, resetting the camera.

This time he set his hand on Dolley's shoulder.

A small shiver jolted through her body. He must be doing it to balance the picture. Not to touch her. Gray's hand was on Abby's shoulder on the other side of the group.

After Liam approved the photo, she and her sisters shooed away Mamma and all the men. They had the kitchen to themselves.

"Did you see Liam's face when he opened the first book?" Dolley couldn't keep the excitement from her voice.

"Hasn't he ever had a true Christmas?" Abby tucked stuffing into a mammoth turkey.

"It doesn't seem like it." Dolley added chopped oranges to the chutney she was prepping. "Is this enough?"

Abby peered into the bowl that included cranberries and pecans. "One more."

"I'm glad we picked up gifts for Liam." Bess peeled potatoes, her face too solemn. "That was a nice thing you did for him."

"Maybe Dolley's looking for tutoring on more than just photography." Abby winked.

Bess didn't smile. "If you are, be careful. Working with someone after you've broken up is horrible."

And Bess's history with Daniel was another great

reason to ignore all the pings and zings that filled her when she was close to Liam. Bess and Daniel still worked together on Carleton House, and her sister was miserable.

"Do you want me to take on more of the Carleton House work?" Dolley asked.

She didn't know how she would get that done, work with Liam *and* finish the projects she'd bid for Jackson, but she hated Bess's sadness.

"I can do this." Bess stood taller. "I just have to take each day a breath at a time."

Both Dolley and Abby hurried over and wrapped their arms around Bess.

"I wish we could do more for you," Dolley said.

"For today." Bess's eyes closed. "Just keep Daniel away from me."

"Absolutely," Abby said.

Dolley squeezed her sister one more time. "We could poison his dinner."

Bess laughed. It was weak, but she laughed. "You're bloodthirsty today."

"I could research something diabolical." Dolley moved back to her cutting board. "Maybe one of your orchids is poisonous."

"No." Bess's hazel eyes glinted with tears, but her spine was straight. "Let's make sure Samuel is comfortable. His cancer treatments are wearing him out."

"Agreed." Abby headed back to her own workstation. "This turkey isn't going to load itself in the oven."

They puttered in the kitchen, creating appetizers and heating up hot apple cider and mulled wine.

Dolley grabbed her camera on the way to the library, where the family had gathered. She set up some shots, trying to remember Liam's advice. First, she took pictures of the antique ornaments on the tree. Focusing on an ornament, she let the lights and branches blur. Then she brought everything into focus.

Flipping back and forth between the pictures, she tried to figure out what each one said to her.

"What are you working on?" Liam's lyrical accent had shivers slipping down her spine.

She held up the camera, afraid her voice would crack like a young boy going through puberty. She had to stop reacting to Liam.

"I like what you're doing." His eyebrows pinched together. "See what happens if you use the rule of thirds."

"Even when I'm purposely blurring the background?"

He leaned in. A hint of his cologne mingled with the piney fragrance of the tree. "Try it."

She couldn't stop inhaling his scent. Lurching away from him, she composed the shot with the angel in the far right of the frame. Surprisingly, the change made the angel more—prominent.

"You're right." She grinned up at him.

He tapped her nose. "Of course."

It was playful, not intimate. But her heart beat a little faster. They were tucked behind the tree where no one could see them.

The smile slipped off his face, and his eyes darkened to a cobalt blue.

"Wait." She had to keep it light. "You can't stop smiling, or I'm not doing my job."

"What job?"

"Helping you celebrate the holiday." She couldn't confess she'd wanted to make this a special day for him.

He shook his head, stepping away. "It's already better than seventy-five percent of my prior Christmases."

"That's…good," she choked out. Only a quarter of his Christmases had been good? "No, that's horrible."

He waved off her concern. "Look," he whispered. "Why don't you see if you can catch your mum and Martin?"

She peeked around the tree. Mamma sat on the floor, her head resting on Martin's thigh. His hand stroked her strawberry-blond hair while she stared into his face, a loving smile played across her lips. Love. That's what she wanted to capture.

She held her breath, focused and clicked.

Her subjects were oblivious, so she kept shooting. Stepping back, she captured a branch of the tree, but focused on Mamma and Martin. The sun shone through the stained glass dome, and blue, red and green beams decorated the floor and their clothes.

With Liam peering over her shoulder, her hands shook a little, and her breaths grew shallow. Her body was too aware of how close he stood.

She took one more shot, then flipped into replay mode. His breath feathered the back of her neck. She stiffened but angled the camera so he could see the pictures.

"Nice." Pointing to the picture with the Christmas tree branch, he added, "Lovely work."

When he came to the pictures with the stained glass beams, he smiled again. "You've a wonderful sense of light and color."

Her cheeks heated. "Thanks."

"And thank you one more time for the gifts." His blue eyes twinkled. "I can't think of a nicer Christmas."

"I'm so glad." His smile made her heart beat a little faster. "Remember, the day's not done. And your goal today is twelve smiles. No negotiating."

LIAM LEANED BACK in one of the library's wingback chairs. He'd tried to head up to his room, but Mamie insisted he spend the whole day with the family. The Fitzgeralds had welcomed him into the fold. Today he just might break his smile record.

He'd had a few gifts throughout the years. If a

school chum invited him home for the holiday, he'd receive a small present. But nothing like what his friends would receive. And that made sense. He wasn't part of any family. He hadn't belonged.

"Is this your first Christmas in the US?" Bess asked, taking the matching chair.

He shook his head. "My producer invited me to her home a few years ago. She lives on Long Island." He shivered. "That was a cold I don't want to experience again."

"I know what you mean. I don't think I would know how to grow anything up north."

Two men headed down the hallway toward the library's open doors. The elder man pushed a walker, the younger had his hand cupped like he would catch the older gentleman if he fell.

Bess's smile slipped off her face.

"Are these the Foresters?" he asked.

"Samuel and his son, Daniel." She nodded, her eyes shimmering with unshed tears. "Samuel's going through cancer treatments."

"Merry Christmas," the older man called, wheeling into the library.

Bess looked around the room, panic in her eyes. She leaned over. "This may be a strange request, but I need your help."

"Of course." He shifted close, not sure what he could do for her.

"It's Daniel." She tipped her head to the younger Forester. "I don't want to talk to him."

He nodded. "Okay."

"If he corners me and my sisters aren't around, please—rescue me."

He touched her hand. "Absolutely."

"Thanks." Bess took in a deep breath. "I'll help Samuel."

Daniel's stare drilled holes into Bess as she hugged Samuel and settled him next to the fire.

Dolley rushed into the room, head swiveling until she located Bess. She wore a festive green jumper and a red-and-green plaid skirt with green tights. Her curls quivered as she moved to the older man and gave him a hug. "Merry Christmas, Samuel." Then she hustled to Bess's side.

Dolley ignored Daniel, too. What had made the man persona non grata?

The man himself came over. "I'm Daniel Forester."

"Liam Delaney." He added a smile, which of course made him think about Dolley. They shook hands, Daniel making it a contest. Liam squeezed back.

Daniel commandeered Bess's abandoned chair. "What brings you to Savannah?"

"I'm filming a documentary. I'll be staying through St. Patrick's Day." Liam picked up his mug of hot cider and sipped. "The Fitzgeralds were kind enough to invite me to dinner."

Daniel leaned forward, his brown eyes filled with suspicion. "They don't have guests during Christmas."

"I know." Liam smiled. This one counted against his goal. "Lucky me."

Daniel's face paled.

A man who looked identical to Daniel carried a tray of mugs and drinks into the room. "I'm the delivery boy. Compliments of our hostesses."

Gray came in, too, and pulled a chair over to where Liam and Daniel sat. He bounced his fist in the palm of his hand. "You and I need to talk, Forester."

"That's my cue." Liam stood. He wasn't going to get in the middle of whatever was going on. "I'll introduce myself around." And keep Daniel away from Bess.

People moved in and out of the library. Dolley whispered to Bess before leaving the room. Cheryl showed up with her son, Josh. Everyone chatted with Samuel first; the man was obviously a family favorite. When Liam introduced himself, Samuel seemed ill but genuinely nice.

Bess left the room, and Daniel started after her.

Liam stepped into his path. "What is it you do for a living?"

"Listen—" Daniel tried to skirt around him, but Liam blocked his way "—I want...no, I *need* to talk with Bess." Panic edged the man's voice.

"No can do, lad." Liam caught his arm. "Miss Bess doesn't want to be bothered by the likes of you."

"But…" Daniel pinched between his eyes. "I have to talk to her. Help me."

"This was from the lass's own lips." Liam did feel sorry for the man. "Sorry, chum."

Daniel reached into his pocket and pulled out a small velvet box.

Liam's eyes blinked wide open. A ring?

"This really can't wait," Daniel pleaded.

Liam had no clue what to do. Would Bess want to talk to Daniel if she knew his intentions? He scratched the back of his head. His knee-jerk reaction was to help the man—but he'd promised Bess. "Sorry, she doesn't want to talk to you. Let me get you a drink."

When they eventually moved to the dining room, Abby and Dolley flanked Bess. He wanted his camera to document the two warriors protecting their wounded sister.

Conversation buzzed as food circled the table. Liam sat between Josh, a lad of six, and the love-sick Daniel.

He swallowed another mouthful of incredible food. "This is delicious. Thank you for having me for dinner."

His appreciation started a string of thank-yous, directed at Abby.

"This was a group effort," Abby insisted.

Everyone toasted the cooks, then settled in to eat. Small conversations floated around the table.

Daniel, his face looking a little green, cleared his throat. "Bess?"

She grabbed her wineglass and took a sip. "What?"

"Can I talk to you?" Daniel stood. "Please?"

She didn't move. "You've said enough."

Everyone stared. Liam set a hand on Daniel's arm.

Daniel held out his other hand. "I love you."

Bess wilted. Dolley put her arm around her shoulders. Abby glared.

"I screwed up." Daniel pushed Liam's hand away and moved around the table. "My family helped me realize how messed up I am."

Gray shook his head. Daniel's mother bit her lips.

"Please, talk to me," Daniel said.

"You broke my heart, and now you do this." She waved at the table. "Humiliate me in front of our families. At Christmas? I don't want you to talk to me. I want you to leave."

"Not cool, bro," Nathan, Daniel's twin brother, whispered.

"Please, Bess." Daniel moved closer to her.

"I hate you." She pushed out her chair.

Dolley and Abby stood.

"You should," Daniel agreed. "I pretty much hate myself."

Bess wrapped her arms around her waist. "Don't hurt me anymore."

"I don't want to." He reached out and stroked her cheek. "Damn it, I want to marry you!"

Bess's hand covered her mouth. She tore past him.

The sisters blocked Daniel's way.

"Let me by!" He grabbed Dolley and set her aside. She squeaked.

It was wrong to hurt Dolley. Liam moved after him.

Abby did a side step.

"Leave us alone," Daniel begged, running for the door. "Give me a chance."

"Should we go after them?" Dolley bit her thumbnail.

Abby wrapped an arm around Dolley's waist. "Maybe they need to talk." But both sisters stared at the door.

Mamma held up her hands. "Let's finish eating. I'm sure we'll know what's going on soon."

"Is this a normal Christmas?" Liam whispered to Daniel's brother as he moved back to his chair.

"More excitement than we usually have." Nathan shook his head. "My twin really screwed up. Maybe the big gesture wasn't the thing."

Liam helped clear the table, wheeling a cart of dirty dishes into the kitchen. The parents had migrated to the library while the younger adults cleaned. And the sisters glanced across the courtyard to the carriage house where Bess lived.

He should head up to his room. He could find

work to do. But Dolley's pretty eyebrows were scrunched together.

"Do you want me to check on them?" he asked.

"She'll come back if she needs our help." Dolley bit her lip as she set a big pot in the sink. "I hope."

"I see Mr. Dan and Miss Bess," Josh, the little boy, called from the sitting area.

Exclamations circled the kitchen.

Dolley ran to the window, pulling Liam with her. "Oh, my!"

Daniel and Bess walked arm in arm, staring at each other. Smiles wreathed their faces. Seemed like Bess wasn't angry with Daniel anymore.

Liam hung back while everyone strained to see what was going on. He really should head upstairs, but he wanted to know how their story ended.

"They're coming inside. Act normal," Dolley whispered, backing away from the window and rushing to the pile of dishes.

The china banged together as she loaded it into the dishwasher. He winced, hoping nothing would break.

The others followed her lead, making busy and ignoring the couple as they walked inside.

Bess and Daniel stopped by the doorway. No one glanced at them. No one except Liam. Their mouths dropped open the longer they stood without anyone saying anything.

He wished he had a camera. He should grab one

since it seemed like there might be some happy news coming.

Dolley looked over at him, her back still to the couple. She held up soapy hands with a *what's going on?* expression on her face.

He shifted closer and whispered, "They're standing there, gobsmacked."

She wiped her hands and scooted around the counter, not looking back at her sister. "Help me."

He followed her into the butler's pantry. She pulled down trays and set champagne flutes out. Then she grabbed marble bottle holders out of a fridge and bottles of prosecco. Her curls bounced as she moved around. "Let's take everything to the library, just in case there's an announcement."

He hefted the heaviest tray. "Lead on."

In the library, the two mothers sat next to each other holding hands. Martin and Samuel occupied the wingback chairs in front of the fire.

"Are they back?" Mamma asked.

"Arm in arm." Dolley nodded. "Thought we should be ready if there's an announcement."

"I should let your family celebrate," Liam whispered, as they stood near the fire.

"No." Dolley's smile was bigger than he'd ever seen it. She grabbed her camera off the mantel. "But you could take pictures."

"Sure." He checked all the settings and snapped a few of the mothers on the sofa. Then one of Dolley. The comfort of seeing the world through the lens had him letting go of the breaths that had clogged his lungs. This was where he belonged. Behind the camera. Interacting with strangers all the time was exhausting.

A parade of people came down the hall, led by Bess and Daniel holding hands. He pulled the camera up, shooting the couple as they smiled into each other's eyes. Would the tears that hung on her lashes translate as joy or sadness?

Everyone crowded around the pair as they moved to the two older couples.

"She's giving me another chance!" Daniel thrust out Bess's left hand.

Liam hoped he caught the delight on everyone's faces. He couldn't stop to look. He zoomed in on the ring and then pulled the focus back to capture Bess, Abby and Dolley together. Light glinted off their fiery hair as the sisters hugged.

The power of family. He took in a tight breath. It was something he would never have.

The prosecco was popped and glasses were filled. He stayed in the background, capturing the families' joy.

Dolley handed him a flute. "Time to celebrate." There was a little quiver in her voice. "Thank you for taking pictures."

"It's what I do best." He handed her camera back. Without it, he didn't know what to do with his hands. He clutched the flute.

"I'm so happy for my sister." Now there was definitely a quiver in Dolley's voice.

He patted her shoulder. He could do that, give her some comfort.

She sobbed, burying her face in his chest.

Whoa. He froze.

He put an arm around her, still patting her shoulder. Her warm scent filled his nose. He glanced around the room.

Gray frowned at him.

He shrugged, not sure what to do with the weeping woman crying into his chest.

"I'm…I'm sorry." Dolley pulled away, brushing the wet patch on his shirt. "She's just been so sad since they broke up."

Her hand on his chest had his body coming to life. A jolt as sharp as a strobe flash went through his belly. Had he read Dolley wrong? Was she attracted to him, or was this just joy for her sister?

He needed to think and regroup. Taking a deep breath, he stepped away from her. "I've intruded enough on your family's holiday."

"You're not intruding." She reached out but dropped her hand.

He smiled, letting her figure out the smile count. He'd lost track. He wanted to stay and revel in the family's happiness, but he was still an outsider. Always alone. He might be invited to their celebration, but at the end of the day, he wasn't a Fitzgerald.

CHAPTER SEVEN

All photos are accurate. None of them is the truth.

Richard Avedon

DOLLEY TUCKED THE tail of her Catering by Fitzgerald shirt into her black pants and pushed open the kitchen door. They were short one server for tonight's wedding. That put her in the lineup.

Abby had the house phone stretched to the end of its cord, trying to reach her address book. "I'll check. Give me a few minutes, and I'll call you back."

Dolley hustled over and handed the address book to her sister. "What's up?"

"Loretta slipped on the ice this morning." Abby furiously flipped through her book. "She broke her arm."

"Was she tonight's photographer?"

Abby nodded, her ponytail bouncing. "Since I gave the bride her name, she asked if I knew someone else."

A thrill went through Dolley's chest. She could do it. She could take the pictures.

Abby punched numbers into the phone. "Blake. How are you?"

Dolley swallowed. Blake was excellent. He'd photographed dozens of Fitzgerald House weddings. He was a good choice.

Please, be busy.

Abby explained the crisis.

Bess pushed open the door, flowers in her hand. "I have the…"

Dolley put a finger to her lips and pointed to Abby.

"What's up?" Bess asked.

"Loretta broke her arm."

"Oh, no." Bess's eyes flared open. "She was today's photographer?"

Dolley nodded, trying to keep her smile off her face. Bess would *surely* suggest Dolley be given the chance. She grabbed a mug and poured coffee.

Abby called another number. Then another. After two more calls, she slammed the book shut. "No one is available last minute."

Dolley waited, looking between her two sisters.

"Dolley?" Abby asked.

This was it. She straightened. "Yes?"

Abby tapped her finger on the counter. "Let's ask Liam."

"Liam?" *Liam!* No. She wanted to be the one her sisters turned to. "He's—"

"—Fantastic! Great idea," Bess said. "When Daniel and I got engaged, Liam's pictures were incredible."

The coffee seared Dolley's belly. Of course her

sisters would think of Liam. He was fabulous. "He's…he's not a wedding photographer."

"You never know." Abby stood. "He's a photographer."

"Let's ask." Bess handed the flowers to Abby. "Here's the cake topper."

"He might not even be here." But yesterday, he'd suggested they touch up photos together, something they'd been working on the last week and half since Christmas.

Ever since she'd cried all over him, their working relationship had changed. He touched her—more. Not like he was making a move. More like her sisters did—like family.

And as perverse as it sounded, *she* wanted more.

She cringed. Maybe since Mamma announced he was an honorary Fitzgerald, he thought of her as a sister.

The lines between their professional lives and personal had blurred. And she didn't know how to keep them in place.

Bess dragged her up the back stairs.

Maybe Liam would say *no*. Then her sisters would get to the bottom of the barrel—her.

They stopped in front of his suite and Bess knocked.

Liam opened the door and looked between them. "How's the form?"

Dolley shook her head. He'd used the phrase once or twice, and she still didn't know what it meant.

He stepped back and held the door for them. "I mean, *what's up* in Yank."

"We're—" Bess waved her hand "—wondering if you could do us a huge favor."

"What would that be?" He looked at Dolley.

"The photographer for tonight's wedding broke her arm," Bess said.

Dolley shifted. This was so inappropriate. They shouldn't ask a famous photographer to take wedding pictures.

He looked genuinely sorry. "That's terrible."

"Could you stand in?" Bess blurted out.

"Me?"

"It's a small wedding. The ceremony is here. Everything will happen here. Ceremony. Dinner." Bess's words tumbled together.

"There's no one else?" Liam asked.

"Abby's called everyone," Bess said. "No one's available."

Liam frowned at Dolley.

She shook her head. "You can say *no*."

He rubbed his chin. "It could be fun. Sure."

"Really." Dolley's chest ached. "Have you ever shot a wedding?"

"Plenty of my school chums." His blue gaze caught hers. "Worried I won't know what to do?"

"No." But why didn't her sisters recognize she could handle this crisis and do a good job for the bride?

"What time am I needed?" he asked.

Bess typed on her phone. A response dinged. "Abby says, thank you, thank you. And the bride arrives at five."

Dolley checked her phone. Forty-five minutes.

"I need to finish decorating." Bess dashed out the door.

Before Dolley could follow, Liam asked, "Can you help me?"

"Me?" Dolley pressed a hand on her breasts.

He stared at her chest.

Heat flamed through her body. Her hand slipped to her side.

"You can make sure I don't forget any shots the bride will want." His gaze refocused on her face.

"I should be able to swing that." She could help Liam, and while he took pictures of the bride and groom eating and toasting, she could serve. "We lost a server, so I'll be helping with that, too."

"Do what you can, then." He grabbed a camera bag and freshly charged batteries. Then he moved into the bedroom and selected two cameras. "Where will this take place?"

"The ballroom. Follow me."

They headed up the main stairs. Her disappointment weighed down each foot like concrete boots.

"I haven't been up here." Liam stroked the railing.

She imagined him stroking her skin the same way. "You're entranced by our woodwork. Why is that?"

"I am?" He shook his head. "I was thinking of

She hurried to his side.

"Lisa wants to make sure we capture all these pictures." He handed her a piece of paper with a lengthy list.

She scanned it. It seemed like the usual. "Okay. I'll make sure you don't forget any. You can shoot the dress."

He stepped next to the hanging wedding dress and worked his way around it. Then he took a couple of shots of the shiny shoes sitting on the floor.

Dolley had been in and around enough weddings to know how to stage the shots. "Ladies, why don't you all toast the bride?" she suggested. "Lisa, let's put you right in the middle."

They obliged. Dolley found a pen and crossed off the pictures. Her phone buzzed. Groom's party's here.

"You're husband-to-be has arrived," Dolley called out. "We'll check on him."

Lisa's face went pink. "Wonderful."

They could get pictures of the groom getting ready while Lisa got into her own dress. "We'll be back."

"Why don't you take the pictures of the bride dressing?" He handed her a camera. "I don't think I should."

"Oh, wow." It was the Rolleiflex. "You're letting me use your camera?"

He was frowning. "Do you have yours?"

"No." She might lie to get her hands on this exquisite equipment. Grinning, she made sure she knew how to run the camera. "I can't wait."

He stared as she handled the camera.

"I'll take care of it like it's my baby," she assured him.

"Sugar, can't you take our pictures?" a bridesmaid asked Liam.

"We want to get all the pictures Lisa requested," Liam said. "And Dolley's very talented."

Too bad her sisters didn't think so.

"Hurry back." The bridesmaid, champagne flute in hand, brushed Liam's sleeve. "I'm Rachel."

Miffed by Rachel's forwardness, Dolley straightened her shoulders. She shouldn't be jealous. Liam could do what he wanted. She was just his apprentice.

"Lisa, how about getting dressed?" Dolley got the okay to take pictures of the bride in her corset. "You look incredible."

Lisa's smile was a beam of light.

"If you get that lovely dress on, we could shoot some pictures of you on the balcony," Dolley suggested.

"Help me, ladies," Lisa sang out.

Her friends tugged, buttoned and fluffed. Then Dolley opened the French doors.

"Watch the ice," she warned, shooting away as they laughed and surrounded the bride. She got a few good ones and one *great* one. "Why don't I get some with just Lisa?"

Lisa leaned on the balustrade and shouted, "I'm getting married."

Dolley moved to the side, trying to capture the anticipation. Lisa turned with another joyous smile. *There.* She pushed the shutter, hoping she was getting the picture she'd envisioned.

There was a knock. Rachel scurried over and opened the door.

Liam.

"Come in out of the cold," Dolley told the bride. She handed the camera to Liam. "How'd it go?"

He was grinning.

Maybe she should count his smiles today. Unless he was smiling because of *Rachel*.

"I had the groom's party on the balcony in their room," he said.

"Great minds."

He frowned.

"Great minds think alike."

He raised his eyebrows. "They do?"

The sexy lilt in his voice hummed right to the center of her body. She sighed.

They headed to the ballroom ahead of the bride. "Make sure I don't make a hash of it, will you, luv?" he asked.

Who would have imagined an internationally recognized photographer would be nervous about meeting a bride's expectations. Liam took pictures as Dolley checked off the list.

When the minister and groom took their places,

he slipped to the front of the wedding guests. The bridal party made their entrance and Liam was in full control.

Once the *I do's* were said and the couple introduced, Dolley helped set up group shots. It was like they could read each other's minds. She would twitch a skirt or straighten a tie before he could get the words out of his mouth. Without his direction, she moved the wedding party members around for symmetry. Then she backed away and stood next to Liam.

He leaned close, their shoulders brushing. "We're good together."

They were. Was that because he'd taught her to see the world through his lens?

After the group shots were done, Rachel put her hand on Liam's back. "Can I see what you've taken?"

Dolley wanted to rip Rachel's hand, with its perfect French manicure, off Liam's back.

Liam shifted away from the bridesmaid. "I'm afraid you'll have to wait until I go through the pictures with Lisa."

Rachel pouted, crossing her arms under her breasts.

"What's next?" Liam moved to Dolley, not even glancing at the bounty of flesh plumped up for his viewing pleasure.

Rachel sniffed and headed to the bar.

"The only required pictures left are the toasts and the cake cutting. You can just roam for a while." She handed his bag back to him. "I need to set salads."

He caught her hand. "You'll be back?"

She squeezed his. "Yes."

He didn't let go.

Tugging her to a recessed door, he whispered, "Working with you is fun. Does this count in my fun quotient for the day?"

He smiled.

Something hot flowed between them. It scorched her lungs, so she could barely draw in a breath.

"Dolley." Longing filled his voice. He pulled her closer.

She broke away. Not a good idea. Was it? It *was* the new year. But starting something with Liam might ruin their working relationship.

The lines grew murkier each time he touched her. And the need to touch him was drawing her in. "I have to…"

"Liam." Rachel was now the *drunk* bridesmaid. "We'd like more pictures with the bride."

He tore his gaze away from Dolley's. "I'll be right there."

Dolley escaped to the service hall. She leaned against the wall, pulling in deep breaths. There wasn't a doubt what she needed to do. She had to sacrifice this attraction. There was so much more to learn. She wanted to be professional, even if her sisters didn't think she could photograph a wedding. A small snort escaped.

Cheryl came through. "Did you just run up the stairs?"

"Something like that." Easing her hands under a

tray of salad plates, she backed through the swinging door and into the ballroom.

Her gaze zeroed in on Liam. He glanced over, but Rachel said something to him and he turned back to the bridesmaid.

She didn't know whether she wanted to stake out her territory and pull him away from the woman or stick to her principles.

It was fun to flirt with Liam. Exciting to think about what they might be like together. But she wasn't messing up this opportunity.

She sighed. It would be principles. Status quo would have to keep her warm at night.

LIAM CHECKED ON Dolley again. He had to stop doing that.

But when he'd held her hand there'd been that… click. That connection. It couldn't be one-sided. What was keeping them from closing the gap between their lips?

Maybe tonight.

Dolley cleared plates. Someone said something, and she laughed. A sparkling sound that made even a curmudgeon like him smile. Marion, the head of housekeeping for the B and B, wheeled out the cake, and the bride and groom headed over. Once this was done, all the pictures on the list would be checked off.

"How are you holding up?" Dolley had somehow snuck up on him. Her hand was warm where it rested on his back.

"These will be the final pictures." He handed her the list.

"Nice." She grinned. "If your documentary career doesn't work out, I think you've found your fallback."

"Not on your life," he whispered. Hell. His feet ached. And all night he'd fought off Rachel. Although, the looks Dolley had shot Rachel gave him hope. No one could have that kind of animosity and not feel something.

He handed Dolley his camera bag. "Could you find my tilt-shift lens?"

She dug out the right one.

He screwed it on. "Why don't you shoot from the other side?"

"I'd love to." Glee lit her face as she pulled the Rolleiflex from its cushioned cradle.

He moved closer while Dolley shifted to the other side of the cake table. Marion handed the cake knife to the bride and groom.

The couple grinned at each other. They both looked so young, it was hard to imagine this was their second time around.

They smashed cake in each other's faces, laughing. He fired off shots, not able to spend the time to frame or stage. Then Marion took the cake apart with the precision of a surgeon.

"Nice work, Mr. Delaney." Dolley handed the bag back to him.

"It was hard. My back hurts."

She chuckled. "Abby has food for us in the kitchen."

"Are you coming down?" he asked. "I can wait."

"Cheryl and I will deliver the cake, and then we're right on your heels." She picked up a tray of dessert plates.

Liam headed to the kitchen.

"Thank you so much for stepping in." Abby dried her hands, came over and gave him a hug.

"You're welcome. It was fun."

"Now you're just being nice." She patted his back and pulled away. "Are you ready to eat?"

"Absolutely."

"You have your choice of short ribs or pasta."

"A little of both?"

"You've got it." Abby brought over a salad and then the entrée. "What would you like to drink?"

He looked at the food. "Red wine, if you have it."

"I'll be right back."

Dolley and Cheryl pushed through the swinging door, laughing.

"Done?" he asked.

"For now," Dolley said.

At the counter they pulled together plates, grabbing salads out of the fridge. Then they sat at the table with him.

"I've forgotten how sore my feet get." Dolley propped her feet up on the chair next to Liam.

"I can't seem to forget. Ouch." Cheryl stacked her feet on the chair on the other side of his. "That feels good."

Abby came back with a bottle of wine and poured Liam a glass.

"Nothing for them?" He waved his glass at Dolley and Cheryl.

Cheryl's smile evaporated. "I don't drink."

There was a story there, but he didn't know her well enough to ask.

"Dolley?" Abby asked.

"I'm still working." Dolley waved a forkful of lasagna in the air.

He leaned forward and snatched the mouthful off her fork.

"Hey!"

"Thanks." He winked and went back to eating.

Cheryl shook her head. "Children, children."

"Not me," Dolley complained. "Him."

"She waved food near my face," he justified.

Abby laughed. "Marion's got cleanup covered."

"Then I will have a glass of wine." Dolley took the glass Abby handed her.

They ate and talked about the wedding.

"The blonde bridesmaid followed you around all night." Cheryl pointed at him.

He shivered. "The lass wouldn't take *no* for an answer."

Dolley raised an eyebrow but didn't say anything.

He wanted to know what was going on in that sharp mind of hers.

"I'll see you later." Cheryl rinsed and set her dishes in the dishwasher. "I'm heading home."

"Have a good night." Dolley wiggled her feet on the chair.

"You've done this before?" Liam asked.

"When Abby was getting the catering up and running, I would pitch in if she needed me. Sometimes she had three events on a weekend."

"She's lucky to have you as a sister."

Dolley shrugged, almost looking embarrassed.

"Your shirt says Catering by Fitzgerald. That's Abby."

She nodded.

"And I've seen Landscaping by Fitzgerald signs, that's Bess?"

She nodded again, the smile slipping off her face.

"Do you have Photography by Fitzgerald?"

She blinked. Like the idea had never crossed her mind. "I…no. I'm the *other* Fitzgerald sister. The one with no talent."

"Christ on a bike. You can't believe that malarkey?"

She gathered dishes and took them to the counter. "Everyone in Savannah knows Abby and Bess have all the talent."

He moved to Dolley and took her shoulders. "You have boatloads of talent. Your pictures are good, and they'll be great."

"No one sees me that way." She hung her head. "Just you."

"Then they're ignorant asses." He tipped her head up, his thumb stroking her silky cheek.

He hated the pain in her eyes. He'd always thought that if he had a loving family, everything would be right in his world.

But Dolley had loving sisters. They had each other's backs. Yet she was miserable. What if family didn't guarantee happiness?

He bent close and whispered, "You're just as talented as your sisters. More."

Her perfume tugged him closer, a scent filled with warmth and amber. He tried to capture the smell, capture the moment. If he wanted to make a memory, it had to be strong. "Dolley."

Her eyes were deep green pools, calling him to plunge in and stay. Her tongue snuck out and licked her upper lip.

He should resist, but her confusion drew him near. It was no use trying to stop. He inhaled her tempting scent and brushed his mouth against hers, a barely-there touch.

She exhaled on a gasp. He caught her breath by pressing his mouth to hers.

He pulled her close. They fit perfectly.

He tasted wine and Dolley, all in one spicy kiss. Someone moaned. Maybe it was him.

Her head tipped back in surrender. Her fingers gripped his hair.

How had they waited this long?

"Stop." Her word was muffled against his mouth. "Please."

He pulled away, gasping. "Incredible."

"No." She shook her head. "No. That shouldn't have happened. It can't happen."

"But…" His fingers tightened on her arms.

She stepped away, her hand covering her mouth. "If we keep going, everything will be ruined. Ruined."

"I don't think so." He stepped closer. She was really worried. "Why?"

"I just know." She closed her eyes. "We can't do that again. You have to promise me."

"Dolley. This isn't one-sided. There's sparks every time we're together."

"It won't work. We won't work." She pushed her curls off her face. "Believe me."

"I don't—"

The door swung open. Abby bustled into the room. "Oh, good, I was afraid you might have already left."

Shifting behind the counter, he hid his fading erection. He stared at Dolley. They needed to talk.

"Still here." Instead of looking at him, Dolley fiddled with the dishwasher.

"I mean Liam." Abby looked between the two of them and frowned. "The photographer you stepped in for was supposed to take my wedding pictures in February. The doctor says she'll still have the cast on."

"I'm sorry to hear that." He glanced at Dolley, but she'd moved to the table to pick up the remaining dishes.

"I know this is an imposition—" Abby bit her lip "—but could you take our pictures, too?"

Dolley's head jerked up. She stared at her sister.

Why didn't her sisters recognize Dolley's talent? "What about Dolley?" he asked.

"Dolley?"

He held up his hand. "Did you think about asking her to take the pictures?"

Dolley swallowed. "Liam, that's not necessary."

"It is. You're talented. I checked out the pictures you took of the bride dressing. Wonderful composition, great use of lighting. And the picture of the bride on the balcony—she'll make that a centerpiece of her memory book."

"I never…" Abby's mouth dropped open.

"And why was that?" Liam asked, incensed.

"Liam." Dolley held up her hand. "Enough."

He pointed a finger at her. "Stand up for yourself."

Her shoulders straightened. "This isn't your battle."

"Stop." Abby took Dolley's hand. "I'm sorry I hurt you."

"Abs," Dolley said. "You didn't know."

"But I should have." Abby hugged her sister.

"You should have insisted we take your photography seriously."

Dolley hugged her sister back, glaring at him over her sister's shoulder.

"I can't take your pictures." Dolley let her sister go. "I'm in the wedding."

The sisters turned, standing arm in arm. United.

An ache filled his body. He wanted to belong in the way they belonged to each other.

Dolley took a deep breath. "Liam, will you take Abby's wedding pictures? Please?"

"Absolutely." To Dolley he said, "Can I borrow you for one more minute?"

Her gaze darted to the clock. "I…I…have to check on…Marion."

She dashed out of the kitchen before he could say another word.

A kiss hot enough to boil a kettle, and she didn't want to explore the attraction between them? He, for one, was not going to ignore it.

CHAPTER EIGHT

If your pictures aren't good enough, you're not close enough.

Robert Capa

KISSING LIAM WOULDN'T happen again. Dolley's fingers rattled on the Carleton House kitchen counter. All yesterday she'd avoided him.

Their interactions needed to focus on photography. With her poor record with men, she refused to cave in to her desires.

Unfortunately, kissing Liam had been her best kiss ever. She sighed. But not worth risking his mentorship for a few days of pleasure.

Thank goodness she had an excuse not to work with him this morning. She was walking through Carleton House with the AV/Wi-Fi techs.

"What's up with you?" Daniel asked, setting his hand on top of her tapping fingers.

"I hate waiting," she lied.

Daniel checked his phone. "They aren't even late. Something wrong?"

"Why would you ask that?"

Daniel's blond eyebrows snapped together. "Because you're the happy, fun-loving sister. Not the frowning, serious sister."

Dolley sank to the floor, her back against the wall. "There's just a lot going on in my life."

"Does any of this nervousness have to do with that slick-talking Irishman who's staying in Fitzgerald House?" Daniel's hands formed fists. "I could have a talk with him."

"No!"

"Hey. Gray and I are part of your family." His grin was wicked. "We could both have a talk with him."

"I don't need you to fight my battles." She stroked a finger over the newly varnished cabinet. Then stopped. It reminded her of how Liam touched the woodwork in Fitzgerald House.

"So you and the Irishman *are* battling." Daniel slid down the wall. "What can I do to help?"

"We're not *battling*."

Dolley was battling her stupid hormones. Warmth flooded her body. She wanted all the things Liam's kiss had promised. "Does Bess know this crazy protective side of you?"

His grin expanded. "She knows *every* side of me."

Dolley nudged him. "Keep it clean."

"Did Bess tell you she's moving in with me?" Eagerness filled his voice.

"Yeah. Yesterday." And Bess's eyes had gleamed as bright as Daniel's did now.

Maybe she should move into the Fitzgerald carriage house. She wasn't bringing in as much money as when she worked for Jackson.

The tech guys finally arrived.

"Good to see you, Vernon." Dolley pushed off the floor.

"Fun to work with you on the B and B again," he said.

They walked through the plans and requirements. "I'd like to use Fitzgerald House's Wi-Fi. Can we boost the signal to cover Carleton House?"

Daniel wandered away as she, Vernon and his team got into the gritty details of bandwidth, security, card readers and locks.

"We decided to run cable between the two houses," Dolley said when Daniel came back.

Vernon nodded. "With the server in Fitzgerald House, you'll have a cleaner signal."

Daniel helped decide on where to route the cable into Carleton House.

"That's all we need for now," Vernon said. "Answer your cell if I call."

"Will do." She headed back to the kitchen and tugged on her coat.

The door opened as she reached for the knob.

"Dolley." Liam filled the doorway, his black hair wind tousled. He smiled. "I've been looking all over for you."

Every muscle tightened. Her pulse accelerated, echoing in her ears. She should be able to be in the same room without wanting to touch him. "What do you need?" she snapped.

His smile slipped away.

Her face flamed in embarrassment. She'd been

hounding him to smile, and now she'd stripped one off his face. And worse, Liam was a guest. "I'm sorry. That was rude."

"Abby thought you could show me the Carleton House dining room."

"Sure." She headed down the hall.

"Thank you." His tone was so formal, no one would guess he'd had his tongue in her mouth. And it was her fault. She was the one acting weird.

She glanced back, but all he did was nod. "Why do you want to see the dining room?"

"When my team arrives, we'll need meeting space. Abby thought Carleton House was the best option."

She opened the dining room door. One wall was torn open to provide a pass-through from the butler pantry. "You'll have to imagine sliding windows through this hole. And a large table and buffet."

"We'd need large screen projection capabilities to review film."

She rubbed her neck. "Would this wall work? We have a picture slated, but we could wait to hang it."

"It might." He nodded, not looking at her. "She also mentioned a second floor parlor."

She led him up the stairs, the rattle of the paper protecting the refinished floors the only sound.

Opening a door, she said, "This used to be the old music room."

"Do you know what furniture will go in here?"

She pictured the lists she and her sisters had created. "A rose settee here. Two burgundy armchairs in front of the fireplace."

She walked the room, shaping the space with her hands. "A sofa. Coffee table in front of that. I found a really sweet secretary for this wall. We're not buying a baby grand, but I have my eye out for a small spinet or harpsichord for right here."

"Nothing but a coffee table?"

"Yes. And with the curved walls, it would distort any projection." She paced the room. "We could bring in a screen and work table."

He moved around, finally stopping in front of her. His stare pinned her like she was a butterfly on a board.

She shifted, her back hitting the wall. "Were there other rooms you wanted to see?"

"That was it." He took another step but didn't touch her. "Why?"

She didn't pretend not to understand his question. "I don't want to mess up working together."

"Why do you think it will?" His eyebrows smashed together above his gorgeous blue eyes. He was too damn easy to look at.

"Because it will."

She was getting what she needed from Liam, knowledge to launch a photography career. This apprenticeship was her ticket out of Savannah and into the limelight. She'd finally break free of her sisters' shadows.

Dating would complicate everything. People

might assume that's why he was helping her. She'd always wonder if she really had talent or if it had just been attraction.

Life would become too, too complicated.

"I think we can do both." He set his hands on the wall on either side of her head.

"I don't." She crossed her arms, ensuring she didn't reach out to straighten his hair.

"You're going to ignore the sparks between us?" He stroked a finger down her cheek. "You can ignore this?"

"We have to." She shivered, turning her cheek away from his hand. "We're adults. That shouldn't be that hard."

"But why should we want things to be hard?" He leaned in. "Kissing you makes sense to me."

She pressed on his shoulders, easing him away. "That's not what I want."

His breath ruffled her hair. They stared at each other.

"No," she croaked.

He held up his hands and backed away. "We're missing out on something spectacular."

He didn't understand. Men grew tired of her. She couldn't allow that to happen when her dreams were on the line.

"Do you want to see any other rooms?" Her voice shook.

"We'll use the dining room." His voice had chilled. "Can you get me prices?"

"Yes."

He nodded, his eyes icy blue. "Thanks for your time."

"It's for the best," she whispered. But Liam was gone.

This time when she sank to the floor, it was because her legs wouldn't hold her up.

LIAM JERKED OPEN his laptop. He'd planned to edit pictures, but couldn't do delicate work when he wanted to punch something. His long walk and stopping in for afternoon tea hadn't cooled his temper.

What did Dolley think would happen if they dated? He'd take advantage of her?

She should know him better than that. He adored her family. Maybe they needed to spend more time together. Then she'd realize they should give it a chance.

He clicked, then clicked again when the icon for his email didn't open. He took a deep breath and clicked one more time.

They'd kissed, she'd rejected him. Big deal. He'd been rejected before. Probably. It shouldn't bother him.

But it did.

His email opened. The first one—Ian asking whether he'd delivered the letters.

He sent back a terse Mission accomplished.

The second email was from Barbara. She'd lined up the rest of his crew. He sent a quick thank-you and dashed off replies to questions from his business manager and agent.

His email dinged, a message from Dolley. Email? Bollocks. Now she wouldn't talk to him?

It was the dining room rental agreement. He scanned the document. The cost was fair. He shot it off to Barbara. Let her look at the clauses and whatevers.

He shut his computer, a little calmer than when he'd opened it. But he still wasn't in the right frame of mind to edit photos.

If he wanted to spend more time with Dolley, he'd have to be sneaky. He wasn't above that. He'd worked angles with the boarding school kids, always figuring out who might take pity on him for holidays.

Pocketing his key card, he left his room. It was time to explore using the Fitzgeralds in the documentary. He wanted to open and close with Fitzgerald information. He could talk about his *shirttail* connection. It was the reason he'd started this quest.

The sisters would assign someone to work with him. He smiled. Dolley.

He pushed through the kitchen door, aware he was taking advantage of his long-term guest status. But Fitzgerald House felt like home.

Abby smiled. "Hi, Liam. Can I do something for you?"

He came up to the counter where she was packing away leftover bars from tea. "I'm wondering if you have any history of your family's Irish roots?"

"Dolley would be your best bet." She nodded over to the table. "Do you remember what happened to the old journals we found?"

Dolley tapped away on her laptop keyboard. She held up one finger, her head never popping up from her task.

Having been in the kitchen enough times, he pulled a mug from the stack, poured coffee and doctored it with milk.

"Can I pour for you?" he asked Abby.

"Sure."

He handed her a mug with a little sugar and a spot of milk.

She sipped. "You're handy to have around."

A snort sounded from Dolley.

He settled into a chair across the table from Dolley, trying to keep a smirk off his face. A plan coming together was a lovely thing.

Furrows formed between her eyebrows. Her hand moved back and forth from the mouse to the keyboard. She chewed her lower lip, a study of concentration.

His fingers clenched. Damn, he wanted to run his thumb along her worry lines and soothe the lips she abused. He wanted to kiss that mouth again. How could she deny them that pleasure? His breath wheezed out.

Her green gaze homed in on him. "A couple more minutes."

He nodded, sipping his coffee.

Abby joined them at the table, a plate of sweets in her hand. "So you're interested in the Fitzgerald family?"

Liam kept his eyes off Dolley so her sister didn't know how interested he was in one particular member of the family. "I want to include your family in the documentary."

"You do?" Abby almost bounced in her chair.

Dolley looked up, eyebrows arching over her entrancing eyes in disbelief. At least she wasn't frowning. Then she looked back at her keyboard, and her fingers flew.

He would make so many bloody mistakes if he typed that fast.

"Done." Dolley shut her laptop with a snap. "What are you looking for?"

Her gaze was like a green tractor beam. He fought against the pull. She'd been firm. Nothing personal between them.

Dolley would have to make the next move.

"I'd like to interview your family and tie James's journey to the Americas into the documentary."

"Why us?" Dolley's head tilted. "Aren't there other families that are more interesting?"

Not to him. "Trust me, viewers will be interested."

"I love this idea," Abby said. "I'd help if I could, but Dolley is our historian."

He kept the smile from breaking across his face. "Excellent."

Dolley crossed her arms in front of her chest. Her frown was back.

He kept his gaze on Abby's animated face. "Do you think I could interview you, your mum and your sisters?"

Abby turned to Dolley, touching her hand. "We could do the interviews when the family is here for my wedding." When Dolley kept frowning, Abby added, "Besides, Liam is helping us out with my wedding. We owe him."

He leaned forward. Abby was a coconspirator, even if she didn't know it.

Dolley eyed him suspiciously.

He sipped his coffee and put on his best innocent look.

She frowned harder.

"This could be good for the B and B," he added.

"Do we have control over what you say?" Dolley placed her elbows on the table and leaned into his space. "I don't want to hurt our *business*."

Did she think he'd forgotten that's all she wanted between them? He tipped his head. "You won't have absolute control, but I can let you review the rough edits."

And she would have to spend more time with him. Splendid idea.

"I know where the old journals are." She moved into the kitchen and took a set of keys off a rack next to the telephone. "I don't know how far back they go."

Liam stood. To Abby he said, "Why don't you give me possible interview dates? I'd like a two-hour block of time."

"Will do." Abby moved to a pad of paper on the counter and added a note.

Dolley waited for him in the hallway, her hands on her hips. "Don't think this changes anything between us."

"This is business. That's what you wanted, right?"

He wanted her thinking about him. About their kiss. "Thanks for the rental agreement. I've sent it on to my producer."

"Oh. Good." She blinked, long eyelashes covering her confused stare.

"Lay on, MacDuff." The phrase seemed appropriate. He waved his arm so she would lead. They were heading into a battle of wills. "I'd like to see these journals."

DOLLEY TOOK THE back stairs, not bothering to see if Liam followed. He was. His scent and footsteps filled the narrow stairway.

What game was he playing now?

She rubbed her temples. He was making her

crazy. Her vow of *business only* sounded childish and stubborn.

They moved down the third floor hallway to a recessed door.

"I didn't know there was a fourth floor," he said.

"It's not for guests." She unlocked the door and entered the narrow stairway. His scent grew fainter, making her want to turn around and take a sniff. Stupid.

She took the last steps in a rush. Flipping on the naked lights hanging from the ceiling, she moved into the room.

The narrow attic was tall enough for her to stand, but Liam had to duck. Maybe he would hit his head and knock some sense in his hard noggin.

"Shouldn't it be musty and dark up here, with cobwebs?" Liam asked.

"In Fitzgerald House? Cobwebs are not allowed. Marion sends someone up here once a month."

Old paintings leaned against the wall. Lamps filled a corner next to the chimney stacks. They might be able to use some of the bits and pieces they'd stored here for Carleton House. And there were trunks. Lots and lots of trunks. Steamers in different shapes and sizes had flat or domed lids. Some locked with ornate iron latches. They were made of wood and leather. Her favorites were the trunks with drawers and hidden compartments.

She opened the first trunk. Clothes. Kept opening and closing until she found one filled with Mylar bags.

She started to tug it to the center of the room.

Liam touched her back. "Let me."

Before she could protest, he picked it up and pulled it to the center. His head rapped against the ceiling. "Damn."

She winced. She really hadn't wanted him to hurt himself.

Kneeling, she opened the lid. When cleaning out the third floor, they'd tried to stop the papers and photos from deteriorating by placing everything in Mylar bags. She'd always meant to discover what secrets the past contained.

Liam's knees popped as he knelt next to her. "This is amazing."

"You might like to look at these." She opened a bag with all the Savannah maps they'd found. Some were still in frames. "We should be wearing gloves, so please handle them by the edges."

"Wonderful!" Liam gently picked up the plot of the city. "It's dated 1850. Look, another dated 1862. Any chance I could take pictures of these? They're better than what I found in the historical society."

"Sure."

She should have remembered there were things here Liam could use. Instead, she'd worried about her attraction to him.

Her shoulders slumped. She wasn't nice. He was

here to do a job. Not everything was about her and her needs.

Digging through the trunk, she found a shape that felt like a journal. Maybe they should have taken the journals to the historical society, but this was their heritage. "This should be one."

He sat, his long legs stretched out next to her. Picking up a bag, he asked, "May I open it?"

"Don't touch the paper." She looked into his eyes. And got lost.

She swallowed. His stare dipped to her throat.

"May I?"

What was he asking? Could he kiss her? She'd already explained why that was a terrible idea.

He held up the bag.

She blinked. God, he was asking whether he could open the book bag.

"Of course." Her voice was as rusty as the light fixtures they'd cleaned for Carleton House.

She shifted, pulling away from the vortex that tugged her close to his lean, wonderful body. Peering into the trunk, she pulled out more bags. She'd always planned to go through the journals, but they'd been busy finishing Fitzgerald House and beginning work on Carleton House. They'd stuffed everything in bags and forgotten them.

By the time she'd emptied the trunk, ten journals, two bags of letters and a pile of household and business ledgers sat between them on the floor.

"May I get the portable?" he asked.

"Portable?"

"Video camera." Excitement glowed in his eyes.

He glanced at her, and their connection clicked in place like finding the last piece of the jigsaw puzzle. She was afraid to breathe, afraid to move because it might be toward him and not away.

She forced herself to look away. "Portable. Of course."

His footsteps echoed on the stairs.

She leaned back, drawing in a full breath. Pathetic.

She checked the other trunks, not sure if someone had stored papers elsewhere.

Bingo. Here were books that looked like diaries. She placed them with the growing pile of documents.

Footsteps echoed on the stairs again, a little slower this time. He reappeared at the top of the steps, and the room shrank. How did his personality fill a space? He was usually quiet, watching, listening. Why was she so aware of every nuance of his expression?

Right now his face glowed. He stopped next to her. "Even if nothing ties into my research, I appreciate you letting me look at the material."

"I should have thought of the journals earlier." She stared at her feet.

He touched her chin, compelling her to look up. He was smiling, a rare gift to the world and to her. "The timing is grand."

He pulled his hand away.

She longed for his touch. How messed up was that?

"I'm thankful you remembered," he said.

She gazed into the depths of his blue eyes.

His smile faded. Something flickered in his eyes, and they darkened.

She didn't know how long they stared at each other. She wanted him to close the distance. Wanted his artist's fingers on her face and in her hair. Wanted his lips, so firm yet soft on her mouth.

"Thanks." He pulled away, bending to dig in the camera bag.

Her breath whooshed out. Disappointment weighed down her shoulders. He was doing exactly what she wanted—so why did it hurt?

"What can I do to help?" she asked. "Hold something for you?"

He attached a battery and checked settings. "Could you sit behind the trunk?"

"You don't want me in the shot?" she asked, appalled.

"Of course I do." He fumbled with switches.

"Umm, sure." She ran a hand through her tangled hair. Then she crouched next to the open trunk.

He peered through the viewfinder. "How long do you think the papers have been up here?"

He adjusted settings on the camera.

"James Michael Fitzgerald arrived in Savannah in the summer of 1830. He built Fitzgerald House in 1837. There was water damage in the 1950s, and there might have been a fire at some point, but when we stored the papers, a lot of the material was still intact."

"What do you know about James's relatives in Ireland?"

"Not much. He was the second son. I think they owned quarries."

He shouldered the camera. "I wonder if they ever came to visit."

She waved her hands at the bags scattered on the floor. "I guess when we go through the books and papers, we might discover whether they did. When we packed these up, we probably should have had everything filmed by the historical society."

"And why didn't you?" He walked around the room. He must have been looking at how to frame the shot. He was such a perfectionist.

"I guess we were being selfish." She shrugged. "We didn't want to give it away because it's ours."

He hit more buttons and pulled the camera off his shoulder.

"Not enough light?" she asked.

"Lighting's lovely."

"So you decided it wasn't a good shot?"

"The shot was great." He grinned. "Thanks."

She scrambled to her feet. "You didn't give me any warning."

"I didn't want you to tense up." He pointed to her shoulders. "Like you're doing now."

"I…" She *was* tensing up. She hated public speaking. Her back felt like there were rocks instead of muscles there. "Well."

He waved a hand at the papers. "What do you think is the best way to go through the material?"

They kicked around ideas and finally decided the attic was a good place to work. "I'll get Nigel to bring up tables and chairs. We'll need gloves."

"You'll help me?" he said.

He'd muttered the words so softly she had to lean in.

"I thought I was your research assistant." She tried to infuse her voice with lighthearted banter. But it just came out breathy.

"I wasn't sure you still wanted to work with me," he said.

She touched his arm. "That's what I don't want messed up."

He covered her hand with his. "Did someone hurt you?"

Oh, no. Not going to happen. She was not telling him how guys used her and tossed her away. "Too many to mention."

"They were fools." His lilt did funny things in her chest.

"Yes, they were." She slipped her hand out from under his.

This conversation was not about business.

Standing, she escaped his irresistible pull. It didn't matter that each day it got harder to ignore her fascination with Liam. She had too much at stake to give into a momentary attraction.

It was up to her to stay in control.

CHAPTER NINE

Your photography is a record of your living,
for anyone who really sees.

Paul Strand

DOLLEY TUGGED HER coat tighter. "I thought the fore-
cast called for warmer weather?"

"Warm on January 10 is still frigid." Bess rubbed
Dolley's shoulder as they headed to Carleton House
for a final walk-through.

Dolley chewed her lip. Tonight, she would ask
her sisters about moving into the Fitzgerald carriage
house. She'd chickened out last night when they'd
all been together.

"How's the attic research going?" Abby asked.

"Good. Great." Dolley's hand tapped a staccato
beat on her jeans. "We work a couple of hours most
nights. We're getting things organized into decades
first."

"I thought you were his photography apprentice?"
Bess asked.

"I am, but I'm also his research assistant." She
stuck her hand in her pocket. "He rented time in
SCAD's developing rooms. Tonight, I'll be a photographer. I haven't done darkroom work since college."

"It's probably like riding a bike." Bess swiped
a card against the reader and opened the kitchen

door. "I can't wait for y'all to see how Carleton house looks."

At night, no workers pounded or painted. The silence was—weird. "I should run back and get my camera. I need to update the blog."

"No." Bess grabbed her arm. "There's only a few things we need to finalize. You can come back later."

The official Carleton House opening was three weeks away. The cleaning crew had worked for the last week chasing construction dust.

As they headed to the front of the house, Dolley knelt and ran a hand against the heart of the pine floors. "I haven't seen the floors since they pulled up the protective paper. They're beautiful."

Bess nodded but shooed them upstairs.

Everything gleamed.

Bess led them into one of the bedrooms.

"Oh, my." Dolley swallowed. The room was pink. Hot pink. "Is this the color we picked?"

Abby shook her head. "No way."

"Bad, isn't it?" Bess asked.

"It's awful." Dolley shook her head so hard her curls whipped her eyes.

"Unless we want a Pepto-Bismol room." Abby grimaced. "Should we advertise it?"

"I have got to capture this." Dolley pulled out her phone and took pictures. It was so pink, her stomach twisted.

"We can call it the Pretty, Pretty Princess room."
Bess touched the wall.

"And fill it with toys." Dolley grinned. "Maybe
a play castle."

"It reminds me of Dr. Seuss," Abby said. "I'm
afraid the Whos will come running out."

They laughed. Dolley snapped a picture of Abby
and Bess bent over, the hideous wall behind them.
These pictures were definitely going on the website.

"We could advertise this as the most atrocious
room in the inn," Dolley said.

"Guaranteed to keep our guests awake," Abby
added.

"Or give them nightmares," Dolley said.

"Daniel already knows this is wrong." Bess
waved them into the hallway. "Come check the
others."

"Did you tell him in bed?" Abby elbowed her.

"Maybe." Bess winked.

Her sisters shared a knowing look. What was
next, a secret handshake for engaged women?

Dolley hung back as her sisters walked down the
hall. She sighed, but it didn't release the ache in her
chest. Being odd woman out of the Fitzgerald sisters sucked.

They double-checked the paint colors in the other
rooms.

"The rest are fine," Dolley said. "When do we
move in furniture?"

Bess checked her phone. "The twentieth."

"We have guests booked through end of March," Dolley said.

"It helps to have Liam and his crew here." Abby looked out the French doors to the balcony. "The wrought iron looks like it has been here forever."

When Liam's crew arrived, he would move out of the main house. Maybe then she wouldn't wander through Fitzgerald hoping to run into him.

She kept waiting for him to kiss her again.

Abby looked at her and frowned. "You're flushed. Are you getting sick?"

"No." She redirected her sisters' attention from her to the room. "We haven't bought tables for the balconies."

"If we move chairs up from the courtyard, we can wait a month or two," Bess suggested.

Abby nodded.

Dolley and Abby added to Bess's punch list, but Carleton House looked ready to take on guests.

They were pulling on their coats before Dolley got the courage to say, "My lease is up the middle of next month."

"They aren't turning your place into condos, are they?" Bess asked.

"No." She buttoned her jacket, not wanting to look in her sisters' eyes. It was embarrassing to ask to move home when she'd been on her own for years. "Since I'm only bidding projects for Jackson, what Liam's paying me just isn't enough to cover the gap. I'm wondering…can I crash in the carriage house for a few months?" The words rushed out. "It would just be while I'm working with Liam. Maybe for February and March. And April, too."

Abby and Bess stepped in front of her. She looked into their faces, fearing she'd see disappointment.

"Of course you'll use the carriage house." Abby grabbed her hand. "I love the idea."

"The apartment's clean." Bess nodded. "And Daniel and I will help you move."

"Can you be packed by move-in day, the twentieth?" Abby asked.

"I figured I'd move next month." Dolley shoved back a curl.

"We've got the opening, my wedding and then St Patrick's Day." Abby took in a deep breath. "It would be better to move everything on the same day."

"I guess." Dolley rubbed her forehead. She might not sleep between then and now, but she could make it happen.

Abby wrapped an arm around her. "It's perfect timing. With you living in the carriage house, you'll be right next to all the action. I can work you like a dog."

"There's something to look forward to." But now that she'd asked, she liked the idea of being back at Fitzgerald House. "I'll start packing."

A KNOCK ECHOED through the darkroom. Liam hung the last picture before opening the door. "Hallo."

"Hi." Dolley peered in. "I'm not ruining anything by letting light in, am I?"

"No." He held the door open, forcing her to brush next to him. Her warm scent tickled his nose.

Working in the darkroom would accomplish two things, developing Dolley's skills and putting her in close proximity.

But being in a small space with her might be frustrating—at least for him. Less than a week into his campaign to have *her* kiss *him* and his frustration level was spiking out of control.

She took a deep breath but wrinkled her nose. "I haven't been here in…years."

"Don't like the smell?" For him, it was like coming home.

"It reminds me of metal cleaner." Dolley shed her coat, hanging it on top of his. She walked over to the drying pictures. "What are you working on?"

"Bonaventure shots."

She moved around the ones he'd already developed. "I don't remember taking you to this statue."

"I've returned a couple of times." Every few days, the cemetery drew him back.

"What would you like me to do?" she asked.

"Would you take a test strip of the picture in the enlarger?"

"Sure, but it's been a while." She looked over the setup. "Is this the filter you want me to use?"

"Yes." He set a timer and stepped back to watch her. "Let's try five second increments."

Her actions were precise as she waited for the bing of the timer. Then she moved the cardboard down so there were five different exposure times. "Done."

"Go ahead and develop it." He moved away from the water baths.

"This is the part I liked." She slipped the blank paper into the developer bath. "What solution ratio are you using?"

They talked about the pros and cons of different chemicals.

"You did your homework before coming here," he said.

"Of course." Her smile flashed in the low red light. "I would hate to fail any pop quiz you throw at me."

"Now I'm going to have to come up with one." He peered over her shoulder as the picture began to form. "This is where the magic happens."

"Oh, it's Corrine." She moved the picture to the next bath and then the next. "How many times have you been back to Bonaventure?"

"Four or five." He was researching a project out there, but he would tell her about it later.

"I didn't know."

After running the picture through the final water bath, they stared at the finished product.

"Were you going for regret?" she asked.

"You nailed it." They were so in sync, why wouldn't

Dolley want to take their…connection to the next level?

"What's your recommendation?" He knew the exposure he wanted to try.

She leaned over the counter. "You want the most contrast, right?"

"Yes." He set his hand on the counter, not hemming her in, but invading her space a little.

Tapping the picture, she sidestepped away from him. "Somewhere between fifteen and twenty seconds."

"Why?"

"At fifteen seconds, we're able to see the details of her face—see the shadow here?" She pointed to an area behind the statue. "But at twenty seconds, we lose those shadows."

"Good. We need to burn in this area." This time he got close because he needed to demonstrate where the burn should occur.

"I was never good at dodging and burning." She looked over her shoulder at him. Her lips almost brushed his chin.

They both froze. Her eyes dilated. Was that the lighting or desire?

Dolley's breath whispered across his face. *Just a few more centimeters to heaven.*

He drank in her scent, her expressive face. Waiting. For Dolley.

"Liam?" Her voice broke the spell.

"Yes?"

She closed her eyes. Her shoulders hunched to her ears. "I...I can't."

"You can't what?" He shook his head. Was she as out of balance as he was?

"Us." She bit her lip.

"You could." He shook his head. "You won't."

She nodded. "Won't."

"What are you afraid of?" he whispered. He longed to touch her soft cheek and run his fingers through her messy curls, but he didn't.

"That we won't work out."

"How can we know if we don't try?" His hands slapped against the counter.

She jerked. "You...you live in Ireland."

"That's just where I store my things."

"What?" She scooted to the opposite side of the room.

"I love Savannah. I love your family." The idea of moving to Savannah took hold and rooted inside him and bloomed. "Why don't we see what happens?"

"I...but..." She shook her head. Her shoulders sagged. "Trust me. We wouldn't work out."

"Trust you?" He backed away, rejected again. "Grand."

He turned to the enlarger, when he really wanted to shake her. "Let me walk you through this."

Locked in a small room for two hours with Dolley hadn't been his smartest idea. It was going to be a long, frustrating night.

LIAM FOCUSED THE camera on the letter in front of him. It was water-stained, and the handwriting was faded but legible. It was from Seamus, Michael's son, and had been sent to James's son, also named Michael. The American Michael was the first generation FitzGerald to be born on American soil. They'd still capitalized the *G* in the surname.

He'd hung the family tree Ian had given him in the attic. It was the only way he and Dolley kept track of the duplicate names. There were too many Seamuses and Michaels.

He started to run his hand through his hair but stopped. He wore gloves to protect the aging paper.

They'd made a dent in figuring out the correspondence dates. Hard, because water damage had destroyed the edges of the letters and blurred the writing.

"Find anything new?" Dolley's question had him jerking straight up.

"I think it's a letter to James's son from a cousin in Ireland." He held it up.

She leaned over his shoulder, her scent wrapping around him. He inhaled. His vow to keep his hands off her made him ache.

"The handwriting is lovely." She tugged on gloves.

He handed the letter to her, relieved when she moved away.

She scanned the page. "Must be the start of the

famine. He mentions that families and young people are starting to leave."

He nodded. "I can't make out the year, but I believe you're right."

She smiled at him. Then noticed the camera. "You took pictures?"

"I might use the letters in the film. It's real people talking about the problems in Ireland." He pointed to the pile of items he'd planned to capture.

"Do you want me to take the photos?" she asked.

"That would be helpful."

They worked side by side. Other than his desire to wrap his arms around her and lay his lips on that pink mouth, they had a good rhythm.

Once she put the camera away, they sat. Dolley carefully worked two stuck pieces of paper apart. Her curls bobbed as she read the first one. She caught her lower lips between her teeth.

Was she a sadist? Didn't she know he wanted to bite that lip?

Her concentration was a thing of beauty. It was why she was such a good photographer. She waited for the picture to unfold. It was something he hadn't had to teach her. Something he constantly had to remind himself of.

She set the letter in the early 1900s pile.

He should stop watching her and get back to his own material.

She flipped to the signature page and then back

to the first page. A smile erupted like fireworks. "I found one."

She looked at him, and her eyes flashed a little greener. Her breasts rose a little faster with each breath.

"Found one what?" He couldn't think beyond wanting her eyes to sparkle that bright for him.

"A letter written in 1831 from Patrick FitzGerald." She held up the letter, and it trembled in her hand. "It's what you're looking for. He's James's father, right?"

He grinned, excitement bubbling inside. "Righto."

"He's my great-however many times grandfather?" She bounced in her chair.

"Five times." He pointed at the tree.

"Hang on." Dolley pushed out of her seat and placed a hand on his shoulder. "Why didn't I think of this before? Family Bible!"

She dashed out of the room.

He sighed. Dolley leaving the room was like the sun had set and taken all the energy with her. He picked up the letter.

Dearest son,
I hope this letter finds you in good health. Your letters telling of finding lodging and the design of Savannah were read and enjoyed by all. And the glad tidings that your ship and shipment of cotton and indigo arrived safely in London is good news indeed. The Captain stopped in

Kilkee to drop letters and created a stir when his boat entered the harbor. It is…

A water stain blurred most words after that, but it gave him a chill. These words were written almost two hundred years ago.

"Here it is." Dolley burst up the stairs, bringing back the sunshine.

She flipped to the page where a lengthy list of births and deaths had been recorded.

"Is this a FitzGerald Bible, or your father's?" he asked.

"Fitzgerald. We don't have much from the Oliver side."

"Good." He checked the first name in the Bible. "Although this looks like the Bible came from James and Michael's mother's side. She was an O'Donahue."

She elbowed him. "And you call me a walking computer."

"You are." He pushed a curl away from her eye. "Was it unusual for your mother to keep the Fitzgerald name?"

"Yes, but I'm glad." Her nose wrinkled. "The daughter keeps the Fitzgerald name until there is a son. Our papa wasn't above using the Fitzgerald name to improve his stature."

"So, Abby will keep her name?" Liam asked. "And all her children will be Fitzgeralds?"

"I never thought about that." She grinned. "Wonder what Gray will think?"

"He'll do anything Abby wants."

She laughed. "I think you're right."

They filled in births and deaths on the family tree.

"It's ridiculous doing this by hand." Dolley shook her head. "We need a computer and a program."

He tipped his head. "Can you say *research assistant*?"

"Can you say *happy apprentice*?" She tapped his lips. Her eyes went wide, and she snatched her hand away.

And he smiled. Slowly but surely, she was touching him more often. "I think that's smile number three today."

"You don't need to count my smiles." She rolled her eyes. "I'm sure I've smiled more than that in the hour I've been up here with you."

"Then I guess you're not doing your job." They were almost nose to nose. *Her move.*

Dolley's tongue snuck between her teeth and touched her upper lip.

Her phone rang.

They jerked like children caught with their hands in the sweets bowl.

She fished her mobile out of her pocket. "Hey, Anne."

He turned back to the paper, eavesdropping. He'd heard her talk to this Anne more than once.

"That sounds like fun. I'll see you around eight." She pushed the phone back into her jumper pocket. "Are you interested in another foray into the pub scene?"

She bit her lip again. Was it because she hadn't meant to invite him, or because she wanted him to accept the invitation?

It didn't matter. "Sure. Bring your camera and we'll work on nighttime indoor pictures."

And he would work on getting her to make the next move.

Maybe Dolley should have taken this night to get some distance from Liam. But when Anne had called, they'd been having—fun. She glanced at him as they headed down the steep steps to River Street.

What if she took a risk and changed their relationship? Maybe Liam would be different. But how cliché was a mentor and apprentice dating? It sounded sordid and definitely not professional.

"Hang on." Liam slipped his camera out of his bag.

She hung back, trying to figure out his picture's focal point. The cobblestones were damp, and the dim streetlights gave her an impression of bleakness. A man moved ahead of them in the dark.

How could she frame a picture to show hope? She pulled out her own camera and zoomed in on the streetlight pushing back the gloom. The glow of the light was a beautiful warm orange.

They exchanged cameras. In Liam's picture, the man was an eerie shadow in the dark street.

He stared at her pictures. "Do you find hope in everything?"

She didn't answer. "Do you see only isolation and solitude?"

"Probably." He chuckled, but it wasn't a happy sound. He didn't seek joy. His dark outlook on life was a good reason not to change their relationship.

"What's my smile goal tonight?" he asked.

She didn't know how to help him change his attitude. "What do you think it should be?"

"Two."

She snorted. "Ten."

"Four?"

"Eight, and I'm not dropping lower."

They stopped one more time to take pictures of the river and the boats docked upstream. "They're not as dreary as your last pictures." She handed his camera back.

"Maybe I need you to remind me every day to look for the joy in life." His blue gaze caught hers and snatched her breath away.

She wasn't capable of being his happiness monitor. She was learning *from* him. If she was good enough, maybe he could connect her to the right people to take her work to the next level.

But that sentiment felt—wrong. She'd come to value her time with Liam.

He held the door for her. "Okay. Eight smiles."

"Don't feel you have to be stingy."

He grinned. "One."

Groups gathered next to the bar. She searched for Anne. "Let's see if she's near the stage."

Anne and a couple more work friends had commandeered a table near the windows, a little back from the stage. Empty glasses filled the table. Anne waved them over.

"I missssss you." Anne gave her an enthusiastic, inebriated hug.

"Been here a while?" Dolley whispered.

Anne giggled. "Yeah."

Hmm. Drunk Anne could be good or bad. Hopefully, she wouldn't be crying in her beer by the end of the night.

She and Liam headed to the open chairs. Liam pulled hers out, so she could sit down. Had anyone ever held her chair before?

After making introductions, she and Liam ordered pints, and the rest of the table ordered another round.

"I love your accent," Anne gushed. "Dolley told me how fabulous it was, but it's nothing like hearing it in person."

Dolley glanced at Liam.

He grinned, holding up two fingers.

She racked her memory. Hopefully, that was the only embarrassing thing she'd confessed to Anne.

There was a rustle of people, and the entertainment moved onto the small stage. One man held a small flute and another a mandolin. A woman carried a fiddle.

Liam's eyes lit up. "Are they playing traditional music?"

"Of course." Sliding her chair around, she faced the stage. She leaned closer to his ear. "The tourists eat it up."

She stayed there too long, absorbing his warmth. When she slid back in her seat, Anne grinned at her. Dolley shook her head.

"Who's driving you home?" Dolley whispered.

Anne pointed down the table.

Faith had a soft drink in front of her. She heaved an exaggerated sigh. "I'm designated driver."

At least Dolley didn't need to retrieve her car and cart Anne home.

The music started. A sad, lilting ballad.

Liam leaned forward, hands on his thighs, his focus on the stage. He could block out everything else. Was that why he was so good at what he did? Did she need to focus more? Take up meditation to calm the racket inside her head?

What if Liam focused on her? A thrill ran down her spine and curled into her center. Ever since their kiss, it was hard not to think of kissing him again. Of being free to touch him and run her fingers in the black silk of his hair.

There was another reason to stay away from him. If she was thinking about kissing him, she wasn't concentrating on what he could teach her.

She sighed.

Liam turned and smiled. And held up three fingers. Almost halfway to the goal. Would they leave when he smiled eight times?

He held up his camera.

She was supposed to be working. See. Lack of focus.

She debated what to shoot. Lights shone from the floor up to the performers. Dust swirled in the beams.

She moved closer, holding up her camera to the woman with the fiddle. The fiddler nodded, her hands flying up and down the neck of her instrument. The bow wove a pattern in the air.

If she kept the shutter open, would she capture the energy of the song? She screwed the camera onto her tripod.

Concentrating only on the fiddler's strong hands against the dark wood of the instrument, she blurred the background. If she captured that power, she would be happy.

Then she did the same with the other musicians. With the flute she wanted to evoke *gentleness* during a sad song. The mandolin, *sweetness*.

She pulled back the focus and framed the trio. They'd morphed into a rollicking reel. Their faces were dewed with sweat. *Energy*. She was still snapping pictures as they ended the set with a flourish.

She moved back to the table.

Liam held out his hand. "Let's see."

She chewed on her lip.

He scrolled through the photos, pausing on the close-ups. "I don't know that I would have done the close-ups, but I love them." His fourth grin of the night. "You've a talent, Miss Dolley Fitzgerald."

Heat rushed through her body. "Thank you."

He pulled release forms out of his bag. "Now for the not-so-fun stuff."

He tugged her to the stage. A few customers were talking to the trio.

The fiddler approached them. "Hallo."

"A countrywoman," Liam said. "Where might you be from?"

"Dublin."

Liam and the trio talked. Dolley listened to their travel discussion. Envy hollowed out her stomach.

"We're here through St Paddy's Day," the fiddler said.

"I'm wondering if you might sign releases in case the pictures my associate took are used in a film and book I'm putting together."

The woman nodded.

Liam handed her the papers and a pen. She took them to the two men.

Dolley's mouth dropped open. Associate? And he wanted to use her pictures?

Liam tapped her chin, making her teeth clack together. "Don't look so surprised."

"You want to use my pictures?" Her voice squeaked.

Another grin swept across his face. "Aye."

"Any chance we could get copies?" the fiddler asked.

Liam looked at Dolley, but she was speechless. "Absolutely," he answered for her. "An email would do."

Dolley stumbled back to the table. It was happening. Her photographs might appear somewhere other than *Bridal Party Today* and the B and B's blog. She sank into the chair, her heart pounding a little. Her dream was coming true. And it felt—fantastic.

Anne shifted chairs, wrapping an arm around her shoulder. She leaned over Dolley and said to Liam, "How are you doing helping our Dolley find a career in photography?"

Liam frowned. "What?"

"She was hoping you'd give her a leg up in the industry." Anne looked between the two of them.

"Anne." Dolley settled her friend back in her chair. "I don't know what you're talking about." Her words were so fast, they ran together.

Anne frowned. "You wanted Liam to get you a job, right?"

"She told you that?" Liam's gaze turned a glacial blue.

"Last fall. Before you'd agreed to mentor her?" Anne blinked and shook her head.

"Anne," Dolley choked out.

"Remember. You told me your big secret. You wanted Liam to fast-track your career." Anne's eyes grew huge. "Secret. I forgot. I wasn't supposed to say anything."

"A secret." Liam's jaw clamped tight.

Dolley closed her eyes. "Liam, it's not as… mercenary as it sounds."

He nodded. His expression was as impenetrable as granite.

All this time she'd worried dating Liam would ruin her chances of learning about her craft. And it was Dolley's own ambitions and her friend's big mouth ruining everything.

LIAM WATCHED DOLLEY'S fingers twist into knots.

His gut burned. It was Kieran all over again.

Did Dolley feel guilty for using him? Did it matter? She'd seen an opportunity and grabbed for it. Was she holding out on him until she could ask about helping her find a job? Maybe this—connection between them was fake. Shite.

No wonder Dolley hadn't kissed him. She was only in it for what he could *do* for her. *Mercenary*. He rubbed at the ache in his chest. She'd used the ugly word. He wanted to get as far away from her as possible. She'd fooled him once. Once was enough.

"Right, then." He pushed away from the table and slung his camera bag over his shoulder. "I'm off."

Dolley pulled bills out of her purse and tossed them on the table. "I'll come with you."

"Stay with your friends." The words came out in a harsh growl.

"No." She leaned down to Anne. "I'll talk to you tomorrow."

Liam strode toward the exit, not waiting. He'd wanted to stay and listen to the music, but his pleasure was gone.

Her light footsteps echoed behind him. "Wait."

He kept going. His legs chewed up the distance. Disappointment was the only companion he wanted right now. That and maybe Jameson.

"Liam!" The click of her shoes moved faster.

He couldn't bear to look at her. He should be making sure Dolley got home safely, but everything inside hated her duplicity. Didn't she know he would have helped her no matter what?

Now everything had changed.

He took the steps up to Bay Street two at a time, his thighs complaining at the pace. But he couldn't shake the echo of her footsteps.

There was a smack of leather on stone. And a grunt. "Ooohh."

Don't turn around. But he couldn't stop himself.

Dolley was splayed over the steps, cradling her bag.

He closed his eyes and exhaled. Then headed down the steps. "Are you all right?"

Tears glistened in her eyes. "No."

He bent and took her elbow to help her off the cold, wet steps.

She winced and stood slowly. Her arm shook under his fingers.

"Can you check my camera?" Her voice trembled as much as her body.

Liam slid the strap over her shoulder, bumping the side of her breast. "Sorry."

His body perked up, and he slapped down his desire. His campaign was through. Pulling out her Nikon, he checked that there weren't any dents. Then he turned on the power, focused, shot pictures of the steps above them. "Everything's savage."

"What?"

"Fine. It's fine."

"It's not what you think. Really. I told Anne about the possibility of you becoming my mentor." Her words ran together. She grabbed his hand and stared into his eyes. "I might have said it would be great if you could help me. But that's not why I wanted to learn from you. You're talented. That's why I wanted to work with you. Not so you would find me a job."

He yanked his hand away but couldn't stop staring at her face. She gnawed on her poor lower lip.

"Please, Liam." She touched his arm.

He shrugged away her hand. "Are you okay to walk?"

She swallowed. "Yes."

He started to climb the stairs but stopped to check on her.

Dolley grabbed the railing and shuffled her feet

one step at a time. Each time she put weight on her left leg, her face contorted.

"Oh, for God's sake," he muttered.

Retracing his steps, again, he stopped next to her. "What did you do?"

"I tried to save my camera, so I twisted and landed on my left side. My hip took a beating." Her words came out in a shaky gasp.

"Hang on." He shouldn't have come to the pub with her. Why hadn't he left well enough alone? He placed one arm under her thighs and the other around her waist. "Up you go."

"Oh." She grasped his neck with her hand.

He'd imagined holding her countless times, but this scenario wasn't in any of his fantasies. How could cuddling her into his chest feel so right and be so wrong? As he climbed the stairs, he tried to make sure he didn't press his fingers into her sore left side.

Obviously, he wasn't meant to be part of any relationship. Even Dolley only wanted to be around him for what he could do for her career.

"Please, forgive me." She set her head against his chest. "It wasn't like Anne made it sound. I just want to do something special with my photography. Is it wrong to dream?"

"It's wrong if you're using me." His head brushed against the curls peeking out from her woolen hat. They were as soft as he remembered. Her warm scent wrapped around him.

"If I was using you, would I have fought so hard

to keep things businesslike?" Her fingers twisted the button of his coat. "Wouldn't I have encouraged a relationship?"

"I don't know what goes on in the computer you call a brain." His anger was fading. He wanted to clutch it tight, so he didn't get hurt.

"It wasn't that way." She touched his face. "It was the day you offered the mentorship. I was so nervous. I have no idea what I told Anne."

He looked down at the curvy bundle in his arms. Mistake. Tears hung on her eyelashes. "Apparently, you told her you like my voice."

"I love your voice." She hiccupped. "I could listen to you all night."

Was that an invitation?

He'd never understand Dolley.

He focused on the sidewalk and not the woman in his arms. He was going to get mental whiplash from her.

"I can probably walk." She tucked her head deeper into his chest. Even through the layers of coat and shirt, her touch had him heating up.

He set her on her feet, if for no other reason than self-preservation.

"I'm sure it's just a bad bruise." She took a few hobbling steps, favoring her left leg. "Trying to walk up the steps was too much. I'll be fine."

He stayed right next to her, wanting to put his arm around her waist, just to help her keep the pressure off her sore side.

Her jaw gritted with determination, but with each step, her shoulders stiffened.

"Oh, devil take me." He wrapped his arm around her waist and took her weight every time she stepped on her left leg.

"Thanks," she whispered through clenched teeth.

"Where do you live?" he asked.

"Just…take me to Fitzgerald House. I'll crash in the carriage house."

"Grand." Everything was *grand*, right?

Her curls brushed his nose, enticing him with the scent that was all Dolley. He tried to hold on to his anger, really tried, but he couldn't. He didn't want the wound from her mercenary talk to heal.

"What did you think I could do for you?" he asked.

"What?" she croaked.

"When you were talking to Anne, what did you think *I* could do for you?"

"I have no idea." Her head rubbed back and forth in the cup of his shoulder. "I guess advice more than anything. It was a nebulous desire. I want to…to be you. Travel and see the world through my camera lens."

"I've done it." He thought about sleeping on the ground in bug-infested tents. Of making acquaintances for a month or two. Of never belonging. "It's not as romantic as you think."

"But you've done it." He felt her sigh. "You make a living doing what you love."

She stumbled, and he tightened his grip. "There's more to living than making a living." But she'd never understand that. She had what he wanted—family, friends, roots.

"Too bad we can't change places," he mumbled.

"Why would you want to be a nobody website designer stuck in Savannah?"

"You need to work on your self-image."

"That's what I am." She shifted, and a moan rumbled through her body.

"I want to get back to the B and B before next month." He swept her back up in his arms. "You're a partner in a successful business. You're incredibly bright and a brilliant photographer."

He felt her head tip back, but he wasn't going to look down at her. If he did, he'd kiss her. How could this woman not understand she was amazing?

"In Savannah, I'm just the youngest Fitzgerald sister. Everyone knows about Abby and Bess. I'm the other one."

He stared at her. Gave in and brushed a kiss on her forehead. "You are so wrong."

He took a side gate into the Fitzgerald House courtyard. Lights spilled through windows and curtains in the main house. The bushes glowed with tiny blue-and-white lights. A nighttime fairyland.

It would be safer to leave Dolley at the foot of the carriage house stairs, but she needed his help. The thump of his steps on the stairs echoed in the night.

He set her gently on her feet. She dug in her purse

and came up with a key chain sporting a fob with the Fitzgerald House logo.

Everything she touched carried the mark of her family's success. How could she think she wasn't a key ingredient to that recipe? He'd heard the three sisters discuss their business. Everyone's voice was heard.

He wanted desperately to be valued like that. Not for his talent, but because he was Liam.

Dolley had no clue how lucky she was.

"Thank you for helping me," she said, unlocking her door.

"You're welcome." He started to turn, but she clutched his arm. He reached out to steady her.

Her face, normally so animated, was solemn. "I'm sorry."

She tugged on his shoulders, forcing him to bend.

Her lips settled against his mouth. Just a soft brush, but enough to set his body churning.

He clutched her, tugging her onto her toes.

Her mouth opened under his.

He should push her away.

Instead, he wrapped his arms under that sweet behind and pulled her so she didn't stand on her sore leg.

His tongue chased hers. There was that taste he craved. All Dolley. He swept kisses along her cheek, running his teeth along the delicate shell of her ear. He blew softly into her ear.

She moaned his name, tugging him back to her mouth. This kiss was deeper, hotter.

His breath rasped in and out.

Her hands roamed down his back, cupping his butt and pulling him closer.

He braced her against her door to take more.

It flew open, banging on the wall and bouncing back. He caught the rebounding door before it smacked her.

She dropped her head to his shoulder and laughed. A laugh that vibrated through her whole body.

"We're barking mad," he gasped. Hugging her close, he let his rusty laugh join hers, their chests rising and falling together.

She wiggled down his body. He held her until she was steady. He hated the cool air that filled the space where they had touched. He leaned against the door frame, not wanting to leave, but knowing he wasn't going to stay. Pity, that.

"Are we okay?" she asked. "I don't want my stupidity to screw anything up."

"We're good." He stroked her cheek. "I'll wander back to my room."

"Thank you for helping me." Her green eyes were huge as she shuffled into the apartment.

He tugged the door closed with a click.

Setting his hand on the wood, he sighed. He'd gotten what he wanted. Dolley had kissed him.

What did it mean? Had she kissed him so he would keep helping her? Was it panic—or real?

CHAPTER TEN

Everything has beauty, but not everyone sees it.

Confucius

"HAVE YOU SEEN LIAM?" Dolley limped into the kitchen. She had to make sure she and Liam were okay.

"Was I on Liam watch?" Abby made a production of checking her to-do list. "Nope. You have that honor."

"Right." Dolley rolled her eyes. Wait. Did Abby suspect something? "I thought...you might have talked to him this morning. That's all," she sputtered.

Abby frowned. "Did something happen?"

"We were at Kevin Barry's, and Anne was drunk. She said something that made it sound like I was... using him." Dolley rubbed her temple, but her headache pounded harder.

"Liam's spent enough time with you to know that's not true." Abby came over and rubbed Dolley's left arm. "Don't worry."

Dolley winced.

Abby pulled away. "What's wrong?"

"I fell climbing the River Street stairs." She exhaled. "And landed on my left side."

"Oh, Dolley." Abby reached out to hug her but stopped. "Would a cup of tea help?"

"Yes." Dolley shuffled to the sitting area and

eased onto the sofa with a groan. "Any muffins left from breakfast?"

"Do you want apple cinnamon or the ginger fig?"

"Ginger fig."

Dolley leaned back on the sofa and closed her eyes. What if Liam had second thoughts? What if he believed she was mercenary? Had kissing him seemed like a ploy, too? Her head throbbed with worry.

"Here you go." Abby set a mug of tea on the coffee table. Then she handed her a couple of ibuprofen and a warm muffin with cream cheese melting on the top.

"You're the best." Dolley swallowed the pills.

"What are you doing here so early?"

"I didn't want to walk to my apartment last night." Dolley shifted off a sore spot. "I crashed in the carriage house."

"You must really hurt." Abby turned to her lists. "Did you get your bridesmaid's dress back from the seamstress yesterday?"

"I didn't have a chance. I might have Technicolor skin for your wedding."

"You're that bruised?" Alarm filled Abby's voice.

Dolley rolled up the sleeve of her sweater. A deep purple bruise covered most of her upper arm.

"Ouch. There's always makeup. Maybe the bruises will fade in two weeks."

"If they don't, Liam will make *me* touch up the photos." Assuming he didn't fire her. "Or I can only have the right side of my body in the pictures."

They both chuckled.

"Don't make me laugh." Dolley grabbed her ribs. "It hurts."

Abby sat on the coffee table and took her good hand. "I should take you to the ER. You could have cracked a rib."

"I'm just sore." Dolley changed the subject. "I saw Mamma's coming down the end of the week."

A smile lit Abby's face. "She loved the idea of being part of Liam's documentary. Personally, I think she wants to adopt the man. We'll do the interview before the wedding."

"Great." *Not.* She didn't want to have to talk on camera. Dolley rolled a little. The bruise on her hip ached.

While she finished her tea and muffin, they talked about Carleton House and timing issues. "I guess I'll see if I can find Liam."

Maybe she should call. Going to his room might make him doubt her sincerity even more. She rolled her shoulders. Mistake. She breathed through the pain.

Even after taking the elevator, she was groaning by the time she knocked on Liam's door.

"Coming," he called.

The door opened. His face was a solemn mask. "Hallo."

His blue gaze stole her breath. She wheezed out, "Hi."

They stared at each other. Sound slipped away.

There was only him. Their chests rose and fell in sync.

He didn't reach for her. Did he regret last night? Or was it happening again? A couple of kisses and another man was done with her.

"Would you like to come in?" he asked.

"Yes." She forced her feet to move in a limping shuffle.

Last time she'd been in his room, she hadn't noticed the clutter of Liam's life. Piles of books overflowed the tables. Flip charts hung from the walls. Notepads occupied the chairs. "Impressive."

"Yes." But he wasn't looking at his work, he was looking at her.

A blush heated her face—darn redheaded genes.

"How are you feeling?" he asked.

"Nervous." She wrapped her arms around her waist, her fingers tapping her sweater. "Embarrassed. Anxious."

His eyebrows popped up. "I meant your side. Where you fell."

"Oh." She stuffed her hands in her pockets. "Sore. I'm growing impressive bruises."

"I'm sorry you were hurt."

They stood in the middle of the room.

"I just—" she said.

"Last night—" he started at the same time.

They both stopped.

"Sit." He cleared a tablet off the sofa.

She sank onto the cushions, easing her foot onto the coffee table.

Instead of sitting next to her, he took the armchair. "Go ahead."

She'd rather Liam go first.

If she apologized again and he thanked her but wanted nothing more to do with her, she'd curl into a depressed ball. Stalling, she asked, "What were you going to say?"

"Ladies first."

"I'm sorry Anne made me sound…like such a scheming bitch." She looked into his eyes, biting her lower lip. "It's not true."

"Do you think I think so little of you?" His voice was low and deep.

"I…I don't know." She rubbed her temple. "I'm not good with men."

"You have more male friends than I do!"

"I'm not good at the—" she waved her hand between their bodies "—romantic part. Men don't like me that way."

"Then they don't see how amazing you are, darlin'." He shifted to the sofa, sitting on her right side. "May I put my arm around you?"

She nodded, afraid if she talked, her voice would crack.

Carefully, he tucked her into his chest. "I don't want to hurt you."

She turned her face into his shirt. "You were upset last night."

"I got over it." He brushed his lips on her forehead. "You kissed my anger away."

She traced patterns on his chest. The ability to touch him felt natural but odd.

"What are you frettin' on?" he asked.

"Why are you so different?" she blurted out.

"Different?" He smoothed a curl off her face. "How's that?"

"You've been around me for almost a month." She looked at her lap. "Most guys tire of me by now."

He tugged her chin up. "I told you, Yanks don't appreciate you."

Cupping her cheek, he dipped his head. His eyes were so serious, it made her breath catch in her chest.

"You're special." His mouth brushed hers.

She tilted her head, wanting more than a soft, tender kiss.

His lips pressed harder, and she opened to him. He delved in and stroked her tongue.

She chased his tongue with hers, tasting coffee and mint and Liam.

He groaned. His hand slipped to her chest, hesitating when she wanted him to be bold.

She pressed his hand to her breast.

"Dolley." His hands tested and massaged. His thumb brushed against her aching nipple. Wrapping his arm around her waist, he pulled her onto his lap.

"Owww." Pain knifed through her.

He cursed. "I forgot. I'm sorry. Sorry."

She let out a shaky breath, tears filling her eyes. "Damn."

His hand stroked her back. "Are you all right?"

She took a shallow, shaky breath. "I will be."

He eased her back onto the sofa. "I should have waited."

"I didn't want you to." She wanted more, but the pain was too much.

Concern filled his face. "Can I get you something? Do you need pills, water?"

"Abby took care of me." She smoothed her finger over the furrows between his eyebrows. "Now what?"

He pressed a chaste kiss on her lips. "Now we work in the attic."

She chuckled. "You say the sweetest things."

As they headed to the elevator, she asked, "Working together won't change, right?" Anxiousness made her voice crack.

"I always thought we could work together and have a relationship." His jaw flexed. "Why don't we take it a day at a time?"

One day at a time. She liked to plan a little further ahead than that. But maybe that was her problem. "Okay. A day at a time."

DOLLEY GRABBED THE box of half-dead plants from her car. It was moving day for her and Carleton House.

No working with Liam on research or photography today. She sighed. And no kisses. His kisses over the last week and a half were the highlight of her day. Year. Decade. She worried she was a junkie, first addicted to his cologne and now his kisses.

Bess and Abby exited the Fitzgerald House kitchen door.

"Moving day!" Abby called from across the courtyard. "Do you want me to grab anything?"

"There are boxes and suitcases in my car." Dolley hurried up the steps as fast as she could. Most of the soreness had eased, but her hip still hurt. Plus, she didn't want Bess to see the plants she'd almost killed.

"What have you done?" Bess's steps pounded behind her.

"How could you see the plants from across the courtyard?" Dolley asked.

Bess shook her head. "I heard them crying."

Dolley handed Bess the box and unlocked the door. "I've been busy."

"No excuses," Bess scolded, taking the box into the kitchen. She pulled out a drooping Peace Lily and African violet. "Oh, my lands."

Dolley left her tending the abused plants. She held the door for Abby as her sister hauled in a suitcase, then headed to the car to grab more boxes.

The car was empty in fifteen minutes.

"I feel like we just moved Bess out of here." Abby sank to the floor.

"We did." Dolley checked to see if any of the trucks had arrived.

"Daniel's just leaving your apartment." Bess looked up from her phone. "Rest while you can, ladies. We'll unload your furniture. The first truck for Carleton House arrives in fifty minutes."

"It's hard to believe this is happening." Abby bounced a little. "Last year Fitzgerald House had unfinished rooms."

They talked about reservations and Abby's wedding and Bess's engagement. She hadn't figured out how to tell her sisters about Liam.

She chewed her nail.

"Not you, too." Abby tapped her hand. "Don't pick up Bess's bad habit."

Dolley pulled her thumb away from her mouth.

"What's wrong?" Bess asked. "Still sore?"

"Yeah." Let them think it was her bruises rather than confessing she was in a relationship with her mentor. She didn't want anyone to think what she and Liam were exploring was—sleazy. She took in a deep breath. It was amazing. He was amazing.

The rumble of a truck in the parking lot had them pushing to their feet.

"Let's do this." Dolley led the way down the steps.

"You're limping," Abby said to Dolley. "Hand out boxes from the truck."

"Okay." Dolley didn't argue.

Gray dropped the truck ramp with a clang. "Are you ready?"

Abby pulled him into a hug. "Always."

Daniel came around from the front of the truck and swung Bess into a hug. "'Morning."

The two couples kissed.

"Enough," Dolley called out, wishing Liam was here to greet her the same way. She climbed into the truck and handed boxes to her sisters. "Do something constructive."

Daniel and Gray pulled out her sofa.

While they climbed the stairs, she moved boxes to the truck ramp. It held most of her possessions. If she left Savannah, what would she do with her things? Her stomach twisted at the thought.

"What can I haul up?" Liam called from outside.

Warmth filled her. "What are you doing here?"

"Helping." He hopped into the truck and closed in on her.

"You're a guest." Dolley chewed her lip.

Touching her cheek, he said, "I want to help. You're not completely healed."

She drew in a quick breath, leaning into his touch. Her heart pounded. After being around him for a while, shouldn't this physical reaction lessen? "Thanks."

"'Morning." His voice was low. It drilled into her core.

Her hand covered his. "'Morning."

Footsteps echoed on the stairs.

They stepped apart.

"I feel guilty pulling you away from your work," she said.

"Don't." His eyes sparkled in the dim light. "It just means you'll have to spend late nights helping me catch up."

He jumped out of the truck and grabbed a box before she could reply.

Swallowing, she stripped off her fleece sweatshirt. It was heating up in here.

They emptied the truck. Boxes and people filled her new living room.

Daniel looked up from his phone. "The first Carleton House truck is almost here."

Everyone headed over to Carleton House, but she held Liam back.

"Thank you." She stood on her toes and brushed a kiss on his lips.

He backed her against the door, his fingers threading through her hair. "I hated the idea of not seeing you all day."

Her mouth dropped open, and he took advantage of her surprise. Their tongues thrust and parried, a mock duel she didn't mind losing.

When he pulled away, she was gasping. Thank goodness she was leaning against the door, or her legs might have given way.

He grinned. "Let's head to Carleton House."

"You're cruel," she muttered.

Working around Liam all day was torture. He

was everywhere, and she couldn't stop admiring his butt as he lifted and carried.

They took a break in the Carleton House dining room. Cheryl set out muffins, and the moving crew hovered next to the trays and coffeepot.

Dolley frowned. "You're wearing blue jeans."

Liam looked down, his golden skin tinged with pink. "Aye."

"I've never seen you in blue jeans." And he wore a flannel shirt.

He shrugged and headed to the tray of treats.

Liam, Nathan and Daniel stood next to each other. And they all wore the same thing. Flannel shirts and jeans. Clones.

Liam always wore black jeans. And she'd never seen him in a flannel shirt.

Bess set a hand on her shoulder. "The truck with the furniture Mamma bought just arrived from Atlanta. Time to do your thing."

Dolley set up in the service entrance. Her memory came in handy on moving day. As people filed by with furniture, she directed them to the proper room. A human *Harry Potter* sorting hat. When she had a break, she checked off items on the paper list.

"That floor lamp goes into the Telfair room," she said to one of the crew. Instead of the presidents' wives theme from Fitzgerald House, they'd named the Carleton House rooms after Savannah's squares.

Liam came in with a bookcase wrapped in a moving blanket. She pulled back the cover and matched the furniture with the inventory in her head. "Second floor hallway opposite Oglethorpe."

He shook his head. "You're amazing."

His appreciation warmed her. "I have a good memory."

"*I* have a good memory. *You* have a computer for a brain."

She rolled her shoulder. A computer didn't sound like a compliment. But he was moving down the hall, and the next piece of furniture waited for sorting.

The crews stopped for lunch. Dolley took pictures for the blog. Then they met the next truck.

"This is very organized." Dolley touched Bess's arm. "Congratulations."

"I'm too smart to organize this craziness. We have Daniel and Abby at our beck and call." Bess had been the sister in charge of bringing Carleton House on line. "I brought them together, and they developed the timelines."

"Next truck is here," Daniel announced.

Workers scrambled to their feet.

"That should be mattresses," Bess said.

The afternoon flew by. When Dolley hadn't seen Liam for almost an hour, she assumed he'd gone back to work. She missed him.

He came through the hallway with an armful of flattened boxes.

Her body warmed. "I thought you left."

"Nope. They had me opening boxes. Tellies."

"The flat screens?"

"Yes."

"If no one has said it, thank you for all your help." She touched his arm.

A smile broke across his face. He'd been doing it so often, she wondered if he knew. He wasn't hanging in the background like he used to.

"I've been invited to dinner." He wove their fingers together. "That's thanks enough, unless you have another way to thank me?"

The warmth she'd felt all day blossomed into a full-blown fire. From starting her day disappointed she wouldn't see Liam to spending the day and evening with him was a wonderful surprise. She could think of lots of ways to thank him. Most involved his bed. "I will. In private."

She stood on her toes and kissed him.

"Hey, you two, you're holding up the line," Gray called, backing through the door carrying one end of a very large box. Daniel was on the other side. "Here's the biggest flat screen."

"Library," Dolley squeaked out.

"Delaney, want to help with this?" Gray glared at Liam as he carried the box past them.

"Absolutely, lads." Liam grabbed the middle and moved away from her with a wink.

Daniel's eyebrows arched as he moved past her.

She bit her lip. Should she follow them down the hall and make sure Gray and Daniel weren't taking this big-brother thing too far?

"Where does this go?" asked a mover, holding an armoire.

"The Orleans room."

Liam would have to hold his own against Gray and Daniel. She had work to do.

LIAM HELD THE Carleton House kitchen door for Gray and Daniel.

The two men had taken turns glaring at him most of the afternoon.

"Hold up, Delaney," Gray ordered.

Liam stopped on the courtyard path. "What can I do for you?"

"Explain what's going on with you and Dolley." Daniel's muscles bulged as he crossed his arms.

Liam stood a little straighter. These men would not intimidate him. "She's an amazing woman."

Gray's blue gaze seared his face. "Yes, she is."

"And she's going to be our sister." Daniel waved a hand between him and Gray.

Gray poked a finger into Liam's chest. "You hurt her, we hurt you."

Liam pushed Gray's hand away. "Did you two gits practice this act?"

"Naw." Daniel slapped his back. Hard. "Just remember. You answer to us now."

How could he forget? Maybe he should ignore Abby's dinner invitation and take Dolley out. He inhaled. She'd promised to thank him for helping them move *in private*.

He followed Gray and Daniel into the Fitzgerald House kitchen.

The sisters worked in different sections of the room. Daniel moved to Bess in the sitting area. Gray homed in on Abby next to the ovens. He glanced at Dolley.

She waved but turned back to setting the table.

"Smells grand in here," Liam said, hating that he was odd man out.

"Lasagna." Abby slipped bread into the oven.

Gray nuzzled her neck. "I love your lasagna."

Abby laughed. "Which is why you asked for it about a dozen times when you knew you could help with moving day."

Liam laughed along with everyone, but he didn't like this. He moved to Dolley and brushed a kiss on her cheek. "How are you feeling?"

Her face went pink. "A little sore, but I'm okay."

Four pairs of eyes burned holes in his back. Too bad. He and Dolley were a couple.

"Anyone want a Jameson?" he asked.

"Sure." Daniel said.

Gray nodded. "I'll help."

They headed to the library. Liam picked up the Waterford decanter, and Gray added ice to all three tumblers.

"I usually—" Liam took it neat.

"Yes?" Gray held up the tumbler.

"Nothing." When in Rome.

Liam carried Daniel's glass and his and made the silent trip back to the kitchen. He wasn't letting

Gray get the upper hand. He and Dolley were dating, and that was that.

Dolley frowned and pointed to his glass. "You take your Jameson neat."

"Gray added ice." He took a sip. "It's not bad."

Her frown deepened.

Abby called them to the table before he could ask what was wrong.

He took a seat next to Dolley.

Abby and Gray rubbed shoulders. Bess and Daniel held hands.

Dolley took his hand and brushed a kiss across his knuckles.

And the tension that had knotted the muscles in his back eased.

"My, my," Abby said, breaking the quiet. "This is a new development."

"Don't start," Dolley warned under her breath.

"I told you." Bess held her hand out to Abby. "You owe me ten bucks."

Gray laughed and held out his hand to Daniel. "You owe me twenty."

"You were betting...on us?" Dolley blinked.

"When you're together there's—" Gray looked at Abby "—sparks in the air."

Liam put his arm around the back of her chair. He pointed at Gray and Daniel. "And I've already been lectured by those two."

"What?" Dolley sputtered. She shook her fingers at the men. "You have no right to interfere."

"We're family," Daniel explained.

Gray and Daniel gave each other high fives.

"Liam," Gray called down. "You're now an honorary member of the wedding party and family. I expect you to come to my bachelor party and groom's dinner."

Liam blinked. "That's not necessary."

"Oh, but it is." Gray nodded. "Right now we're outnumbered by Fitzgerald women. You'll even the odds."

Abby elbowed her fiancé.

"Let me rephrase," Gray spit out. "We're outnumbered by *gorgeous* Fitzgerald women. And Daniel and I would love to have a talk with you."

"That's better." Abby batted her eyelashes.

"No talking!" Dolley pointed her finger at Gray and Daniel.

Liam laughed. "You're all cracked."

"After dinner we're doing a bourbon tasting," Daniel said. "Come with us."

"I've never had bourbon," Liam said.

"You're in the South," Daniel said. "Time to expand your liquor knowledge."

"That sounds…interesting." Liam sighed. Now he wouldn't find out how Dolley had planned to thank him.

DOLLEY DRAGGED HERSELF into the second floor parlor Liam was using to interview her family. Mamma, Abby and Bess stood near the fireplace.

"I'm sorry I'm late." Dolley moved to Liam and whispered, "I don't think you need to film me, just Mamma, Abby and Bess."

"Of course you'll be in this interview."

She chewed on her thumbnail.

Liam touched her hand.

Her eyes widened. She *was* picking up Bess's habit of destroying her nails.

"Are you nervous, luv?" He set his hand on her shoulder.

"Me?"

"You're tremblin' like a bird cornered by a cat."

"Maybe." Dolley bit her lip. "A little. I'm better behind a camera."

"You'll be fantastic." He took both her shoulders in his hands. "Forget the camera. Just talk to your family and me. Deep breath."

She inhaled and exhaled. "I'm sorry. I've always had a tiny bit of stage fright." Tiny was a lie.

"It's only you and me talking." He wrapped an arm around her shoulders. "Mrs. Robbins, if you would take the middle chair," Liam directed, "then your lovely daughters can be next to you."

Bess rolled her eyes. Abby grinned. Mamma laughed.

Dolley twisted her hands.

"Call me Mamie." Mamma touched Liam's arm. "Since I married, I barely answer to the right name anymore."

Dolley sat and tugged her skirt down. A flash

went off and her head jerked up. "I didn't know you were taking pictures, too. I could do that."

"Relax." Mamma patted Dolley's leg. "Try and have fun."

Was Mamma remembering Dolley's valedictorian speech? She'd stumbled through her remarks and then run to the bathroom and thrown up.

She swallowed. That memory wasn't conducive to talking in front of a camera.

"I don't usually have so many lovely women all in one room," Liam said.

Everyone but Dolley laughed. Where was the closest bathroom?

"Abby, luv, could you change places with Bess?"

Abby grinned. "Sure."

Abby stood and Bess slid over.

Dolley closed her eyes and focused on her breathing.

"Good. Great. Now the colors are mixed up a bit," he explained.

"Thank you for taking the time to talk about your ancestry." Liam took a chair next to the camera. "I want this to be a dialogue. I may bounce around with questions, but don't worry. The magic happens in the editing room."

"I'm not sure how much we can tell you." Mamma's shoulders rose and fell.

"Why don't we start with what you know," he said. "When did your ancestors come to America?"

Everyone looked at Dolley.

She swallowed. Whatever knowledge she had about the Fitzgeralds evaporated.

"Dolley?" Liam's bright blue gaze captured hers. He mouthed, *Talk to me*.

Her breath shook as she inhaled. "James Michael FitzGerald landed in Savannah in the summer of 1830. His wife, Fiona, didn't arrive until 1833." She smiled. "From the letters we've found, it appears she stayed with the Irish FitzGeralds while her husband started up his business."

"Fiona had definite preferences as they built Fitzgerald House," Mamma said. "I used to love the stories Great-grandmamma told about Fiona. She was a woman who knew what she wanted."

"I guess it's genetic," Bess said, under her breath. They laughed.

"What else do you know about Fitzgerald House?"

"It took two years to complete." Dolley forced herself to ignore the camera and talk to Liam and her family. "Now that we have samples of Fiona's handwriting, we can tell she made most of the notes on the original architect's drawings."

"In the beginning, the kitchen was a separate building, where the family patio is now. I've got recipes." Abby grinned. "Fiona's currant scones, shortbread cookies and Welsh cakes."

"Grandmamma told me the moss roses on the side of the house were brought from Ireland by Fiona,"

Bess added. "The palm tree in the sunroom is very old. It might have been Fiona's or her daughter's."

"The matching vases in the ballroom came from Ireland," Dolley added. "I saw a note in one of the letters."

"Oh, and the smaller tea trolley," Mamma murmured.

"The silver hairbrush set was Fiona's daughter's, wasn't it?" Abby asked.

Dolley frowned. "I think it was her grandson's wife, Clara's."

Liam unfolded the family tree, and they discussed what they knew of each of their ancestors.

He asked, "James arrived before the potato famine?"

"Yes." Dolley nodded.

Mamma tapped a finger on Dolley's hands. They were balled into fists in her lap. She forced her fingers to uncurl.

"Your ancestors were a little different than most, having come from money."

"Based on the letters you brought us and what we've found, James had an inheritance he put to good use," Dolley said.

Liam's eyebrows arched up, but the camera wouldn't catch that. "He was wealthy. A rather different journey than that of the countrymen and women who escaped Ireland during the famine."

A prickle of unease wormed its way down Dolley's back. "I don't know if every immigrant was poor." She spoke only to Liam. "I do know James was a good businessman."

Liam nodded. "Not so hard when he had the money."

"It wasn't a crime to have money back then," she snapped.

Mamma set a hand on her shoulder.

Didn't Mamma understand what Liam was doing?

"James Fitzgerald went into shipping when he immigrated, right?" Liam asked.

Everyone nodded.

"James bought a small shipping company based out of London and established the American ports," Dolley answered. Where was Liam taking these questions? "The warehouse he owned in Savannah burned down in the mid-1940s, but by then the family fortune was declining."

"My mother remembered playing in the warehouse." Mamma talked about the bank and shipping company. "Now it's all gone."

"When James immigrated, Georgia was a slave state," Liam said. "Did the family own slaves?"

Dolley sank back in her seat and looked at Mamma. She hated the tone of Liam's questions.

"I never heard of any," Mamma said.

"I think they would have been noted in the ledgers," Dolley said. "Freedmen worked in the warehouse." She visualized the journal pages. "But there are lots of Irish surnames in the ledgers."

Liam sat straighter. "Did he make a point of hiring his countrymen?"

His brilliant gaze was like an electrical current zapping her every nerve ending. It stole her breath.

She ripped her gaze away from him and forced the pages of the journal to flip through her memory. "I…I think there were mostly Irish surnames. He might have."

Liam handed her copies of the journal pages.

"Yes. Here," Dolley said, excitement bubbling inside her chest. "These are the household staff. O'Connor. Flanagan. Tolan. O'Gara. I wonder if this O'Gara is related to the current owners of the pub."

"I remember a housekeeper named Flanagan." A soft smile filled Mamma's face. "She used to sneak me cookies."

Mamma reminisced about the staff and Fitzgerald House until they all fell silent.

"That's it, ladies." Liam grinned. "Thank you so much."

Dolley stretched. She checked her phone. My goodness, they'd talked for two hours.

"I understand you're taking Abby's wedding pictures." Mamie laid her hand on Liam's arm. "Thank you for stepping in."

"You've made me feel so welcome. It was the least I could do." He covered Mamma's hand with his. "And since Dolley is my apprentice, she'll help pull the pictures together."

"I heard she was a little more than that." Her eyebrows arched. "We'll talk at the wine tasting."

Bess slipped by Dolley and whispered, "You're in for it now."

"Liam, you'll join us for dinner?" Abby asked.

"That would be lovely." He unscrewed the camera from the tripod.

Abby walked out with Bess. Mamma gave Dolley one more look before she left.

They were alone. Finally. "What is the focus of your documentary?"

"The Irish in Savannah. In the South." He bent to pack the camera.

She crossed her arms. "Then why all the questions on wealth and slaves? Are you trying to make our family look bad?"

"Of course not." But he stayed bent over his bags so she couldn't read his eyes.

"Look at me."

He stood up. "Yes?"

"What is the...the premise of your documentary?"

He ran his hand through his hair. "It's...haves versus have-nots."

She shivered like he'd doused her with ice water. "And the Fitzgeralds are the *haves*?"

He paced to the fireplace and back. "Yes."

His answer doubled her over, like he'd hit her in

the stomach. "I can't believe you'd do that." She waved her hands. "Are you going to tell the audience we lost the fortune and we deserved our financial downfall? We *deserved* to have to turn our home into a business?"

He rushed to her side, taking her hand. "That's not the story I plan to tell."

"How can I believe you?" She jerked her hand away. "This is all we have. You paint us in a... greedy light and we might lose everything. I won't let you do that."

"I would never..."

She shook her head. "I trusted you."

He tried to catch her shoulders, but she ran to the door.

She was a fool when it came to men. What if the documentary hurt her family? Hurt the B and B?

Nausea burned the back of her throat. Not from speaking on camera. This time because of Liam.

LIAM PACED HIS ROOM. His walk through the squares hadn't soothed his temper.

He'd made a hash of things. Dolley had looked at him like he was lower than a snake.

Even if his documentary was about rich versus the poor, that didn't mean he would cast the Fitzgeralds in a bad light. They were generations away from James FitzGerald's journey to America.

She'd never made a documentary. She didn't know how to structure a film. He had. Besides, this was *his* documentary. He would tell the story of the Irish in Savannah his way.

He dropped into the desk chair. If he did, Dolley might never speak to him again. Her family would push him away.

He twirled the documents he'd brought in to the interview. Dolley had been right about the names on the ledgers; they were familiar. He'd seen them on Savannah businesses and noted their Irish names as possible people to interview.

The chair creaked as he sat up. The names were right from the ledgers he and Dolley had reviewed.

Maybe his story wasn't about *haves* versus *have-nots*. Maybe there was more. Maybe it was about the Fitzgeralds helping their countrymen.

Dolley would know. She might even be able to connect him with the descendants of the families who worked for James and Fiona Fitzgerald.

And maybe—he'd get back in her good graces. Because right now he doubted if she would let him hold her hand.

Can we talk? he texted. His fingers rattled against his phone as he waited for her answer.

Later. Working wine tasting.

Perfect. In a public setting, she couldn't snarl at him.

He grabbed the sheets and headed to the library.

Mamie stood next to the anniversary couple he'd met last night. She waved as he walked in.

At least Dolley hadn't poisoned her mother against him. He exhaled. Losing the affection of the Fitzgerald family would cut a hole in his heart.

Dolley cleared dirty dishes. She raised an eyebrow and hefted the tray.

"I could carry that for you," he offered.

"I don't need your help." She headed to the kitchen.

He traipsed behind her.

"I'm working." She bumped the kitchen door open with her hip. "I know you think I work only for you, but I don't. I have other responsibilities."

"That's not fair."

The dishes clanked as she set them down next to the sink.

"Fair?" She drilled a finger into his chest, green eyes blazing. "Coming from you, that's rich. Fair is telling me how you were going to paint my ancestors. Fair would have been letting me know that we were the bad guys, so I could tell my family not to talk to you. Fair would have been explaining your *premise* before we signed those damn releases."

"Ouch." He grabbed at her hand.

She stepped out of his reach. "I have things to do."

"You can't spare a minute?" His temper was igniting, and he yanked it under control. "Sixty seconds?"

She scraped leftover food into a bin. "What for?"

Had they really kissed multiple times? They were so out of sync, it was like they were on different planets. "I want to explore another angle. Another premise."

"Rich versus poor isn't enough for you? You found another way to humiliate us?"

"Dolley." Frustration infused her name.

She hung her head and exhaled. "One minute."

"I want to find these people's descendants." He spread the papers in front of her and pointed at the names. "There's too many to be a coincidence. I think James and Fiona helped their countrymen. Help me find them."

She stared at the paper. Silent.

Was he losing her? Losing her family?

"If it's true James and Fiona helped their countrymen, that's the story you'll tell?" Her eyes swam with emotion.

"I would never hurt your family." He moved around the counter, turning her to face him.

She chewed her lip. "It was your questions..." Her voice trailed off. Vulnerability filled her face.

"Trust me." He touched her chin, wanting to kiss her worries away.

"I'm not good at trusting men." She stroked his cheek.

He caught her hand, relieved she would reach out to him. "Maybe if we work together on this, you'll start to trust me."

"Maybe." Her arms circled his waist.

He pulled her close and brushed a kiss on the top of her head. "Thank you."

His world righted. They'd better be able to verify that James and Fiona had truly helped the immigrants. Because if he couldn't convince his producer this was a viable story line, Dolley would hate him.

Then he'd lose the Fitzgeralds. Not acceptable.

DOLLEY KNEW THE exact moment Liam entered the kitchen. The air changed. Just like before a lightning storm and the hairs on her arm stood on end. She forced herself not to rush to his side.

She wanted to trust him.

He bent and brushed a hello kiss on her mouth.

Licking her lips, she tasted whiskey. "You've been into the Jameson."

He held up a tumbler, the ice rattling in the glass. "I have."

Gray pushed open the courtyard door, shedding his coat. "I know I just left Boston, and it was snowing, but it's cold here." His gaze zeroed in on Liam's glass as he headed for the fire. "That looks appealing."

"Warm up and I'll fetch a glass." Liam headed to the door but turned back. "Daniel, what about you?"

Daniel stood in front of the fire with his arm around Bess's shoulders, like they were joined at the hip. "I'll take the same. Thanks."

Dolley watched Liam go. She'd seen him do small things like pouring wine or helping her sisters and the staff all the time. He'd even acted as bellhop when Nigel or another staff member wasn't around.

He'd woven himself into the fabric of the B and B, and she couldn't imagine life without him. Doubt crawled through her like a virus. Was there a purpose behind his kindness?

"Anything I can do?" she asked Abby, unable to stand still.

"Get water for us?"

Dolley filled the pitcher and added lemons and ice.

When Liam backed through the door and headed to the sitting area, she stared at him.

Bess came to the table with a stack of plates. "Look at those three men."

Her sister's whisper gave her an excuse to study him longer.

Liam fit right in. The guys were all about the same height, six-one or six-two. Both Liam and Gray had black, wavy hair, but Liam's was longer, more artistic. In contrast, Daniel had blond hair, also long. All three men wore blue jeans and sweaters, Gray's dressier than Daniel's. Liam had a leaner look; his tight jeans made his legs look like he was a runner.

Liam stood back a little, keeping his glass close to his mouth and observing the two men. What was he thinking?

An arm caught her waist. The scent of Mamma's familiar perfume had her shoulders softening.

"Lost in thought?" Mamma asked.

She wrapped an arm around Mamma so they were linked. "Maybe a little daydreaming."

Mamma shot her gaze over to the group of men. "He's quiet. Almost sad."

"He is." She added, "A couple of times I've given him smile goals."

"And you and he are…dating?" A shimmer of anxiousness filled her mother's voice.

"We haven't gone out much, but, yes." She sighed. "I've tried to get him into the pubs, but he loves the quiet."

"And you love your crowds." Mamma rubbed her back. "He lives in Ireland."

"I know. Galway." Dolley turned. "Did you ever want to see where our ancestors came from?"

"Not really. After I married your father, there was never the money. Then when I went to help Aunt CeCe in Atlanta, it would have been hard to find the time."

"But now Aunt CeCe has full-time help."

Mamma nodded. "After I told Martin about the interview, he suggested we go to Ireland."

"He's so good for you." Mamma deserved to have fun. "When is Martin coming to Savannah?"

"By Thursday. That's when Gray's family are coming in."

"Ahhh, we're presenting a united front." Dolley laughed.

Mamma brushed her hand one more time on Dolley's back. "Since I haven't met the Smythes and they were rough on Abby the first time they met her, I want us all to be here."

"You're protecting Abby?" Dolley laughed again.

Liam turned.

"Abby will come after them with her longest chef knife," Dolley said.

"No one disses my children."

Another laugh rolled out of Dolley.

This time everyone in the room turned.

"What's going on over there?" Bess demanded.

"Nothing." Dolley wiped a tear from her eye. "Mamma broke her own rule."

Mamma shook her head.

Dolley pointed her finger at her mother. "You used slang."

"Mamma!" Abby put her hands on her hips, glancing at Liam. "We do not use slang around guests."

Liam slapped a hand to his chest. "Don't blame me. I don't even know what that word means."

"To show disrespect. Often by insults or criticism," Dolley blurted out.

Horror filled Daniel's face. "Did you memorize the dictionary?"

Liam tapped his temple. "Photographic memory."

Now everyone laughed. Well, Liam only grinned, but that was like a rolling belly laugh from him.

She headed over to plant a kiss on his lips.

Before she could move, Abby called out, "Let's eat."

Dolley slipped into the seat next to Liam.

He took her hand and it felt right. She leaned in. "I'm glad you're here."

"What are you two conspiring about?" Bess asked. "You're not going to run around shooting pictures, are you? Dolley's been bad enough since she bought her new camera."

Liam held up his hands. "My camera's upstairs."

Dolley kept her head down and took salad.

"Dolley?" Abby said.

"I'm not holding one right now, am I?" It was on the mantel.

"Let's keep it that way," Mamie said. "I'd rather not ruin a lovely dinner."

"I admire Dolley's dedication to her art." Liam passed Dolley the tureen of borscht. "You should, too."

Dolley's cheeks heated to the color of the soup she ladled into her bowl. Her head jerked up. "It's okay."

"No, it's not." His blue laser gaze scanned the table. "Your family should know how talented you are."

Everyone stared at her.

"Liam—"

"Dolley," he interrupted. "They should acknowledge your talent and drive."

She pressed on her roiling stomach. It hadn't settled down since the interview.

"Thank you for the reminder." Mamma moved around the table and hugged Liam's shoulders. Then she kissed Dolley's cheek. "I've grown accustomed to thinking of her camera as an irritation. I'm ashamed of myself. I appreciate you reminding us that Dolley is an artist."

"Thank you, Mamma." Dolley closed her eyes. Her chest heaved. Mamma had just called her an artist. But only because Liam had held a mirror up to their behavior.

Mamma squeezed her shoulder before moving back to her chair.

Did she even think of herself as an artist?

"I'm sorry, too." Bess tipped their heads together. "That would be like you booing whenever I moved dirt."

"Or when I bake," Abby added.

Dolley swallowed. "I'm still learning my craft."

"Don't belittle yourself." Liam slapped a hand on the table, and the silverware jumped. "You've talent and skill. Especially your pictures of people. One that I don't have."

Her family stared at him.

Dolley took a hasty sip of wine. This was what it was like to have someone in her life who had her back. This was what her sisters had found in their fiancés. What Mamma had found with Martin.

She was finally part of the sisterhood. Tears hung on her eyelashes.

"Thank you," she whispered to Liam. Louder, she said, "Is someone going to pass around Abby's stroganoff? Talk about an artist."

Her joke broke the tension. The food circulated again. Conversation picked up.

"Never let anyone diss your talent," Liam whispered.

She laughed. "You asked me to trust you."

He nodded.

She squeezed his hand tight. "I do."

Liam's smile burst open like sunlight after a thunderstorm. "I won't let you down."

Her heart beat a little faster. She was trusting Liam with her family's legacy and her dreams. *Don't let this be a mistake.*

CHAPTER ELEVEN

Every artist dips his brush in his own soul and paints his nature into his pictures.

Henry Ward Beecher

"TAKE A SHORT BREAK, GENTS." Liam changed the lens on the camera. "We're almost done."

Gray, Daniel and his other groomsmen from Boston, Phillips and Doug, moved to the balcony and lit cigars. True to their threats, they'd included him in all the wedding activities. And grilled him about his intentions toward Dolley.

Who did that anymore?

He had no clue what his intentions were. But when he was around Dolley and her family, it was like his life was in focus.

Unfortunately, since the day of the interview, he'd barely seen Dolley. When he'd been free, she'd had a rush website job. Then he'd buckled down to flesh out the documentary's new story line.

Dolley had located descendants of the people listed in James and Fiona's ledgers and journals. He only knew this because of the notes and texts that flew between them. He'd hoped the various wedding events would bring them together, but that hadn't happened.

They lived mere feet from each other, and he hadn't set eyes on her since the groom's dinner two nights ago. Too long for his needs. Tonight, even though he was taking the wedding pictures, he planned to spend time with Dolley. Please, God.

He took a couple of shots of the four men, cigar smoke curling around their heads. Better than the picture he was going to suggest.

"Are we done?" Daniel asked.

He snapped a few more. "For now."

He headed to the opposite wing of the house. Knocking, he called out, "It's Liam."

Bess pulled the door open. "We're decent."

He peered into the room. "I'd say you're not just decent, you're beautiful."

Dolley toasted him with a half-empty champagne glass. "You say the sweetest things."

Her grin had the strain in his body evaporating like mist in the morning sun. How could her smile give him…peace?

She wore a dusky rose dress, short and tight. Her green eyes glittered like emeralds. Her curls were tamed into an attractive do. Pity. He loved her wild curly locks.

Bess's dress was a paler rose color. Her long hair was piled on her head. Her eyes were a dimmer shade of green, but still shone like gems.

But Abby was the star of the bouquet of beauties. Her fairy-tale gown sparkled, and so did her green eyes. A couple of freckles spotted her bare shoulders.

Had Dolley taken a picture of Abby's shoulders? That would be a nice shot.

He smiled at Dolley. "Don't mind me. I'll just get some pictures."

"I've shot Abby's dress and her getting ready." Dolley brought over her camera. "And the makeup and hair people working on her."

"You make it sound like I had a giant overhaul," Abby complained.

"They were perfecting the glorious being that is you." Bess tipped her flute at her sister.

"I love my sisters!" Abby pinched her lips together.

"Don't you cry!" Bess came over with the champagne bottle and topped off her glass. "There's no crying once you've had your makeup done."

Abby sniffed back her tears. "I know."

"I'll take more champagne." Gray's sister, Courtney, was tucked in a chair over in the corner, a bored expression on her face.

She was just as pretty as the Fitzgeralds, maybe prettier. She had Gray's bright blue eyes and black curly hair that fell to the middle of her back. But she would never be stunning like Dolley or her sisters, because she didn't have...spark.

Bess topped off Courtney's glass. "Sure."

He snapped a picture of Courtney's pouting face.

"I wasn't ready." She straightened and pasted on an insincere smile.

He snapped a few more but knew the first picture was the reflection of her true personality. Too bad. Her brother was...real. And nice.

He moved around the room, and Dolley's gaze followed him. It was like the stroke of her hand on his back, comforting and exciting. He stood over the pile of sparkling heels, tipping one on its side.

Dolley and Bess relaxed on a small love seat, their bare feet resting on a coffee table. Since they were watching Abby, he took a couple of candids. Then he zoomed in on Dolley's face. She had so much life and energy.

He would have to remember that it was the bride's day today. Not Dolley's.

Mamie, along with Gray's mother, Olivia, Debbie Forester and Marion all entered the bridal boudoir.

"I'd like to get pictures with the mothers." Liam nodded to Dolley. They were going to tag team as much as possible today. She caught up her camera and stood a little apart from him.

Abby walked to the women. When Abby wrapped her arm around Marion and Deb, Olivia looked a little stunned.

Liam understood that these women were as much a part of the Fitzgerald family as Abby's sisters. He'd even caught Marion scolding Abby.

He and Dolley took group photos in the room and then moved everyone to the balcony.

"I don't understand why Dolley's taking our pictures," Courtney complained. "She's not a professional."

"Actually, I am." Dolley's voice was even.

"She's my apprentice." Liam shifted the women around. "And very, very good."

"Really?" Courtney drawled. Under her breath, she added, "That's what they call it these days?"

Dolley was facing him, so he caught her eye roll.

"Ignore her," he whispered. "You take charge."

Maybe Courtney would eat her words.

"Mamma and Abby, first," Dolley said, changing her camera's settings.

Dolley had a flair for portraits. After she shot their poses, she added Olivia and then Marion and Deb.

Liam stepped in. "Now, all the sisters."

Courtney took her time joining the group. He would have everyone in this picture and eliminate until he had only the Fitzgeralds, because joy should be what was reflected on everyone's faces, not disdain.

Dolley handed her camera to him.

He whispered, "It's too bad everyone can't be happy today."

Her glance shot to Courtney. She whispered back, "When Abby and Gray first started dating, she caused problems. He'd been dating her BFF."

He frowned.

"Her best friend forever. BFF."

"Ahh."

After taking all the group photos, he packed his cameras. "I'll see you upstairs."

Abby's grin sparkled. "Okay."

In the ballroom, he framed pictures of the guests, tables and the arbor. Finally the mothers were escorted to their chairs. The string quartet changed songs as Gray and the judge entered and stood by the arbor.

On the bride's side of the aisle, women wore hats. On the groom's side, the younger women wore something Dolley had called a fascinator. High fashion and stiff backs were evident there. Would the two groups mix during cocktail hour?

Courtney came down the aisle first. He snapped the obligatory pictures of the couple. Dolley came next. He focused on her radiant face, finally remembering that wedding pictures should include the dresses. He did the same for Bess.

He twirled to catch Gray's expression as Abby appeared. The groom's mouth dropped open, and a smile split his face.

Samuel Forester escorted Abby down the silk-covered aisle. He didn't use his walker, so their pace was slow, but Samuel couldn't have looked any prouder than if she was his own daughter. He kissed her cheek and murmured something only Abby could hear.

The ceremony flew by. He traversed the room, trying to stay inconspicuous. After they were declared husband and wife, he was delighted to catch Abby's mouth form an O as Gray dipped her into a kiss. Then he swung around and snapped the witnesses laughing and applauding.

He lined up the groups for the family pictures. Dolley's grin never left her face. When she could, she helped by changing cards or lenses. If she wasn't in a series of pictures, she grabbed a camera.

It was like she could read his mind, always ready with the right camera or adjusting the groups to suit him.

If she could read his mind, she would know he wanted to strip off her dress with his teeth. What would she think of that?

He needed to focus. There was the cocktail hour, dinner, cake cutting and the dance to get through.

"It's time for you to take a break," Dolley insisted. "Amy will bring your plate to my table."

"Can you sit with me?" They were tucked behind a pillar.

She touched his face. "I thought I would cover while you took a break."

He leaned in. "I want more time with you."

"And I want the last dance with you." She smoothed the lapels of his suit.

"I want that, too." And more. "In my room?"

"Oh, yeah."

Grinning, he brushed a kiss on her upturned mouth. "I'll be back."

Her eyes blinked open, but her gaze was blurred.

He loved that he could fog her mind, because she was sure messing with his.

After he finished another fine meal, he moved next to Dolley.

She shot the cake cutting. "Got it."

She handed his camera to him. "How was dinner?"

"I missed you."

Her face softened.

Bess ripped Dolley away from him. "First dance. Come on."

He was so used to being alone. Used to watching other people have fun. But being with Dolley was...different.

That was a thought for later. He still had six weeks to enjoy Dolley, the Fitzgeralds and Savannah.

While the couple shared their first dance, he circled the dance floor.

"Abby and Gray want the bridal party and their parents to join them on the floor," the DJ announced. He pointed to the Foresters. "That incudes you, Mr. and Mrs. Forester."

Liam took pictures of each couple. When he turned his lens to the smiling faces of Dolley and Phillips, Phillips held Dolley way too tight and his gaze was glued to her cleavage.

Liam flipped on the flash and shot a picture right in Phillips's eyes.

"Hey!" Phillips loosened his grip on Dolley.

Dolley laughed. "Sorry, sorry."

Thankfully, the song ended. He was close enough to hear Dolley say, "Thank you," to the lecherous man.

She stopped next to him. "That wasn't necessary."

"He was staring down your frock."

Her head bobbed up. "What?"

"He was looking down the front of your dress," he said through clenched teeth, leading her away from the dance floor. "I'd assumed we were… exclusive."

Her face cycled through joy, relief and then came irritation. "We are. But what you did was not appropriate."

"It was from my side of the camera."

"Men," she muttered.

"Come on, Dolley, let's dance." Nathan, Daniel's twin brother, grabbed her hand.

"See you later." She squeezed Liam's hand. "Remember I want the last dance."

He kept an eye on the Forester brother. Ready to shine the flash in that man's eyes, too.

DOLLEY SHOULD HAVE been checking whether Abby needed anything, like a good bridesmaid. She glanced over at Liam, inhaling, but couldn't draw in a full breath.

All she could think about was dancing with Liam. It didn't matter if they danced right after Abby and Gray left or thirty minutes later. She wanted Liam's arms around her.

"Come on." Bess tapped her on the shoulder. "Abby and Gray are leaving."

Thank goodness.

Bess looked at her funny.

Shoot. Had she said that aloud?

The guests waved Abby and Gray out of the ballroom.

She didn't have to turn to know Liam stood behind her; the air changed when he was near. She grabbed his hand. "Last dance?"

His blue gaze promised so much more. "Absolutely."

The DJ played a slow ballad. Liam pulled her close, and they rocked to the song.

"I've wanted to hold you all night," he whispered in her ear.

He twirled her, and she tipped her head back. Lights flashed and sparkled off the chandeliers. "My sister's wedding was beautiful."

"So are you." He eased her head back and into his chest.

Her knees went weak. Liam was as intoxicating as champagne.

He held her up. "You all right?"

"Yes." More than all right. She was where she wanted to be. In Liam's arms. It may not last, but right now she had him.

At least for tonight.

His arms pulled her close as they swayed to the music. "Oh, not just tonight, darlin'."

His words added to the heat bubbling inside her. "I have to quit mumbling."

Guests gathered their things and said goodbye. Bess and Daniel swung by on the dance floor.

Her sister winked. "We're taking off. See you two at brunch?"

Dolley nodded.

The music ended. Liam laced their fingers together. "Ready?"

She nodded, unable to push words past the lump in her throat. They were really going to do this. What if she...disappointed him?

He gathered his camera bag. "I think I got some good pictures."

"You rarely take anything *but* a good photo."

"I need to keep you around."

Her breath escaped in a whoosh. Did he mean that, or was it foreplay talk?

They avoided the departing guests by escaping to the back stairs.

In the narrow staircase, he pressed her against the wall. His hand cupped her chin, tugging her face up. "Here's something else I've been thinking of doing all night."

"Me, too." Her hands wrapped around his neck.

His mouth crashed down on hers as if he couldn't wait another second. Tongues collided, his taste an addictive combination of whiskey and cake. He cupped her ass, tugging her into perfect alignment with his erection.

His bag bumped her side, and she didn't care. "Oh, my," she said.

He rolled his hips against hers.

"We need to get to your room," she whispered.

"Now." He took her hand.

They hurried down the remaining stairs and stopped at his doorway. He fumbled the key card more than once. So cute. And her confidence built.

"Finally." He yanked her inside, and the door locked behind them. Moonlight drenched the room. She reached out and stroked his shadowed face.

"Why did we wait so long?" She kicked off her shoes. One flew under the desk, the other behind the sofa.

"This last week, I've barely seen you." He toed off his own shoes. "Before that, I wasn't sure you liked me."

She tugged off his suit coat and tossed it over the desk chair. "But I did. I just didn't want to ruin my shot at a mentorship."

"Not going to happen." He spun her around and dragged down her zipper. Nothing could cool the heat flaming inside her. "I love working with you."

"Me, too." Her voice shook.

His fingers smoothed along her shoulders, pushing away the dress. His hands trailed to the small of her back. His lips took the same path. "Your skin is so gorgeous."

With a little shimmy, her dress slid off, pooling on the floor. Stepping out of the circle of fabric, she kicked it away.

His hands slid around her, cupping her breasts as he pulled her into his chest. His thumbs brushed her nipples, forcing them into aching peaks under the silk of her bra. He nuzzled her neck. "Anticipation is a wonderful thing."

Each touch of his fingers drove waves of liquid heat to her core. Gripping his thighs, she leaned her head back.

He kissed her, thrusting his tongue to meet hers. His erection surged against her bottom.

It wasn't enough. She twisted so her chest pressed against him. But nothing relieved the ache building inside.

She fought the buttons on his shirt, fumbling and pushing to get at his bare skin.

"Let me." He ripped his shirt over his head and tossed it toward the sofa.

With his hands on her arms, he backed her toward the bedroom.

Her fingers caressed his chest, thumbs finding and brushing his flat nipples.

His groan filled the room. "I want to be inside you, luv."

"That's the plan." But her voice shook. The back of her legs hit the edge of the bed.

"I love the undies." He brushed a finger along the top of her pale peach bra and ran it down the center of her belly to the matching thong. "The color suits you."

"When I put them on—" she shivered "—I was thinking of you looking at me."

She inched up on the bed until her back hit the pillows, her elbows propping her up.

He shucked off his pants, shoving his socks off with a sharp push. She waited for the boxer briefs to drop. There was a lovely bulge tenting the fabric.

Instead of joining her, he hurried into the bathroom. Light leaked into the room, chasing away some of the shadows.

Tossing condoms next to her, he crawled on the bed and straddled her legs. "I want you naked."

She clutched his hips. "We're on the same page."

"It's going to be your needs first, because I don't want this to end too early." He slid his hands behind her back and popped the hooks on her bra.

Her hands clutched the comforter as he peeled her bra away.

He stopped and stared.

Embarrassment heated her cheeks...probably her whole body. "I thought you were in a hurry."

"I want to admire you."

"Liam," she whispered.

He traced a finger from her chin down to the top of her breast and then repeated the action on her other breast. "What?"

"You're taking too long."

"I love looking at you. I love your body."

His constant use of the word *love* had her breath stuck in her chest. "You're not hard on the eyes, either," she said, keeping things light.

He slipped lower, licking her nipple until it formed a tight aching bud. Then he took it in his mouth, working it with his tongue and teeth.

"Oh, yes." His touch made her drunk.

"Liam," she gasped, stroking his head, his shoulder, anywhere she could.

Her nipple popped out of his mouth, glistening. "I'm right here having the time of my life."

"I want to touch you," she pleaded.

"I don't think so."

He planted kisses between her breasts and worked his way south. Down her belly, lingering to circle her belly button with his tongue. His fingers clamped on her hips as he kissed his way across her stomach to each hip bone.

And headed lower. Her breath caught in her chest. She couldn't think. Only feel. Everything pitched inside her like a boat caught in the surf.

He brushed a soft kiss on the inside of her thigh as he tugged off her thong.

"I can't take much more," she panted, trying to sit up.

"You'll have to." He pressed her back to the mattress. "You smell good," he growled.

She couldn't reach him to touch. Could only arch her back as he pressed his mouth to her aching center. Fireworks flared behind her eyelids.

He tortured her for hours, days. Whenever she would get close, he backed away.

"Not yet. Not yet."

She couldn't take this. She grabbed his shoulder, pulling him up where she could touch him.

Slipping her hand inside his briefs, she wrapped her fingers around him. A groan rumbled through his chest as she stroked him.

"Enough," he growled.

Liam rose on his knees, pushing down his shorts. There was a crinkle of foil, and then he was finally, *finally*, taking his place between her legs.

"Now." She grabbed hold of his lean hips. "Please."

Pressing a kiss to her mouth, he entered her slowly. "I want to savor this. Savor you."

"You're killing me."

He laughed. A rolling laugh that shook his chest and vibrated inside her.

"Liam!"

His blue eyes darkened to black as he held himself above her, his arms straining. She tilted her hips up to help him slide to the perfect union.

His hair slipped over his eyes as he worked his hips up and down, finally pushing home. The tendons in his arms popped out in deep relief.

She took a deep breath and breathed in Liam. His musk, the scent of their bodies together. Another addictive scent. She circled her hips, her breath catching.

"Stop, luv. Give me a minute here." His head dropped next to her ear, and he took her earlobe between his teeth and nipped. A bite she felt all the way to where their bodies joined.

When he slid home again, everything—exploded.

Sparklers flared behind her eyelids. *Yes!* She moaned, afraid the wedding guests would hear her in the ball-room.

"Another," he whispered.

He rolled across his bed, taking her with him. Shifting so they stayed connected, he sat with the pillows stacked behind him.

"Come here." His voice was a rocky command she couldn't disobey.

She straddled him, resting her hands on the head-board, and undulated as he directed her body.

His blue eyes grew black, and his chest heaved as she took him deeper. His fingers bit into her hips.

She didn't care. Her life had boiled down to each stroke of his body inside hers.

Tingles rolled through her again and she splin-tered into a thousand raindrops.

He thrust and held her as he came with her. Wave after wave tossed her around. She collapsed with a groan, and his arms were steel anchors holding them together, keeping her from disintegrating.

"I've got you. I've got you," Liam murmured.

He rolled so they lay on their sides.

She forced her heavy eyes open. "Hi."

"How's the form?" He cupped her cheek and stared into her eyes.

A weak laugh bubbled up. "Your form was fan-tastic."

He frowned. "Are you all right?"

"I'm more than all right. I'm fabulous."

"That you are, luv. That you are." He brushed a kiss on her forehead before sliding to the edge of the bed. "I'll be right back."

She should dress and run across the courtyard to her apartment. But how could she move? Her eyes shut. She just needed to rest—a bit.

And drifted off to sleep.

CHAPTER TWELVE

There are no bad pictures; that's just how your
face looks sometimes.

Abraham Lincoln

DOLLEY HOOKED HER arm with Liam's as they entered the ballroom. There were a few people mill-
ing around, but no Abby or Gray.

"You're grinning." Liam's whispered breath in
her ear had tingles dancing along her skin.

"It might be gloating," she whispered back. She
planned to enjoy their new *couple's status*.

He covered her hand and squeezed. "After last
night, I might never need a smile goal again."

Bess waved at them. "Don't you two look like
Reggie after he's caught a couple of bunnies? You'd
better tone it down, or Mamma will be asking questions."

Liam frowned, but it morphed into a smile. "Ah,
Reggie is that behemoth white cat?"

Bess nodded.

Dolley stuck her tongue out at her sister.

But she didn't mind the teasing. She loved finally
being on equal footing with both sisters. Well, close.
Abby had just gotten married, and Bess was engaged. But this was the first time she'd had a man
to show off to her family.

"Where are the bride and groom?" she asked.

"Abby's on her way," Bess said. "She loved their bedroom."

She and Bess had filled Abby and Gray's bedroom with flowers, candles and rose petals. She let out a little hum. "It was so romantic."

Gray's sister walked in the room.

Bess leaned over. "I swear, Courtney pouted all week."

"I'm afraid she won't like her candid shots." Liam stroked Dolley's back. "What can I get you ladies to drink?"

"Mimosa," Bess said.

"Make it two," Dolley said.

Liam headed to the drink setup area.

"So…" Bess asked.

"So…" Dolley responded.

"Anything new with you two?" Bess bumped her shoulder.

Dolley pretended to lock her lips.

Bess's eyebrows arched. "Come on. How was it?"

She was too close to her sisters. Yet normally, she would have shared. Why was Liam different? "Bess."

"It's been a while since you've had someone in your life." Bess touched her hand.

"Wonderful. Incredible. Unbelievable. Pick one."

"My, my." Bess waved her hand like a fan. Then

her smile slipped from her face. "What happens when he heads back to Ireland?"

Her sister's words struck her heart. "I don't know. I can't see that far ahead."

Bess rubbed Dolley's back, soothing the tension there. "That's…hard. Don't let him hurt you."

Liam came back with their drinks. "Where's Daniel?"

Bess took one of the flutes from him. "He's picking up his parents."

"I took some pictures of the Forester family they might like." Liam tipped his coffee mug to their glasses.

"I know they would love copies." Bess sighed. "Thank you."

"Samuel looked stronger than at Christmas." Dolley leaned into Liam, just because she could.

"They lowered his chemo dosage for the wedding," Bess said.

While they chatted, people flowed into the room in a steady stream. Even now they formed clumps of Boston society—Gray's guests in one corner and Abby's in the other.

When Mamma and Martin arrived, they circulated through the groups. Dolley was content to stay with Liam. For once she didn't want to flit from group to group.

Abby and Gray made an entrance, and everyone applauded. Then the servers laid out the buffet.

"I can't believe I'm hungry after eating steady for a week." Dolley took a place in line.

"Maybe it was last night," Liam breathed in her ear.

She turned and grinned up at him.

Courtney stared at her from the back of the line. Her face was screwed up like she'd just swallowed a basket of lemons.

Who cared? Courtney would go back to Boston. Dolley would only have to put up with her presence occasionally.

"This all looks wonderful." Liam handed her a plate. "Abby didn't make this, did she?"

Dolley glanced over at her sister. "She's a control freak, but last night's caterers did the food today."

She added egg strata to her plate along with fruit.

He leaned over. "You might need more fortification than that, luv."

His whisper stole her breath.

"I will?" she choked out.

His eyes twinkled. "I thought we'd start working on your sister's wedding pictures this afternoon."

"Oh." Her sigh had a curl fluttering around her face.

"Why, Miss Dolley, what did you think I was implying?" he asked.

She flounced to an empty table, looking over her shoulder with a smile, and said, "Not that."

Liam chuckled. His laughter was a gift. He set his plate down. "Do you want coffee or tea?"

She couldn't help grinning. No one had ever cared for her the way Liam did. "Coffee, please."

He brushed a kiss on her forehead. "Be right back."

She watched him walk away, almost pinching herself. Liam Delaney had picked *her*.

"What is it with you and your sisters?"

Dolley turned. Courtney stood next to the table with her plate of food.

"What do you mean?" Dolley asked.

Courtney jerked her head at her brother. "Your sister seduced my brother, and he invests millions in your family business."

Dolley's mouth dropped open. She snapped it shut with a click. "He gave us a loan."

Courtney waved her statement away. "And now you're seducing this Irishman, so you can learn the art of photography?"

"What? No!" She pushed up from the table but kept her voice down. "You have a twisted mind."

"Right." Courtney drew out the word, making it sound ugly.

"Is that how people in Boston treat each other?" Dolley snapped out.

"It's what you Fitzgeralds do. Use men to get what you need. Even Bess is hooking up with a hot contractor, and he's the one working on the house that *my brother bought*." Courtney shook her head. "Why can't guys see through women like you and your sisters?"

"You…you…you're so wrong." Why couldn't she think of better words to defend her family?

Courtney shook back her dark curls. "Everyone's saying it." She moved to the table where her family sat.

Dolley slumped into her chair. *Everyone?*

It felt like a thousand eyes drilled into her back.

She should have been able to eviscerate the Boston Bitch. Why couldn't Gray's own sister see how in love Abby and Gray were? And Courtney had no idea the heartbreak Bess and Daniel had overcome.

Liam set a mug of coffee next to her plate.

"Thanks," she mumbled.

"What's wrong?" He touched her shoulder.

She chewed her lip. "Courtney was spreading her poison."

"Don't let her ruin this wonderful day and meal." He dug into his food.

She picked up her fork and started to eat, but everything had lost its taste.

Was she using Liam? Had she allowed their relationship to progress because he'd been so angry after Anne had made her sound like a mercenary?

Her stomach rolled. Was she just as bad as the men in her life who'd used her?

Courtney had jumped to that conclusion. Would everyone in the photography world assume she'd slept with Liam just to get ahead?

"This is delicious." Liam held up his fork. "Try it."

She opened her mouth and let him feed her a

bite of French toast, giving him an unenthusiastic "Mmm."

The sparkle had gone off her day. Maybe it would be better to call it quits with Liam. Then she might salvage some professionalism.

Liam squeezed her leg. "I've got this weird sensation in my chest."

She grasped his hand. "Are you okay?"

"It's happiness." He touched her face.

Her breath whooshed out. How could she break up with him? "You make me happy, too. Thank you."

"No." He stroked her cheek. "Thank you."

But Courtney's ugliness hung like a cloud over her happiness.

"BARBARA, HOW'S IT GOING?" Liam put his mobile on speaker.

"You sound…chipper. Is something wrong?"

He laughed. "Everything's splendid."

"Who is this, and what have you done with Liam Delaney?"

"Har-har." But energy flowed through his body. He was alive for the first time in his life.

Last night had been incredible. He couldn't wait for a repeat. Although he'd hoped Dolley would have worked with him this afternoon, she'd begged off. Pity. He needed to work, but he also wanted to spend more time with her.

He pushed away from the attic table and paced to the center of the floor.

"Tell me more about your new premise idea," his producer said.

"You didn't really call me on a Sunday to ask, did you?"

"Maybe."

"The Fitzgerald helped a lot of Irish immigrants. I've interviewed a few of the descendants. Thought I would start the film with the general Irish migration, then talk about what the immigrants did in the south, the way they celebrate, and zero in on how James Fitzgerald and his son, Michael, helped their countrymen succeed. I'll tie everything back to the families that remained in Ireland."

"And you've found enough descendants to keep the film interesting?" she asked.

"Yes. Dolley even found a letter from the Irish FitzGeralds asking James to help immigrants from Clare." It had been a great find.

He heard Barbara's fingernails tap on her desk. "I'm still thinking about this change."

He swallowed. He hoped Barb wasn't going to make a liar out of him. He needed this new story line to work. "We found more letters between the Irish and American Fitzgeralds."

"And the Fitzgeralds have signed all the releases?"

"Yes. I interviewed them last week."

"Good." There was more tapping. "I think I'll come down with the crew."

"It would be great to see you." She hadn't come on location in years. Was she checking up on him? "Do you want me to make a reservation?"

"You read my mind."

Liam got the specifics. "I'll let you know if they're full."

"I've one more request. We need to get a website up for this film. I should have started this a while back, but the designer quit."

Liam sat up. "Dolley's a website designer."

"The woman who works with you also designs websites?" Glee filled her voice.

"And does them well from what I've seen."

"I don't suppose she'd consider designing a website under our current agreement."

"Barbara," he admonished.

"It would keep the budget in line."

"She's talented." And gorgeous and sexy. "Why don't I show her what's been done for prior films and see if she has any ideas. Then you can meet when you're down here."

"Excellent."

The chair squeaked as he leaned back. Dolley needed help with a job, and he wanted to spend even more time with her. That was a win for him.

CHAPTER THIRTEEN

Every picture tells a story.

Proverb

DOLLEY PAUSED AT the bottom of the attic stairs, gripping the railing like it was the only thing between her and a hundred-foot fall.

Liam was up there. Waiting.

After the wedding brunch, she'd pleaded exhaustion. He called last night wishing her a good night's sleep. She'd almost raced across the courtyard to be with him.

Courtney's accusations had stopped her.

She'd stayed awake half the night debating whether she should give up her apprenticeship. Her fists clenched. Give up Liam.

If she gave everything up, she'd have to go back and work for Jackson. The idea of a lifetime designing other people's websites…sucked. She wanted a career. She wanted to work with Liam. She wanted Liam.

But was she using him? Her head ached.

Taking a breath, she headed up the steep stairs.

Liam waited at the top, grinning. "I missed you last night." He pulled her computer bag from her shoulder and set it on the floor.

She couldn't lie. "I missed you, too."

He laced their fingers together, reeled her close and kissed her.

Coffee, mint, Liam and passion. She clutched his shoulders, her legs weak from his kiss.

He pulled her into a hug and sighed. "Let's get to work."

She took a deep breath and locked her knees. She couldn't lose this, lose him.

"I loaded the files into the work area you set up." He stroked her back. "Get to work."

"Slave driver." Dolley grinned.

She went through the steps they'd perfected working on Lisa's wedding pictures. Copy the file so she didn't destroy an original. Open it. Delete if no good. Enhance if necessary. Save.

It could have been monotonous. But she was working in the field she wanted to make her career. And seeing her sister's wedding pictures, having a hand in making them the best they could be, had her body relaxing.

"I love this one," she said to Liam.

Gray and Abby were sitting, her head on his shoulder. Gray grinned down at her. Abby smiled up at him. Their feet were propped on a spare chair, and Abby was barefoot.

"I had an idea on how to change that up." He started to take over her computer but stopped. "Try going to black and white."

She made the change.

"Add back their eye color."

He'd worked with her on this with Lisa's pictures. She made the changes. In the shades of gray, Abby's green eyes and Gray's bright blue popped.

He leaned closer. "Now her lips."

She did. Then did the same with Abby's bright pink toenails.

"I love it!" She turned to look at Liam and barely missed bashing his nose.

His breath heaved out, fluttering her curls. His stunning blue eyes stared into hers.

"Dolley?" His gaze dropped to her lips.

Longing flooded through her like a crashing wave.

She closed the distance between their mouths, slipping her tongue between his lips. And the world narrowed to only him.

He pulled her so she straddled his lap and trailed fiery kisses from her chin to her ear and down to her collarbone.

Her hips rolled, settling onto the thick ridge forming under her. When he merged their mouths together, her fingers furrowed through his hair.

Breaking away, he buried his face between her breasts. "We're supposed to be working," he gasped.

"Mmm-hmm." How could she ever think about giving him up? She combusted each time they touched.

"Don't suppose you want to head down to my room?" he asked.

More than she wanted to breathe. "As tempting as that sounds, I suppose we should keep working."

"You Americans. You don't know how to enjoy life."

This from the man who rarely smiled? Although, he had been smiling all morning.

He set her back on her chair. And brushed a kiss on her lips.

She ran her fingernail down his nose. "Have any plans tonight?"

"I hope so." A grin made his eyes glitter.

She kissed him again. Because she could. "Let's get to work."

They turned to their computers. "Speaking of work, are you interested in designing the website for the documentary?"

Her body stilled. "A website?"

"My producer is looking for a new designer. I thought of you."

Of course. No one thought of her as a photographer. Not even Liam, apparently. "What are you looking for?" she choked out.

"I'll shoot you addresses of some of the previous work. They're not especially creative. I know you can impress Barbara. You're so talented."

His compliment sounded...canned.

But she needed the money. Masking her hurt, she said, "I'll take a look."

"You have access to all my photos, so I won't have to sort through anything. I'll give you clips, too. And Barbara's coming next week so you can show her your ideas and negotiate a hefty payment."

"Sure." Her throat tightened.

Liam had everything lined up, didn't he? How long had he been planning this? Since he found out she was a website designer? She'd trusted him and instead of considering her for a photography gig, he'd gotten her a *design* job.

She closed her eyes and let out a sigh. Who was using whom in this relationship?

DOLLEY CHECKED THE TIME. "I'm heading to Carleton House."

Abby smiled. "Have fun."

"Would you turn off the beaming smile, already? You're blinding me."

Abby was back from her week-long mini-honeymoon. She and Gray planned a longer honeymoon in late April after the craziness of St. Patrick's Day.

"I can't help it." Abby threw out her arms and did a little spin. "I'm so happy!"

"I have no clue who you are." Dolley added a splash of milk to her tea and headed to the door. "First you come home with a tan—a tan! We're redheads. Now you're spinning in the kitchen."

Abby did another pirouette. "I married the man of my dreams, Carleton House is open." Her grin brightened. "And Gray is making tentative plans to convert the carriage house into my restaurant."

Dolley jerked on her coat. "That must have been some honeymoon. He wants to fund the restaurant?" What would Gray's sister say about that? "I thought it was weird having guests move between the two houses."

"It's so great! At breakfast this morning, people shared tables, and based on the laughter, they liked it. Two couples decided to visit Tybee together. Who knows, we may be creating lifetime friendships in our B and B."

Their B and B affected people's lives. Dolley wanted the guests' visits to run smoothly. She did her best to handle the registration system, Wi-Fi, room electronics, business center and now the gift shop.

Abby filled the guests with fabulous food. Bess wowed them with the beauty of her gardens, plants, flowers and orchids that decorated the two houses.

She'd always thought her sisters made the bigger contributions, but maybe it was the package. Maybe she was a key contributor, too.

"I think you're crazy. But a good crazy." She gave Abby a hug. "See you later. I need to get to this meeting."

She was nervous about meeting Liam's crew and producer. Whenever he talked about Barbara, respect filled his voice.

She swiped her card over the reader and entered the Carleton House kitchen. A massive coffeemaker filled one counter.

They'd really done it. They'd converted another mansion into a B and B.

"Hello," a young woman called, grabbing a coffee mug. "You're Dolley, right?"

"I am." She'd checked in the newlyweds. "Melanie?"

"Yes." The bride smiled.

"How's your stay?"

"Awesome. I wish we could be here another week."

"I can arrange that for you," Dolley offered with a grin.

"Oh, I wish. We both have to go back to work." She heaved out an exaggerated sigh. "See you later."

Dolley headed to the dining room, where Liam and his team had begun meeting yesterday. The production company was based in New York, but Liam's team was international. One woman was from Sweden and the rest from all over the States. And of course Liam was from Ireland.

She'd barely left Chatham County.

At the door she drew in a deep breath and knocked.

"Come in," an unfamiliar female voice called.

"There she is." Liam scrambled from his chair. "Dolley, come meet everyone."

He was dressed in black, looking long and lean.

But she knew about the muscles hidden under his clothes, because ever since the Monday after the wedding, they'd been together every night except last night.

A projector sat in the middle of the table. Along the walls hung Liam's flip charts and the Fitzgerald family tree.

On another wall was a chart listing the names they'd discovered in James's shipping company ledgers and Fiona's household journals.

Liam put a hand on her shoulder, but as soon as they approached the table, it slipped away. He introduced the four people in the room. Jerry, Tom, Sonjia and Barb.

Barb was stunning. A personality with—force. She was a study in black. Black blouse, black skirt, black stockings and black flats. Sharply cut black hair curled around her chin.

Dolley's hand brushed her uncooperative curls.

The only non-black accessories were Barbara's red-framed glasses and a red silk shawl thrown over the back of her chair.

Barb moved to the pass-through, grabbed the carafe and poured coffee. Leaning against the counter, she was a slim silhouette against the warm wainscoting and wood counter. "You and your sisters run the B and Bs?"

"We own the B and Bs," Dolley clarified.

"Right, right. That's what I meant."

"The three sisters are incredibly talented," Liam added, talking only to Barbara. "It's been lovely to watch the family work together."

"I can't imagine working with my two sisters."

Barbara rolled her eyes. "We'd beat each other bloody within a month."

Dolley blinked.

"Did you bring your website ideas?" Liam asked, filling the silence.

"That's why I'm here, right?" Could she sound more stupid?

"Good, good. Let's get to it." Liam headed to the other side of the table.

Dolley flipped open her Mac.

"Tom and I are going to take background shots." Jerry picked up a clipboard with a list written in Liam's handwriting. Tom grabbed a camera bag that was bigger than the video camera Liam had been using.

Barb pointed at a stack of papers. "Don't forget releases."

Dolley connected her computer to the projector. "I've looked at some of your websites and gotten a sense of what you've used before. I'd be interested in knowing the hits you're getting on the sites."

"I'd be interested in getting more hits on *all* the sites." Barb sat back at the head of the table. The power chair.

"The last designer wasn't very creative," Liam said.

"You got that right," Barb said. Liam's boss had a slight accent. Brooklyn?

Liam sat to Barb's right, and Sonjia was at the

opposite end of the table with a pad of paper covered in notes.

Dolley took a seat next to the projector.

"This is a mock-up of the website's first page."

The page loaded with pictures of Savannah she'd taken from Daniel's sailboat last summer. "The concept is to take the visitors through what the immigrants would have seen as they landed in port."

Barb sat up, her dark eyes gleaming. "Show me more."

Liam stared first at Barbara's face and then her hands. What was that about?

"I've also included the letters between the brothers and copies of the household journals." She'd included pictures she and Liam had taken on their *rambles* through Savannah. "I thought the page links could be set up in a timeline."

"Great idea." Liam looked at his producer.

Dolley took them through the few pages she'd developed.

Barb nodded. Liam nodded back, shooting Dolley a smile every now and then.

"I like it." Barb slapped her hand on the table.

Liam grinned. "I thought you would."

The producer speared her with a dark gaze. "Can you shoot me a bid?"

"Absolutely." Dolley unplugged and packed away her equipment. Happy, but something wasn't right. Her gut was churning. Was it because Liam hadn't said anything about her photography? "I'll get it to you this afternoon."

He walked Dolley into the hallway. Glancing back through the open doorway, he whispered, "Nice work."

"Thanks. I'll see you later?"

He glanced back again. "Barb's only here one more day."

He shifted so they weren't visible from inside the room and touched his lips to hers. "I'll let you know when I get clear. Abby's bringing over lunch and dinner for us, so…"

He might not be available. She got it. But they'd only spent two nights apart since Abby's wedding. She rolled her shoulders. "Let me know."

She headed to the carriage house apartment to work up the bid. And what was different about Liam clicked. He'd been looking for cues from Barb on how to react to her work.

The light bulb exploded in her head. He always looked for cues from people. He changed to match his environment. He'd worn black because his boss wore black. He was looking to Barb to see if he should be enthusiastic about her designs, even though when she'd given him a dry run he'd been thrilled.

Around Gray and Daniel, he mimicked their uniform of flannel shirts and blue jeans. Good lord, he'd even started drinking his Jameson with ice.

He was a…a chameleon!

Her stomach flip-flopped. Now that his environment had changed again, what did that mean for the two of them?

LIAM STRETCHED. "We've made good progress finding families that James and Fiona FitzGerald helped." He had one more day to convince Barb that this approach would work.

"I prefer the rich-versus-poor angle that you first proposed." Barb took another sip of her coffee. "It would make good polarizing drama."

He pulled over the coffeepot. Barbara drank caffeine all day. And he wanted to keep her happy. A happy producer made an easier work environment.

"I can make the distinction between how the rest of America treated the immigrants and what the Fitzgeralds did for their countrymen." Topping off her cup, he said, "Dolley can incorporate some of the information into the website."

She nodded and sipped her cup. "What do they put in their coffee down here? It's fantastic."

Heart? "Abby trained in New York before she returned to the B and B. She was the sous-chef at Maurice's." That fact would impress a foodie like Barb. "They got a Michelin star when she worked there."

Dolley had had such pride when she'd told him that fact. And when Barb mentioned beating her sisters bloody, Dolley's face had filled with horror. These two parts of his life were definitely...

different. He would just have to balance their differences and play to both of their strengths.

"I can't wait to see what she serves for dinner." Barb took another sip of her coffee. "Lunch was great, too."

And that was as good a compliment as Liam ever heard from his tough producer.

"I've some film of the Fitzgeralds." He'd done rough edits. "Do you want to go through it, since they might become the core of this story?"

He handed Sonjia the rough cut he'd made at a script for this segment.

Barb kicked off her shoes, stacked her feet on the chair next to her and said, "Roll it."

The two-hour interview had been cut to fifteen minutes. Still too long.

"The Fitzgeralds photograph well," Barb said.

"They're a lovely family."

"And from what I saw at the wine tasting yesterday, you've slipped right into the flow of their B and B."

"They've been...kind." Treated him like family. "Even invited me to their Christmas celebrations." His best in years.

"I did, too." Barb pointed at him.

"It's a lot warmer here than New York."

"Isn't that the truth?" She concentrated on the questions and answers, watching to the end. "I like it, but it's too long."

"I know. More work to do." He just hadn't been

able to cut Dolley's answers. She glowed on screen. Her sparkle wasn't as strong in a photo as in real life, but film was her medium.

The tape stopped. A final shot of Dolley's smiling face. The twinkle in her eyes had him staring a second too long.

"So," Barb drawled, "she's our research assistant."

He nodded. "Plus, she's taking pictures that can be used for the book, website and the film."

"You don't have to defend her to me." She set her feet on the floor. "If her ideas play out, I might hire her to clean up and develop all our websites."

"Really?"

Barb shrugged. "It depends. Is she always this good? Or is she inspired because she's so smitten with you?"

Sonjia snickered. "I hear that's not the first time that has happened."

"What?" He'd never worked with Sonjia before.

"I checked with some of your previous crew members, wanting to know how you like to work. They warned me women can't resist your sad Irish eyes." She snickered again. "And that was a direct quote."

"Women love our Liam. It doesn't hurt that he's the whole package. The face, the body and the accent." Barb slipped on her shoes. "I need a break."

"Is this approach a go?" He swallowed.

Barb tapped the table. "Yes."

Excellent. He would have Dolley continue to search the ledgers and journals to uncover other families the Fitzgeralds had helped.

He grinned. A perfect excuse to consult with her tonight.

"DONE." DOLLEY EMAILED the website bid to Barb.

Maybe she should do what both her sisters had done. Create a company to isolate her work from the family business.

She pushed away from her apartment kitchen table. She didn't want to spend her life creating websites. She wanted to travel and take pictures.

From the window, she stared at Bess's gardens. The gray fog from the morning still hadn't lifted.

Staying in Savannah wouldn't accomplish Dolley's dream. And building other people's websites wouldn't, either. She almost resented that Liam was the one who'd suggested it. He'd thought he was doing her a favor.

But she did need the money.

She paced the small living room. The apartment still felt like Abby's place, even though Bess had lived here a few months.

Bess now lived with Daniel. Abby and Gray had moved into the Carleton carriage house.

And Dolley was in transition. Unfortunately, she'd wasn't sure what she was transitioning to. She hadn't even hung any pictures. How could she call herself a photographer?

The nice thing about living at Fitzgerald House was she could go bother Abby. She tossed on her jacket, slipped on her shoes and dashed across the courtyard.

The kitchen was quiet, but a fire burned on the hearth. Abby couldn't be too far away. She shucked off her coat and made a tea. The door swung open. Dolley glanced up from the sitting area. "Hey, Cheryl."

Cheryl waved. "Are you looking for Abby?"

"Yeah." Dolley scrunched up her mouth. "I'm... out of sorts. Thought I'd come and whine."

"She won't even hear you." Cheryl whipped her hair into a ponytail and pulled on an apron. Then she headed to the sink to wash her hands. "She's still in the clouds."

"It's obnoxious." Dolley heaved out a sigh.

"You can bitch to me. I'm making pasta for Italian night."

"Cool." Dolley moved to the counter.

Cheryl measured out yellow flour, eggs and salt into the mixer.

"How's Josh enjoying school?" Dolley asked.

Cheryl grinned and talked about her son. It was soothing to have the hum of the mixer and Cheryl's chatter competing with the voice inside her head that was telling her she wasn't getting what she needed from this apprenticeship.

Liam was getting his research from her, but what was she getting to improve her photography skills? The last pictures they worked on had been of Abby's wedding.

"Do you want to tell me why you're frowning?" Cheryl asked.

Dolley shook her head. "It's hard when no one can see my dreams but me."

"I know that story by heart." Cheryl shut off the mixer and peeled the dough off the beater. "I think that every time I'm cleaning a toilet."

Dolley laughed. "I'm glad I saw you wash your hands when you came in. And you really are turning into an excellent chef."

Cheryl grinned. "I'm spending more and more time in the kitchen. So there's hope."

Dolley headed to the cupboard to check on Abby's stash of cookies. "Is that your dream?"

"My biggest dream is to make a good life for Josh. He's my center." Cheryl scattered flour on the stainless steel counter. "But I could see myself cooking full-time."

And apparently so could Abby. Because Cheryl had been the one who'd done the cooking and baking while Abby and Gray had been gone. Cheryl's dream was flourishing.

But no one thought of Dolley as a photographer.

That was her fault. It was time to start acting like one. "Thanks for letting me pout."

"Anytime." Cheryl grinned. "You could knead pasta. I get a lot of frustrations out when I do."

"I'm good." Or she would be as soon as she grabbed her camera.

LIAM SLIPPED HIS phone out of his pocket. Where was Dolley? She hadn't responded to his last three texts.

There was a knock on the dining room door.

"Come in," Liam called.

Amy stuck her head inside. "Can I clear your dishes?"

"Sure. But leave the wine." Barb waved her hand at the remains of their dinner. "And tell the chef it was great."

"I will." Amy loaded a couple of trays and pushed them through the pass-through. "Italian night is always a hit."

"Do you eat like this all the time?" Jerry rubbed his stomach.

"You'll have to check out their wine tastings to find out." Liam smiled.

"I'm going to download today's film in my room." Jerry headed to the door.

"I'll help." Tom pulled up a chair.

"I'm done for." Sonjia gathered up her notebooks. "I'll head up, too."

"Nice setup." Barb tipped the last drops of the wine into her glass. "Too bad they don't have Scotch."

"Would Jameson do?"

"They really do relish their Irish roots." She laughed. "Sure."

"Grab your jacket. We'll go to the main house." And maybe he'd find Dolley.

"I didn't notice the gardens when I came through last night." Barb tugged up her collar. "They're nice."

More than one compliment out of Barb's mouth was pretty amazing.

He bumped his room card against the Fitzgerald House library door.

Shedding his coat, he took Barb's and hung them on the coat tree.

"Lead the way." Barb held out her hand.

"They keep the whiskey stocked in here." He poured two glasses. Neat. Barbara's choice.

"Will you need a crew when you film in Ireland?" she asked, settling into one of the chairs set in front of the glowing fire.

"If there's budget troubles, I know someone I can tap for a day or two."

"That sounds dirty, Mr. Delaney." She sipped. "Ahhh. Nice way to end a long work day."

He sipped, too. And took a deep breath but couldn't find his balance. Dolley was missing from the equation.

He steered the talk to Barb's family and their holidays. Barb liked to rail about her son, but the love shone through.

"He's convinced that we *must* take a snowboarding vacation this spring break. *All* his friends are going to Colorado."

"It sounds like fun," he said.

"I'd rather come here. I don't suppose they have an on-site spa. I'd never leave the building."

"None that I know of, but they have connections all over town. I'm sure they'd set you up."

"I won't be here that long. You have the project well in hand."

"Glad you feel that way." Because he hadn't until he'd come up with the last brainstorm.

Bright hair moved past the library door. He was up and moving before he could excuse himself to Barb. "Dolley?"

"Liam." Her cheeks were rosy with the cold. Her curls were tangled and falling in her eyes. "Are you done for the night?"

"Yes. Barb and I are having a bump." He took her icy hand. "Join us."

"Sure." Her grin was huge. What had made her so happy?

"Hi, Barb." She headed to the decanter and poured a short shot. Tossing her coat over to the sofa, she stood next to the fire. "This feels wonderful."

He wanted to warm her hands. But a quick glance at Barb had him sitting back in his chair.

"Your bid looked good, so I've sent it to the number crunchers." Barb took another sip.

"Thanks. If they have questions, they can call."

"Where were you off to?" Liam asked. When his question sounded strange, he tried again. "I texted you a couple of times. Were you…"

He left it open-ended, because he wasn't sure what he was asking.

"The fog had me grabbing my camera. I was down by the harbor."

"Let's see."

They sat together on the sofa, and she pulled her camera out of its case.

"Well, kids, I'm topping this off and taking it back to Carleton House. I'll see you in the morning." Barb slipped on her coat and left.

"Didn't you know there was Jameson in the Carleton House library?" she asked.

"I'm so used to grabbing a glass here, I never thought about it. And I wanted to run into you."

"Oh." Her green eyes looked vulnerable.

He touched her cheek. "Show me your work."

"There's a lot that should be trashed," she warned.

"Never apologize." He waited as she scrolled through the pictures.

She'd started at The Waving Girl. The fog curled around the statue's feet, almost obscuring the dog he knew was there. He'd taken his pictures in the sun. This was more…ominous. Like the girl was warning the ships away. He couldn't wait to see the picture full-size.

"Some of the later immigrants you're talking

about might have seen her waving. She was a fixture at the harbor in the late 1800s through 1930."

She'd moved around the statue, shooting up and also down.

"I like the fog rolling off the water," he said.

"I do, too." She chewed on her lip.

He had to force himself to focus on the pictures and not her mouth.

These pictures were darker than Dolley's normal outlook. He hoped his dreary view of the world hadn't rubbed off on her.

She'd found an abandoned boat listing in the water. The paint was peeling. It was juxtaposed against a shiny yacht motoring downriver.

"These are…incredible. The best work you've ever done." And each picture got better and better. "What emotions were you going for?"

"It was—" she pushed her curls away from her face "—everything. Frustration. Perseverance. Despair. Solitude."

"That's not your normal reaction to life." He let the camera drop in his lap and took one of the hands she twisted from her lap. "What's wrong?"

"I…I don't know." She stared at their hands. "I want more."

"More?" From him?

"I don't want to be the other Fitzgerald sister or a website designer." She swallowed. "I'm a photographer."

"I know, darlin'." He waved at the camera sitting in his lap.

"You do?" Her jaw stiffened. "You didn't introduce me that way today."

"I didn't?" He thought back to their morning meeting. "I…I guess it was because we were there to talk about the website."

"Or was it because that's how you think of me first? Website designer. Gopher. Research assistant." She pulled her hand from his and crossed her arms.

He was stepping onto boggy ground without a safety rope. "You're talented at everything you do. Photography. Researching. Running a B and B. Website design. Kissing. Making love."

Her stiff shoulders softened. "Good answer."

"I'm sorry if I didn't highlight each of your many talents." He brushed a kiss across her knuckles. When that wasn't enough, he pulled her into his chest.

"So you texted me earlier." Her cheek was resting against his chest.

"Aye." He tightened his arm around her. "Don't take this wrong, but I want you to find more descendants of the immigrants who worked for James."

She snorted. "Of course you do."

"But I only ask, knowing how amazing you are at everything you do."

"Suck-up."

"And I really want to see you develop some of the

pictures you just took. They are almost as amazing as you."

She brushed a kiss on his lips. "Good save."

"One more request." He stroked a finger down her cheek. "Barb and I talked about documenting the making of the film for the book. I'd like you to take those pictures."

"Really?" Her body quivered against his.

There was that energy, the life that filled her so full, she couldn't help but vibrate in his arms. Her grin was a twenty on a scale of one to ten. "I would love to."

"Wonderful." Putting a little leer in his voice, he asked, "Interested in working out the finer details in my room?"

"Oh, my. Do you make that offer to all your research assistants?"

"Never."

She drew a pattern on his chest that had his body tightening up. "The carriage house is closer."

He grabbed her hand. "Let's go."

CHAPTER FOURTEEN

Seeing is not enough; you have to feel what you photograph.

Andre Kertesz

LIAM WAITED AS the team set up for the Murphy interview. The family immigrated in 1905. The wife had worked for the Fitzgeralds as a cook, and her husband eventually became a supervisor in the warehouse. Now their descendants owned and managed Savannah real estate.

And the Murphys had produced meticulous records of their journey from Ireland to America and their early life in Savannah. A great find.

His phone vibrated in his pocket. The patriarch of the family wasn't here yet, so he took the call.

He kept his voice low. "Hey, Barb, what's up?"

"We've got a couple of publications interested in doing pieces on your documentary."

"Wonderful. What do you need from me?"

"I'll email you their contact info. They might ask a few more questions, but I've given them background. They've requested pictures."

"Sounds great." His heart beat a little faster. He could use Dolley's Waving Girl picture. Get her some exposure while they did publicity for the film. "I'll contact them as soon as I'm done."

He was pulling the phone away from his ear when he heard a click.

Dolley lowered her camera, a grin painting her face. She smiled a lot lately. And so had he.

"I'm naming that picture *Documentary Maker at Work*."

"Or taking a phone call."

"That, too." She tipped her head to the group. "I never knew the Murphys were connected with my family until you had me do the research."

"Your family touched a lot of lives."

"Thank you." She inched closer. "For showing me how…exceptional my ancestors were."

He touched her arm. "I can think of other ways to thank me."

"Me, too." She looked over at the crew. They were oblivious to their conversation. "My place tonight?"

"Seems reasonable." He sighed. "Although I might have to do some publicity work. I'll keep you posted."

"You do that, Mr. Delaney."

"You're okay if I send in pictures we both took, right?" he asked.

"Some of my pictures?" Her eyes lit up like fireworks. "You bet."

"I know just the photographs I want to send them." After Dolley got recognition for her photos, how bright would her eyes gleam?

After finishing with the Murphys, Liam shoehorned in talking to both interviewers and sent off a series of pictures, both his and Dolley's.

By the time they were together in Dolley's carriage house apartment, he wanted an ale and Dolley.

He pulled a bottle from her fridge and leaned against her living room doorway. Dolley bent over her laptop. Her curls bobbed as her fingers flew over the keyboard.

A peacefulness warmed him like a blanket. He was where he belonged. Savannah. The Fitzgeralds. Dolley. Not just for this project, but maybe the long-term.

"I did some publicity today and gave them your email. You can add the online article links to the website." He handed her his beer, and she took a sip. "Hopefully, you'll have the info tomorrow."

"That will work. I've almost finished the website's first pass." She pulled up the home page. "I'll add an announcement or reviews section. I've seen that on a couple of the other sites."

He stared down at her.

Looking up, she asked, "What?"

"It's time to pack it in for the night." He reached for her computer.

She whipped it away. "I want to impress the people I'm working for."

"You always impress me." He pushed the coffee table back with his foot and knelt in front of her. His hands stroked her thighs. "I think we should take the night off."

"You work more hours than me." Her breasts brushed his shoulder as she set her computer on the table.

A touch of her body and his headed for high alert. "Not tonight."

She wrapped her legs around his waist and pulled him closer. "What did you have in mind?"

His hands wormed under her jumper, pushing it over her head. Her bra was hot pink. There would be matching knickers under her jeans. "Nice."

"I got *hot* watching you work today." She worked on the buttons of his shirt.

He tugged off his shirt. "If you're hot, I'll help you shed your clothes."

Her eyes sparkled with laughter. "You're so useful."

"I know, darlin'." He kissed her.

She tasted of beer and Dolley and all things that were home. He could imagine living in Savannah and spending his life coming home to Fitzgerald House and being a part of the whole family. Learning their language, being part of their jokes.

It was all he'd ever wanted. Being part of something. Belonging.

He nuzzled under her ear, a spot guaranteed to have her squirming her lithe body against his.

"I love the way you kiss," she moaned. "I love the way you touch me."

He froze. *Love?*

That would suit him just fine. He loved the

Fitzgeralds, loved Savannah and he was falling in love with Dolley. She was the icing on this particular cake. A little bit spicy and always a surprise.

After he had been an emotional tumbleweed all his life, the Fitzgeralds were giving him roots. He wanted whatever was growing between them to take root and bloom.

He kissed her hard. Fumbling, he flipped open her jeans, then stripped them off her legs, tossing jeans and socks behind him. The only thing left between him and heaven was her skimpy hot-pink thong.

He pulled her up to his mouth, soaking the silk that kept him from paradise.

She moaned, the sound drilling into his groin. "Liam." She tried to pull him up.

"Let me." The material was pushed aside, and he kissed her core. Heat and honey flowed over his tongue as he licked the heart of her.

"I want *you*," she pleaded.

He whipped away the silk, and she was bare to him. Bare and beautiful. He ached to join with her, but wanted to capture this moment.

He snatched her camera off the coffee table.

"What are you doing!" She curled into a ball, giving him a delightful view of her bum.

"Please." He touched her shoulder. "I want you to see how…lovely, how full of life you are."

She uncurled her body, her lip tucked between her teeth. "Liam, I…"

He kissed her until they both gasped for air.

She slumped against the sofa. "If these ever end up on social media, I will kill you."

He grinned. Standing over her with the camera, he shot a close up of her face. Her eyes sparkled with arousal. Her curls, tousled by his hands, covered half her face. He dropped to her lips, swollen from his kisses.

Then he focused on her breasts, the skin flushed. Her tight nipples gleamed from his mouth.

His breath turned to pants.

Zooming out, he captured her whole body. One arm thrust above her head, nipples erect, slim hips waiting for him. And in that moment, that perfect click, her face…knowing. Seductive.

His hands shook as he set the camera down. "What you do to me," he whispered.

Dolley slid to the edge of the sofa. "Enough."

His trouser button was dealt with. She reached under his boxers and wrapped her fingers around him.

He groaned, clapping his hand on hers. "Too much."

Shifting, he shucked off pants, boxers and socks.

She wrapped her lips around him.

His fingers burrowed in her hair. "Dolley!"

He pulled her up and sat her on the sofa.

After donning a condom, he set her legs on his shoulders. Finally, he entered her, driving home.

She clutched at the sofa, her head rolling back and forth.

"Yes," she cried.

Her body clung to his as he pounded into her, unable to hold back or slow down.

She came apart around him, and he rocketed to completion. He panted, driving into her one more time.

Her head lolled back.

His legs wobbled. How could being with Dolley keep getting better and better? If he took a picture now, he'd title it *Satisfied Woman*.

He kissed her ankles and slipped them from his shoulders. And collapsed at her feet.

Dolley opened one eye. "Hey, handsome."

He should clean up, but he couldn't find the energy. He laid his head on her thigh. "Hey, yourself."

"That was…different."

He snatched up the beer sitting on the end table and gulped down half the bottle. Then he handed it to her. "Different good or different bad?"

Her fingers ruffled his hair. "Absolutely fantastic."

He sat on the floor between her legs, wrapping them so they draped down his chest. He didn't want to lose their connection. His body quivered with aftershocks. "I'm knackered."

Her legs bounced as she laughed. "I feel like I could take on the world."

He inhaled. "I'm for bed."

"I think I'll work a little more."

"It's after ten."

She pushed on his shoulders. "Get some sleep. A lot of my best creativity happens after midnight."

"But lots of your best moves happen before."

Another dazzling laugh shook her body. "Only with you."

Did she mean that? Was what they had special to her, too? He didn't like the idea of going to bed without her, but he understood the creative process.

He hauled himself up from the floor and brushed a kiss on her upturned nose. "Don't be too late."

DOLLEY PUSHED HER hair off her face. The adrenaline that had sustained through the first hour of work evaporated. Time to crawl into bed. With Liam.

She gave herself a hug. This was the first man she'd dated who hadn't given her the boot after a few dates, and it felt...incredible.

She started to shut her laptop, but her email dinged.

It was after midnight. No one would expect her to answer.

She touched the top of her laptop ready to shut it, but couldn't. She would just peek. It was probably junk mail.

She clicked and scanned the subject. It was one of the articles about Liam and the documentary. Had Liam talked about her family? About Savannah? She couldn't resist reading what the interviewer said about the film. She could take a quick look, link the article to the website and then head to bed.

When the site opened, the first picture that loaded was her Waving Girl in the Fog. Dolley's mouth dropped open. Her photo was in a major magazine.

She shimmied a little, her joy too strong to sit still. She'd assumed Liam would use some of the pictures they'd taken around town. Her photo was in the article.

She clicked on the picture, and her fingers froze over her mouse. "What?"

She stared at the attribution: *Photo: Liam Delaney and Dolley Fitzgerald.*

Liam had had nothing to do with the photo. Why had he claimed her picture?

She checked the entire article. Of the seven pictures, four were hers and three were Liam's. They were all labeled Liam Delaney and Dolley Fitzgerald.

She chewed her thumbnail. The reporter must have made a mistake. Liam wouldn't take credit for her pictures.

What had he said earlier? *You're okay if I send in pictures we both took.*

She'd expected to receive credit for her own pictures.

She closed her eyes and scanned the contract she'd signed with the documentary company. *Nothing about photography.* It only gave them rights to the pictures she took while documenting the film. Not rights to her other photos.

The Waving Girl was one of the best pictures she'd ever taken. Acid burned holes in her stomach. Now Liam's name was on it.

She'd trusted him. The breath she inhaled shook. She'd shared her dreams with him, and he'd stolen her work. Betrayed her.

She tore at her curls. He knew how much photography meant to her. The thief slept in her bed. She wanted to toss off the covers and throw him out of her apartment—out of the B and B. Out of her life.

"Damn it!" Unfortunately, the B and B was better off *with* Liam and his crew than without them. They might be able to rent the rooms around St. Patrick's Day, but kicking him out would jeopardize a month of rentals for a minimum of four beds.

She couldn't sleep next to him. If she did, she'd be tempted to cover his lying face with a pillow.

Curling up on the sofa, she wrapped a throw around herself. He had everything she wanted: travel, a career in photography, even the documentary. Why did he have to steal her dreams, too?

A single tear slid down her cheek. She sniffed back any others. It was all the grief she could afford to release, because if she lost control, she might have to acknowledge she'd started to fall in love with a bastard.

She tossed, turned. Every few minutes a voice inside her head screamed, *Why!*

Finally, she marched into the bedroom. She didn't care if it was two in the morning. She shoved his shoulder.

He rolled over, never waking.

She pushed again. "Delaney."

"Mphfgh," he mumbled.

She leaned into his ear. "Wake up!"

His arm flailed. "What's wrong?" His voice was scratchy with sleep.

"Why did you do it?"

"Do what?" He rubbed his eyes. Shaking his head, he sat up. He looked so at home—*in her bed*. He stared at the clock. "Come to bed."

"Why did you do it?" She forced herself to ask again. "Why did you steal my picture?"

"Steal?" He flipped on the end-table light, wincing at the brightness. "Darlin', I don't have a clue what you're talking about."

Her stomach flopped. "I got the link. Is that why you had the interviewer send it to me? So I knew that you took credit for my pictures?"

"I've never stolen a picture in my life." His lips formed a straight line. "I told them to put our names on the pictures."

"How can you take credit for a picture you never took?"

"Because we work together." He pushed his hair back. "Because I helped you edit your photos. My name will give you a leg up." He threw the covers back and sat up. "That's what you wanted, right? My help in getting your name out there?"

"Any picture I take, you can claim?"

"I asked you today." He pushed off the bed and stood. "You were bloody excited."

"But…" Is this how it was done? When she'd agreed to be an apprentice, he could do something this…this vile?

He came closer. "I thought you'd appreciate using my name to get noticed. We worked together on all the pictures I sent in."

"Because you made one small suggestion for a change in a picture I took?" She couldn't keep the doubt from her voice.

Her legs gave out, and she collapsed onto the bed.

"You're my apprentice." He sounded so damned reasonable.

Swallowing hard, she whispered, "I assumed it would be my name."

He sank next to her on the bed. "I thought you knew what I was asking this afternoon."

She should get up, get away from him. But everything inside crumbled. "I didn't."

He swore. "I'm trying to help you."

"It doesn't feel like it." Her throat ached from holding back tears.

"Luv." He slid closer and tugged her head so her cheek rested on his bare chest. "I was thrilled when my mentor did the same thing."

She should pull away, but her muscles had filled with lead.

"I'm sorry you misunderstood." He hesitated before brushing a kiss on her forehead.

She wanted to believe him.

He wrapped his arm around her waist, anchoring her to his warmth.

"I wanted to do something nice for you." He tugged her onto his lap. "And now I've hurt you."

She couldn't talk. If she did, the stupid tears would fall. She burrowed into his chest.

He rocked her like she was a child. Maybe she was just as naïve. Is this really how things worked for an apprentice?

"Let's get you in bed."

He tucked her in. Shutting off the light, he slid in behind her. He brushed a kiss on the top of her head. "Sleep, luv."

She stared at the curtains, unable to shut her eyes.

He thought she'd misunderstood.

But these were *her* pictures.

Had he done it on purpose?

She hated her doubts. Hated that she wasn't sure an apprenticeship equated to taking credit for her work.

Hated that she just might be falling in love with Liam. Her chest tightened. And if he wasn't telling the truth, this was betrayal.

HAD HE MISLED HER? Liam wished he had Dolley's phenomenal memory to replay their conversation.

Sharing credit wasn't a bad thing. He'd done it before.

But Dolley's sparkle had vanished in the last two days.

Sonjia rapped on the table. "Are you with us?"

"Yes, right."

She slid a piece of paper down to him. "Here's today's shooting schedule."

Before he could review the list, his phone buzzed. He turned his back on the morning staff meeting.

"We're getting excellent buzz on the interviews," Barb said without saying hello.

"That's good." But he couldn't fake enthusiasm for something driving him and Dolley apart. "Did you look at Dolley's latest website mockup?"

"Fabulous. Where has she been hiding all this time?"

"In plain sight in Savannah." He heard the pride in his voice. Dolley was talented at everything she did.

"I've gotten the go-ahead to offer her a job," Barb said.

"You have?" He straightened. Would Dolley take a job working for Barb? Would that be good or bad for their relationship?

"She's got more creativity than any website designers we've worked with before," Barb said. "I want her working for us and not our competition."

"Good luck." After Barb hung up, he set his phone on the table.

Maybe a job offer would get him and Dolley back on track. Because for the last two days he felt like he was on trial, with a guilty sign hanging around his neck.

Her withdrawal hadn't stopped them from being together the last couple of nights. But he hated the speculative looks she shot his way.

Last night he'd dreamed he lived in Savannah—with Dolley. Her large extended family had visited their house and he was host. The Foresters, Cheryl and her son, the people from the wedding had all shown up in his dream. He'd awakened with a smile.

He wanted that dream to become reality.

Everything clicked into place. This was where he belonged. Savannah. With the Fitzgeralds. This was what he wanted. To be part of the craziness and joy surrounding their family.

He turned back to the table.

"How's the script?" Sonjia asked.

He forced his head back into the work at hand. "I've made changes. Tell me what you think."

He grabbed the correct folder.

She flipped through his handwritten notes. "These are good. I'll finalize and print."

"I think we should tape down on River Street, while the crowds are light," Jerry said. "Then we'll have a comparison with the holiday crowds."

Liam checked the shooting schedule for the day. "Are we trying to get there today?"

"Dolley thought an evening shot would have more atmosphere. I've slotted it for tonight."

"Okay."

Tom flashed some media badges. "We've got what we need to film the crowds for the actual holiday."

Things were coming together like a perfect picture materializing in a darkroom.

Him. Savannah. The Fitzgeralds. Dolley.

Yes.

DOLLEY MADE THE final adjustments to the documentary website. The pages winked from the three monitors she had active in front of her.

The site would continue to change, but Barb's staff was capable of handling updates.

She pushed away from the desk she'd set up in the apartment's extra bedroom. Bending forward, she stretched her aching lower back.

What was Liam doing now? She checked the printed schedule on her desk.

He should be finishing a staff meeting. Then there was an interview with another family helped by James and Fiona Fitzgerald.

Lately, all she'd worked on was the documentary. Liam had bumped her hours again. She'd poured hours into his research, helped with scripts, suggested spots to shoot and he took credit for her work.

Her photos had been out for two days, the pictures the world thought were a collaboration between her and Liam.

She swallowed the sour taste in her mouth. He'd never mentioned her in the article. Maybe her talent wasn't strong enough to stand on its own.

The purpose of pursuing the apprenticeship had been to escape her sisters' brilliance. Nothing had changed. She still faded into the background, except now she was stuck in Liam's shadow.

Her thoughts were ugly. Was she only dating Liam for what he could do for her new career? It made her sound like a…a gold digger. A user. Like the men she'd dated. And exactly what Courtney had accused her of being.

Snatching her mug from the desk, she took a swig. Cold.

In the kitchen, she flipped on the kettle. Why couldn't she focus on how generous Liam had been with his talents and mentoring and stop wanting more?

While the water heated, she picked up a travel magazine. On the cover, a bikini-clad woman rested on the beach. The blue of the water was achingly beautiful. A rock set in the upper left drew the eye to the distance.

Other than beauty, she didn't get an emotion from the picture. Liam would have tossed it. She flipped through the pages. Instead of reading the articles, she examined the pictures. Some had been taken by a photojournalist, some articles had both a reporter and photographer.

She could do both. The blog had taught her how to keep her audience interested. Longing whipped through her. When she pictured her life in ten years, it included a passport filled with stamps from countries she'd never heard of and pictures of people and places where she didn't speak the language.

First, she had to get a passport.

The kettle boiled, and she added water to the teapot, then filled her mug.

Back in her office, she took one more pass through the website and checked the mobile version. She was happy with her work and she'd beaten the deadline by two days.

Time to ship it to Barb.

Just as she hit Send, her cell rang.

Liam? She kicked herself. How needy was she?

Instead, it was Barbara. "Hi, Barb."

"Dolley. How's it going?"

"I just sent you the website for approval."

"Wow. You're good. Don't forget to copy Samantha."

Dolley smiled. "Already done."

"Excellent." There was a small tapping noise in the background, like a fingernail on ceramic. What was up?

"I really like your work," Barb said.

"Thank you."

"How would you like to take on all Wonderment, Inc.'s website work? Full-time."

A small thrill pulsed through her. Barb liked her work enough to offer her a job.

But it wasn't the job she wanted. Her body slumped.

"We'd help you find an apartment in New York. You'd have full control of the websites. I understand you made security change suggestions on the hosting service."

Butterflies danced in her belly. "You'd want me to move to New York?"

"That's where the job is," Barb said. "I'd like you to look at our old sites and revise them to get better hits and accessibility. You'd spend time in our LA office, too."

She couldn't get over the idea of moving to New York. And working between LA and New York. Her head spun like she wasn't getting enough oxygen.

"We also have a London office. But we'd want you to get your feet wet on the North America productions first."

London? She let her head sink onto the back of the chair, her phone clenched in a death grip. "I...I..."

"Why don't I send you the list of websites so you know what's in front of you? And I'll send you this quarter's projects." Barb added, "We've done this all with contract help, but I've convinced the partners it's better to bring you onboard, and you can create your own department."

"I'd have staff?"

Barb laughed. "When I send you the list of sites, you'll understand why. We have a lot of upcoming projects."

"I appreciate the offer."

"Then let's talk money." Barb named a figure that had Dolley tucking her head between her knees.

When that wasn't enough to stop her head spins, she slid out of the chair and lay flat on the floor.

"Say you'll think about it," Barb said.

"I'll think about it." She rubbed the tension in her jaw. "This is a busy time for my family's B and B. Is it okay if I let you know after we get through St. Patrick's Day?"

Barb's fingernails tapped out a rapid beat. "Sure. Why not."

"Thank you, again." She needed time to figure out her life.

"Great. I'll get Samantha to send those lists."

"Thank you."

After Barb hung up, Dolley let the phone slip out of her hands. New York. LA. London. The cities had slipped off Barb's tongue as easily as if she traveled there every week.

She stared at the ceiling. It was part of her dream. But only part.

Could she start from there? Leapfrogging off this opportunity?

And what about her sisters and the B and B? It wasn't like what she contributed was that unique, but they would have to hire someone to do the book-keeping. And the new reservation system was coming online after they survived the March craziness.

What would Liam think of her job offer? She sat up, wrapping her arms around her legs. Would this mean she would see more him or less? Wonderment produced all his films, but that didn't mean he would always do that.

She didn't want whatever she and Liam had begun to end. She'd never dated a man this long.

Her head pounded with questions.

Swiping her phone off the carpet, she called Abby. "We need a sisters' meeting tonight."

CHAPTER FIFTEEN

The photographer is like the cod which produces a million eggs in order that one may reach maturity.

George Bernard Shaw

"YOU'D LIVE IN NEW YORK?" Bess chewed on her thumbnail.

"Yes." Dolley tapped her sister's hand and then paced the kitchen's sitting area. She'd been stewing about Barb's offer all day. "Although she talked about working with their LA team and possibly the London group."

"New York." Abby's eyes were huge. No smile creased her normally happy face. "You would love living there. You'd fit in."

"I don't know about that." Dolley waved a hand over her jeans and red top. "Everyone who works with Liam thinks black is the ultimate wardrobe choice."

"So you'd stand out." Bess leaned forward from her spot of the sofa. "You'd add a spark of color to their dull worlds. People would circle you like you were an exotic plant. Or a light and they're all moths."

Dolley shook her head. "Don't moths eat clothes?"

Bess waved her hand. "You know what I mean."

"But what about what we're building here?" Abby asked.

"You and Bess are the creative forces behind Fitzgerald and Carleton House." She sank down onto the sofa. "What I do can be done by other people."

"We're a team." Abby's strawberry-blond ponytail shook back and forth. "And you're a valuable member of Team Fitzgerald."

Dolley rolled her eyes. "I can monitor whoever we hire to pick up my slack. With Fitzgerald and Carleton House both running, our cash flow is stronger. I'd stop taking a draw."

"You're an owner." Abby rubbed her temples. "I can't picture the B and B without you."

Dolley's stomach flipped. Would they want to buy out her B and B share? Her legacy?

Bess grabbed her hand. "I love seeing you every day."

"You're both too busy with Gray and Daniel to miss me." But Dolley swallowed. She saw her sisters almost every day. Even if it was hard living in the shadow of their accomplishments, they were her best friends. "All your gooey love eyes are making me sick."

"What does Liam think?" Abby asked.

Dolley pulled on a loose thread on her jeans. "I haven't talked to him yet."

"But you two are…" Bess wiggled her fingers.

"I wanted to talk to you first."

And there was the difference between her older sisters and her. They had someone they loved who would always be first in their lives. Gray and Daniel put them first, too.

She wasn't sure where she and Liam stood or where they were going.

"So, what was the apprenticeship for?" Abby's forehead furrowed into a frown.

Dolley popped off the sofa again, unable to sit. "For my photography."

"But they aren't hiring you as a photographer," Bess said.

"No." She shook her head. "But once I get my feet under me, I might be able to launch a career in photography in New York."

Except she'd looked at the website list Samantha had sent. She had months of work ahead of her. And that was without the new projects.

Abby let out a puff of air. "Have you hated being tied to Fitzgerald House?"

"I…" Dolley shifted on her feet.

"I didn't realize." Abby's face fell. "I'm so sorry."

"I love working with you." Dolley didn't want to hurt her family. "It's just… I want to travel and take pictures instead of build websites."

"But isn't that what you'd be doing for them?" Bess asked.

Dolley swallowed. "But it would be in New York."

"So Savannah is the problem," Abby stated.

"Abby, you lived in New York." Dolley pointed at Bess. "And you went to college in a different town. I stayed here."

"And we've never taken vacations." Abby twirled her wineglass between her fingers, but didn't take a sip.

"I love Savannah," Dolley whispered.

"Then why don't you want to stay?" Bess asked.

Why? "Because I'm the *other* Fitzgerald girl." Dolley pressed her fingertips to her head. "I'm your sister here. Not Dolley Fitzgerald."

Abby rubbed a hand on her back. "That's not true."

Dolley tipped her head. "Even Martin assumed I didn't have any talent."

"He doesn't know you," Abby said. "Everything you do, you do well."

"Don't whitewash it." Dolley shook her head. "No one ever praises me like they do you guys."

"But you're so talented," Bess insisted. "What you do with the website and the blog is magic. No one else could do what you do. And your pictures are stunning."

She snorted. Liam had taken credit for her best work.

"Liam always tells us how good you are." Abby poked her shoulder. "Why do you think your website work isn't creative?"

"It just isn't." Dolley paced back to the fireplace. Her sisters were being kind.

"You're so stubborn you can't see your own talent." Abby's lips pressed together.

Dolley stared at Abby and Bess. "I learned that trait from my older sisters."

"When do you have to let them know?" Bess asked.

Dolley pushed back a curl from her eye. "I asked to have through St. Patrick's Day."

"Oh, sit down," Abby said. "Drink your wine."

Dolley took a seat, but left her wine on the table. Her stomach was churning.

Bess took her hand. "What do you want to do?"

Had either of her sisters ever asked that question? Sure, they'd used the same phrases, but it was always about Fitzgerald or Carleton House decisions. They'd never once asked what *she* wanted to do with her life.

Could she give up working with her sisters, give up Savannah, all for a dream that might never come true?

She blurted out, "I don't know."

LIAM FLUBBED THE script he and Sonjia had crafted—twice. His concentration was shot.

Where was Dolley? She'd sent a text saying she would meet the crew on River Street. It wasn't that her taking pictures of these shoots was that crucial; it's that he hadn't seen her all day. He wanted to know how her conversation with Barb had gone. What she'd thought about the job offer.

"Why don't you rearrange these sentences?" Sonjia suggested. "They're twisting your tongue."

He tried it. Repeated the phrase that he'd mucked up. "That works."

"Ready for another go?" she asked.

He nodded. "Once more."

Jerry re-shouldered the camera.

Tom held the microphone and counted backward from five. The last two numbers were hand signals.

"It's a quiet night on Savannah's River Street, but by March 17, a quarter of a million people will invade this city."

He walked down the steps where Dolley had tripped, where he'd carried her back to the B and B. Walked and talked about the original shipwrecked Irish immigrants. The shipping industry. The flagstone that had come from England as ballast and colonists had reused to pave the streets.

He stopped, then looked at Sonjia.

"Good," she said.

Moving down the street, they set up again. Would Dolley know where to find them?

This time he talked about the Fitzgeralds. "James Fitzgerald's warehouse stood here. He was instrumental in helping his countrymen and women get their start in America."

They retaped the segment. Then he practiced while Jerry panned the nighttime scene of River Street.

"Sorry I'm late." Dolley's voice came from behind him.

He spun toward her, a smile blooming on his face.

"I was starting to worry." He scanned her face. Her eyebrows were furrowed. "Are you okay?"

She crossed her arms and rocked back and forth. "I'm not sure."

He took her elbow, stilling her. "What's wrong?"

Dolley glanced over at his crew and the people who'd stopped to watch the filming. "Later."

"Okay." He cupped her chin, letting his thumb trace the apple of her cheek. He didn't like the confusion in her eyes.

She pulled out her camera and took shots of Jerry and Tom as they prepped. Then focused on him and Sonjia while they reviewed the next scene.

They worked their way down the street, taping and shooting. The final shoot was in front of Kevin Barry's Pub. They were late enough that the music had started. Liam hoped the microphone would pick up the sound as he talked about the history of Kevin and the pub.

"That's a wrap." Sonjia smiled. "Convenient that we ended right in front of a pub."

Liam laughed. "Karma?"

"Good planning," Sonjia said. "Want to stop for a pint?"

"I'm in," Tom said, wrapping a cord around his arm. Jerry nodded.

"My plan," Sonjia said. "You buy the first round."

With the light no longer blinding him, he could

see Dolley hanging in the background. She shook her head.

"I'll take a rain check. Anything you want me to haul back to the B and B?"

Jerry handed off the camera bag. Dolley took another from Tom. Then his crew disappeared into the bar.

"You sure you've got that?" he asked Dolley.

"It's not heavy." She headed toward the steps up to Bay Street.

She was too quiet.

"Do you want to talk now?" he asked, dreading her answer.

"Let's get rid of the equipment."

They waited for a few cars, then crossed Bay and moved through the historic district's serene streets.

"You're good at that," she said, breaking their silence.

"At what?"

"Telling the tales. Making people understand what you're talking about." She pointed behind them. "I can only imagine how much more sincere you will come across on camera."

"The gift of the Irish." He shrugged off her compliment, but warmth filled him. People had admired his work before, but not someone close. Dolley's compliment meant more.

"It's a collaboration," he added. Was that pressing the issue on the photos too much?

"I mean it. I know you photograph well, I've

taken hundreds of pictures of you. But I'm guessing the camera will pick up your…intensity. Sincerity?" She searched for the right word. "Passion. It's your passion."

This time he didn't shrug it off. "Thank you. It means a lot coming from another artist."

She kicked at a rock in the sidewalk. "I'm a website designer, not an artist."

Was that why she was so quiet? Instead of being happy about the job offer, Barb had offended her? He gritted his teeth. "You *are* an artist."

She shook her head.

If she didn't know how good she was, how could he convince her? He thought having her picture in the publicity pieces would help, but that effort had fallen on its face, hadn't it?

They headed into Carleton House. "I'll drop the bags in my room. Do you want to come up? Or head to your apartment and I'll join you?"

"I…I think I'll have a Jameson." Her gaze darted any place but looking him in the eye. "Join me in the library."

"Sure." He took the bag she'd carried. A chill shook his body. Didn't she want to be together tonight? Was she getting ready to tell him to bugger off?

His chest tightened. He couldn't lose what they'd started to build. He'd finally found a home. His fingers clenched the railing's smooth wood.

He couldn't lose everything now. No feckin' way.

He set the bags in his room. Running his fingers through his hair, he took a deep breath. There had to be something he could do to keep Dolley from jettisoning him from the life he wanted.

He paced the length of the room and stared out the window at the gardens starting to bud. He wanted to be here to see them bloom.

There had to be a way. He wasn't letting the Fitzgeralds get away.

In the bathroom, he splashed water on his face. He'd watch, wait and figure out what Dolley needed from him. It was what he'd always done to survive.

Carleton House was quieter than Fitzgerald House. No one passed him on the stairs as he headed down. On the main floor, he waved to the cleaning staff working in the dining room.

The doors to the library were open, but Dolley was alone.

She'd curled into an armchair in front of the flickering fire. Her shoes were on the floor, her feet tucked under her. A tumbler dangled from her fingers.

But it was her face that kept him from entering the room. Her eyes, normally dancing, were shadowed and dark.

She glanced up and nodded. No smile.

Nervous, he headed to the sideboard and poured a shot from the decanter. Taking the other chair set in front of the fire, he said, "You look so solemn."

A weak smile flashed across her lips. "Thinking."

"Barb said she loved the website, so what's wrong?" He held out his hand, needing to touch her. If Barb hadn't offered her a job, he didn't want to say anything.

She reached between the two chairs, but only their fingertips met.

Her hands slipped away, slapping the leather chair with a soft woomp. "Barb offered me a job."

He slid the chair closer and touched her hand. "That's good, isn't it?"

"As a website designer." She spat the words out. "The only good thing is the job would have me living in New York. I'd work between there, LA and probably London."

Ice formed in his belly. "You'd leave Savannah?"

"Yes."

"But—" he dropped her hand and paced to the fireplace "—this is your home. This is where your family lives. Barb should let you work from here."

Her green gaze sharpened. "You knew about this?"

"She mentioned it this morning." He pressed his temple. The dream of being part of the Fitzgerald family was slipping away. "You can work remotely, right?"

"You think I want to be a website designer?" She set her glass down with a clang and stood.

"I know you want to be a photographer, but you've been doing designs, right?"

She crossed her arms. "You don't think I can cut it as a photographer?"

"No." He hurried to her, catching her elbows. "I mean, yes, you can. Of course you can."

She backed away from him.

He held up his hands like she was a hot stove. He was losing her. "I mean, you're already a photographer."

She raised her eyebrows.

"I put your picture in the articles because they're good," he said.

She pointed a finger at him. "And your name came first. I wasn't even mentioned in the article."

"How many times do I have to apologize? I tried to help you."

She held up her hands, shaking her head. "When you think of me working, what comes to mind?"

"Land mines," he said under his breath. He was going to step on one and have it explode in his face.

"What?"

"I…I don't try and put you in a…pocket. I see you first as a…Fitzgerald, a successful businesswoman. A woman who's part of an incredible family."

She closed her eyes. "Don't."

He closed the gap that was growing between them. "I also see you as a budding photographer, absorbing everything I can teach you."

"Budding. Student." Her words choked out.

"And talented." He reached for her again.

Pain-filled green eyes looked up at him. "No one sees that but you."

"Because everything you touch is gold. And, yes, you're an amazing website designer." His words poured out. "But that's because of the creative way you view the world. You see the world through the lens of an artist."

She sank back into the chair. "Like I said, no one sees that but you."

"But they will."

"Not if I move to New York and design websites."

"Then don't." His hands formed into fists.

"But…"

"Tell Barb you'll take the job but only if you can stay here." With him. "You can head up there when necessary."

"But…"

He wasn't going to let her line up her arguments.

"Stay here. With me." He knelt at her feet. "I've fallen in love with your family, with Savannah." He clutched her knees. "I think I'm falling in love with you."

Her mouth dropped open. "You…you're what?" she squeaked.

He huffed out a breath. "I…I think I'm falling in love with you. Stay here with me and your incredible family."

Her eyes were big green marbles. She gripped the chair arms as if her body would blow away in the storm. "I…I…"

His heart pounded in his chest. "I know you feel something."

"But…" She pushed deep into her chair. Trying to get away from him?

He rocked back to his feet. "I thought you might feel the same. Was I fooling myself?" His voice growled a little.

"Liam. I…" She wouldn't look him in the eye.

She was pushing him away. He shook his head.

He'd misread her. Made tactical errors. Let his need for what she had, what he could be a part of rush him into a confession he wasn't even sure was true. Did he love Dolley?

"I don't know what I feel." She wrapped her arms around her stomach and curled into a ball. "I don't know what I want. I don't know what's good for me."

"We can work together."

"I'd always be in your shadow."

"But how can you leave your family, your friends?" What else could he use to convince her that she shouldn't move to New York? "Don't throw us away. I can't lose another family."

"Family?" Her eyes flared open. "This is about my family, not me."

"What?" Panic churned in his chest.

"I'm just a…a way for you to become part of the Fitzgeralds." Her breath shook. "You don't want *me*. You want…*them*."

"Dolley." He pounded on his forehead with his

fist. "We're good together. I can teach you more. We'll figure it out. But not if you move."

"I'd be your apprentice. Always overlooked. You'd use me to get what you've always wanted... a family." Injured green eyes looked up into his. "That's not what I want. I...I deserve more. When would I get to travel? When would I get my dreams? I want my own career. Not just to be an extension of yours."

"I thought we were a team. I care about you!"

"Not enough," she whispered.

Pain ripped through him. He wasn't enough for her. She wanted travel and recognition. She wanted to rip up the roots anchoring her to Savannah and leave.

If she left, where did that leave him?

She didn't care about him. She cared about what he could do for her career. He didn't matter.

"You only wanted me for what I could do for you." Shaking his head, he moved to the door, his feet and heart heavy. "I'm never enough."

WHAT JUST HAPPENED? Dolley laid her cheek on her knees. Was Liam right?

She'd been confused about Barb's job offer, and Liam had shown his true colors. Just like every other man she'd dated, he was using her to get something he wanted. A sharp pain wracked her body. This time it had been her family.

No one wanted *her*. And his offer to stay and live

in his shadow? How could she become a recognized artist like that?

Her throat ached like she'd swallowed a wad of paper and it was sucking up all her spit. Grabbing her glass, she took a sip. The whiskey burned a path to her stomach.

She pressed her palms into her eyes. No one would use her again. She and Liam were through.

How could he even say *I've fallen in love with Savannah, with your family?*

If he did love her, it was a distant third behind her family and Savannah. Her body ached like she'd been pummeled in a boxing ring.

But she was in love with him. Her chest shook. How stupid was that?

The front door opened, footsteps echoing in the hall.

She rubbed her wet cheeks against her sleeve and grabbed her coat, not wanting a guest to find her. Escaping through the courtyard door, she wound her way through the patio furniture and headed to her apartment.

Habit had her glancing up to Liam's room. A shadow against the second-floor French door made her freeze.

He stared down at her. Even from here, she could see his clenched jaw and hooded eyes. The connection that sizzled when she looked at him—was gone. Pain hollowed out her heart.

She didn't know how long she waited for a sign from him. Ten seconds? Ten minutes?

He jerked away from the window and turned his back.

It was a sucker punch, knocking the breath out of her. Rejected again.

She stumbled to the apartment, tears filling her eyes. She would not cry.

Fumbling with the lock, she pushed inside and collapsed on the sofa.

She hadn't done anything wrong. Now she was the bad guy? How had that happened?

She had a right to be confused about accepting Barb's job offer. She had a right to question whether Liam was using her to acquire a family.

She had a right to have someone love her like her sisters and her mother were loved.

Abby, Bess and Mamma weren't loved because they were Fitzgeralds and lived in Savannah. There were no conditions on Gray's, Daniel's and Martin's love.

The only man who'd cared enough to date her, wanted her *for her family*.

She deserved more.

CHAPTER SIXTEEN

A picture is a poem without words.

Horace

LIAM COULDN'T RIP his gaze away from Dolley.

For the last week, Dolley had done what they'd paid her to do—document the making of *Savannah's Irish Roots.* Their personal conversations were limited to directions and questions.

He tried to swallow the lump in his throat. They were through.

She'd accused him of using her to get to her family. Didn't she understand everything was connected? Dolley, the Fitzgeralds, Savannah. He couldn't think of one without the other.

She'd pushed him away as easily as she was going to dump her family and town.

Maybe she wasn't who he'd thought she was. Maybe family wasn't as important to her as it was to him. Maybe she'd only wanted him to get her a leg up in the business, hoping he'd rocket her to fame.

He inhaled, breathing in freshly mown grass. Bollocks. He was being unfair. He was the one who'd mucked things up—not Dolley. He'd panicked.

He moved closer to the Fitzgerald family plot in Bonaventure Cemetery. The sisters hadn't known it existed until he'd searched the records.

Tom said something to Dolley, and she laughed, but it was only a half-hearted chuckle.

Liam's gaze snapped to her.

Her eyes were shadowed, deeper set in her face than they'd ever been. Her smile—nonexistent. If he suggested she count her smiles, she'd probably castrate him. This cold-shoulder routine twisted his belly in knots. Even the crew shot them questioning looks.

"Ready?" he asked Jerry. One more scene and they'd be done for the day.

"Another minute," Jerry said, changing out a battery.

Dolley pulled a lone weed from between the markers. She didn't look up as she said, "Thank you for finding them."

"Eventually, you would have looked."

"Sometimes I think you care more about our ancestors than we do." She crouched and turned her camera to the small statue. It marked the grave of one of James and Fiona's grandchildren. "I don't know if we would have made the effort."

Was her comment another jab at him? He couldn't tell anymore.

"The documentary made me feel close to them." James and Fiona had become his family. He held up a hand. "You've made an effort. Last time I was here, the place wasn't maintained."

Now the weeds were gone. The sign saying Do

Not Maintain had been removed, and flowering bushes lined the plot.

"After you told us about their graves, Bess hauled us out here." Dolley sighed. "We had lunch while we worked. Just like great-grandmamma, I guess."

"It looks nice." He wanted to touch her. He missed the feel of her skin under his fingers. Missed kissing her and talking about their days. And he missed sinking into her body and having her melt around him.

"Why are you shooting out here?" she asked, still focused on her camera.

They hadn't talked about schedules or story lines for a week. And they hadn't talked or worked on her craft, either. This was the longest conversation they'd had in seven days.

"I plan to go back to Ireland and film in front of Michael's grave. Show the differences and the similarities between the two brothers."

She stood and looked at him with sorrow-filled eyes. "Was this documentary always going to be about my family?"

"No. It was going to be about Savannah's Irish roots. Then I thought it was about haves and have-nots. But you made me push deeper. It changed. Now it's about what your family did for the immigrants." He stepped closer, so the crew wouldn't hear. "I've changed, too."

She took a step back.

"May I?" He held out his hand. He'd promised

to help her with her art and hadn't fulfilled his part of the bargain.

She handed him the camera.

The emotions in the stills slapped him. Loneliness. Solitude. Sorrow. She'd shot the pictures in unforgiving black and white film. The sunlight shining on the plot wasn't warm, but harsh and ugly. Raw grief stared up at him.

The pictures were—incredible. But not his Dolley. Not the joy he'd come to rely on.

His fault.

She chewed her lip, waiting.

"What were you looking to expose?" His words croaked out.

"I…" She stared into his eyes.

"Pain. Grief."

She nodded.

"They're amazing."

"Really?" Confusion slipped over her face like a mask.

"I hate them." He touched her cheek, couldn't stop himself.

She closed her eyes and relaxed into the cup of his hand for a few heavenly seconds, then jerked away. "You hate them?"

"Because they aren't you. You always find the good in life." He shook the camera. "This view is *my* outlook on the world—not yours."

She stared at the headstones. "It's sad that we didn't take care of their resting place."

"I hate that I've done this to you," he whispered.

She stared up at him. "I'll get over it. Over you. I always do."

"Can we talk? Tonight?"

She shook her head. "No."

"We're ready," Jerry called.

Liam took a breath, trying to shake off his sorrow. He had a job to do.

Before coming to Savannah, filmmaking had been his life. Before he'd met the Fitzgeralds. Before he'd been with Dolley.

Now he wanted more.

He didn't know how to win her back. After analyzing what had gone wrong, he knew what his problem was. He'd thought his sense of belonging came from Dolley's family and Savannah. But it didn't. It was Dolley. She was the one who forced him to smile. She was the one to brighten his day.

He was in love with her. *Her*.

And he'd made the woman he loved miserable. If he couldn't have a life with Dolley, maybe he could help make her dream of travel and photography come true.

WATCHING LIAM WORK each day was like pouring salt on the hole in her heart. Dolley moved behind Jerry, making sure she didn't step into the frame.

She zoomed in on Liam's face. The makeup Sonjia had applied didn't disguise the shadows under his eyes. Those eyes blazed as he talked about James and Fiona. Even though she stood to the side of the camera, it was like he spoke only to her.

They repeated the take two more times, but finally wrapped for the day.

Dolley packed up her camera and filters.

Liam stopped next to her. "We haven't worked together for a while. I'd like to go back to Corrine's statue and see these bushes you said would flower. See what you can do now."

His offer broke the wound in her heart open again. She hated the idea of spending even more time with him. And working together on her photography was too intimate.

But she'd be a fool not to get a few last hints on how to improve her art. "I could use the walk."

"You drove?" he asked.

"Yes."

"Can I catch a ride back to Carleton House? Then the crew won't have to wait."

"Sure." She closed her eyes. They could work together, but she didn't have to talk to him.

"Thank you." Liam talked to Jerry and came back with his camera bag.

"Do you ever go anywhere without your cameras?" she asked, forgetting that she'd planned to keep their conversation to a minimum.

"Not often. And if I do, I regret it." He pulled out a Nikon she hadn't seen before. "Like when I came down to Christmas breakfast without one and had to run back upstairs."

Christmas. That was aeons ago. She'd been like a puppy, trying to make Liam happy.

She stopped at a statue of an angel all crusted in black. Flowers bloomed at the base of the monument, bright spots of pink.

Liam knelt next to the ornate black iron fence. He took a breath before clicking the shutter. What was he after?

Without words, they exchanged cameras.

He studied her work. "Go in tighter. Make sure the cracks in her face show."

She scrolled through the shots he'd taken. "Were you capturing repeating patterns?"

"I've been taking them for a couple of weeks. I thought it could be a series."

Once he gave back her camera, she tightened the focus so each pit and crevasse in the stone told a story. The shutter clicked as she captured several images.

Even as she reviewed the shots, she knew they were better than the ones she'd taken earlier. When would she do the right thing by instinct instead of needing to be told?

Maybe she would never be more than a hobbyist. She handed her camera to him. "You were right."

"These are good." He tapped the final picture. "Don't be afraid to show the imperfections. Life is filled with flaws. They make the world and people more interesting."

Was he trying to tell her something she didn't

know? Liam's flaw of using her to acquire a family could not be ignored.

She had to move on from their relationship. If she could never have what her sisters had found with Gray and Daniel, then she would have a career that made her happy.

And to do that, she needed to learn everything she could from Liam. She had two weeks.

They took pictures of Corrine and the river until it was closing time. The azaleas were a cloud of pink behind the statue.

Even she could tell her emotions had changed since he'd looked at her pictures of the angel earlier today. So had his.

"This is peaceful," she said.

"Something you never thought you'd see in one of my pictures?" A somber smile flashed across his face.

He'd stopped smiling again, and she didn't have the energy to remind him.

"No. You're always so…intense. I mean your pictures. They're intense," she stuttered.

He handed her camera back. "And these pictures are, if not hopeful, at least content."

So a photo didn't have to reflect the chaos inside her. If she could figure out how to wall up her own disappointment, maybe she could succeed.

No, she *would* succeed.

"Hi, Liam." A worker drove toward them. "Time to get moving. I need to close up."

"Will do, Paul."

They packed up their cameras. "How does he know your name?" she asked.

"Paul's kicked me out of the cemetery a few times."

They were together every day. When had he had the time?

"This is one of my favorite spots in Savannah. I can't stay away." Liam matched his stride with hers. "Thank you for sharing it with me the first day we came out here. The last set of pictures you took are good. I'd like to add a section to the website on the cemetery. If we give the photos proper attribution, could we buy some of your pictures?"

"You don't have to pay me." She waved her hand. "Not when we're taking pictures together."

"You're a professional. You should be paid for your work." He stopped. "Don't forget that."

A professional. She never thought of herself that way. It took Liam to make that clear.

"I won't." Dolley bit her lip, forcing back the tears. She would never forget him.

"THANKS FOR CALLING BACK, EVAN." Liam pushed out of his chair and headed to the balcony off his room.

"Are you giving up fame and glory to work for me again?" Evan asked.

"You were too demanding a boss." But years ago, Evan had given him a shot. "I do have a promising apprentice you might like to hire on her way out of the starting gate."

"I thought you'd sworn off apprentices." Evan's laugh was deep and filled with gravel.

"I had, but she's good." Dolley would be the last person he mentored.

"You've got me intrigued. Loner Liam working with someone. Shoot me some of her work."

"I can do better than that. Check out this blog. Most of the pictures were taken *before* we worked together. Dolley Fitzgerald. She has a lovely writing voice."

"You know I like photojournalists."

"They keep your costs down." Liam gave him the website address. And waited.

He could hear Evan on his keyboard.

"Where are you right now?" Evan asked.

"I'm in Savannah at the B and B. What page of the website are you on?"

"Some of the construction shots. Ooh. That's nice."

"Dolley maintains the blog and takes the pictures. She's talented."

"I'll take a look at the blog and call you if there's anything we can test her on."

"Thanks." He paused, then added, "I'm also calling Amelia."

"My competition?" Evan huffed. "Give me a couple of days before you do."

Liam nodded. "I will."

After ending the call, he gazed across the dimly lit courtyard to Dolley's dark apartment. He wanted to tell her what he'd done but couldn't. Even though they'd worked together this afternoon, she wouldn't want him knocking on her door.

He'd screwed up. But maybe, just maybe, his conversation with Evan would make her dream come true.

"DOLLEY!" ANNE WAVED from a table in the back of the pub. Green shamrocks hung around the bar, and the bartenders all wore green derby hats.

For the first time ever, she wasn't in the celebrating spirit.

Dolley wove her way through the crowd. She'd forgotten how noisy O'Gara's could be. The St. Patrick's Day visitor invasion had begun. Both Fitzgerald and Carleton House were full. This was her last free night for the next week.

"It's been ages since I've seen you." Anne wrapped her in a bear hug. "I thought you were ignoring me."

"The film world works long hours." Dolley took off her coat and settled at the tiny table. It was time to get back to real life. Reconnect with her friends and figure out what she wanted to do about the job offer.

"I'm glad you called." Anne leaned over, raising her voice. "What are you drinking?"

Dolley looked at Anne's bright green drink. "How is that one?"

"Good." Anne flagged down a server. Held up her drink and two fingers. "You need to catch up."

Dolley dredged up a smile. Anne filled her in on company gossip, but nothing soothed the malaise that had suffocated her since she and Liam had ended things.

Getting dumped had never set her back this long. She'd always granted herself twenty-four hours to wallow, and then she'd jumped back in to the swing of life.

"How's Connor?" she asked Anne.

"Incredible." A dreamy smile stretched across her friend's face. "I went to North Carolina last weekend."

"You've been dating since October?" Five months. "You've never dated anyone that long."

"I know." Anne tilted her head. "I think... I think we lasted this long because it started out long-distance. We learned so much more about each other before we slept together. All the phone calls, emails and notes. He's so thoughtful."

Everyone around her was falling in love. Jealousy licked at her like a long-tongued snake, but she pushed it away. "Are you happy?"

Anne nodded. "We've discussed my moving to the Triangle and living with him."

Dolley caught Anne's hand. "That is serious."

"Very. I've talked to Jackson about working remotely." Anne wrinkled her nose. "He wants to make me a contract employee."

"Of course." Dolley rolled her eyes. "Are you going to do it?"

"Maybe." Anne wore a goofy grin. "Any new developments with your gorgeous Irishman?"

Dolley hadn't told Anne about Liam. That was a first. They'd always shared their dating stories. Now there was nothing to tell. "It's been interesting working on this film. I've learned so much from him." Learned not to trust a man willing to sleep with her.

Zoom in on the flaws. Maybe there was a life lesson there. Liam had flaws galore. He was too serious. He loved her family and Savannah more than her.

"When we were at Kevin Barry's, he watched you." Anne tapped her nose.

"He did?" She tried to act shocked.

"I thought he would have made his move by now."

"No." Move made and done. She swallowed. "We just work together."

"Well, that's a goldarn pity." Anne's fingers bounced along with the music.

Dolley finished her first drink. She couldn't talk about Liam anymore. "I have a job offer."

She talked Anne through Barb's offer. Her voice grew hoarse from shouting. When had the pub setting become so uncomfortable?

"A year ago, your bags would have been packed,

and you'd be waving as you drove away," Anne said. "What happened?"

Liam.

"It's not what I want." Dolley sighed. "It's still website design, not photography."

"What about the B and B?" Anne asked.

"My sisters will be fine if I leave." Maybe. She rested her head in her hand. "I always wanted to leave, but now that I have the chance, I don't know what to do. My family built the B and B from the ground up. Together. Can I really just leave?"

"Your mother isn't involved anymore."

"She and Aunt CeCe bought half of the furniture for Carleton House."

Maybe she would never escape Fitzgerald House. Maybe she didn't want to. Maybe she wasn't strong enough to start a new career.

Someone tapped her shoulder. "Dolley, want to dance?"

"Jerry?" If he was here, was Liam? She scanned the room but didn't spot him in the sea of bodies. "Anne, this is Jerry. He's working on the documentary."

They talked for a few minutes, then Jerry asked her to dance again.

"Sure."

He pulled her out of the chair and guided her to the packed dance floor. They moved to the music. All she heard was the booming bass, loud enough to mask the lyrics.

This was what she wanted. She could lose herself in the crowds and noise and have a drink with a friend.

"Is everyone here?" she yelled to Jerry.

"Just Sonjia, Tom and me," he shouted back. He pointed to a table near the floor.

She waved at Tom and Sonjia. Then spun in a circle, bumping into the dancers next to her. Hopefully, Jerry hadn't seen her disappointment.

Had Liam fallen back into his old habit of working every waking hour? Hadn't she cured him of that problem?

The song ended. She started to move off the floor, but Jerry caught her hand. "One more?"

She shook her head. "I need to head home."

"Okay. See you tomorrow."

At the table, she gathered her coat and purse. "I've got to go."

"What?" Shock filled Anne's face. "It's barely eleven."

"I've got twelve- to fifteen-hour days facing me next week." Maybe by working until she was exhausted, she'd fall asleep without thinking about Liam. Maybe she'd forget how she'd loved being with him, how holding his hand made her smile. How she'd screwed up and fallen *in love* with him.

"I miss you, girl." Anne gave her a hug. "Let me know if you need a break during hell week."

Dolley wove her way through the crowd. She rolled her shoulders. She'd wanted to get back to her real life. Working and then hitting the clubs. Having fun.

But nothing fit anymore. She didn't belong here. Maybe she didn't belong anywhere.

"I NEED DOLLEY FITZGERALD'S contact info," Evan said to Liam after he answered his mobile.

Liam glanced across the library. A week before the holiday and the B and B was full. Dolley helped Cheryl with the wine tasting. A man chatted with her as she poured red wine into his glass. She laughed, but he wasn't fooled. Her smile never lit her eyes.

She wore a deep green frock with tights. The green made her eyes look huge. And her golden-red curls danced around her face. He wanted to crush her curls with his hands. Crush *her* in his arms.

"You were impressed?" Liam asked Evan, heading out the library door.

"Very."

"Let me get some place where it's not so loud." Liam entered a small empty parlor, and the noise faded.

Besides having Evan review her blog, Liam had sent the editor some of the photos they'd taken together. "What did you think?"

"Are you sure she's just starting out? Some of those shots in the cemetery are breathtaking. And I love the statue of the girl waving in the fog."

Liam's grin ached, like he hadn't smiled much

lately. Without Dolley acting as his Fun Mentor, he forgot. "Hire her. You won't regret it."

"I thought I could give her a test assignment," Evan said. "She has such great pictures of that cemetery, an article on Bonaventure would be a good trial."

"I'll text you her contact info." Liam sank onto the small sofa. "Do me a favor. Don't mention my name." Dolley might resent his help.

"Why the hell not?" Evan asked.

"Tell her you found her blog."

"I'd think you'd want credit, but all right."

Liam slipped his phone into his pocket. He could head back to Carleton House and work on rough edits.

Since he barely slept anymore, it was better to work than stare at the wall. Or worse, sit and drink Jameson and watch Dolley's apartment. That was just...creepy.

He'd make one more plate of food and go back to work.

When he walked into the library, one of the two sisters from Mississippi waved. "Liam, come back and join us."

Was that Judith or Darlene?

"We saved your seat," said the other sister.

"Had to fight off the masses to keep it for you," the darker blonde said.

He was almost positive she was Judith.

Dolley glanced over, her stare icy. He didn't fool

himself that she might be jealous. Probably just wanted him gone.

"I need to get back to work." He moved to the buffet. Tonight's offerings were all Spanish, including Spanish wines paired with tapas.

"But it's almost St. Patrick's Day." Judith came up beside him and added a stuffed date to her plate. "Party time."

Was that a snort from Dolley? He glanced behind him.

Dolley pulled an empty wine bottle off the table. She jerked. Slipping her phone out, she looked at the number and frowned.

He ducked his head, not wanting to appear too interested.

"Do you have dinner plans?" Darlene asked. When had she snuck up behind him?

"I can't." He topped off his wineglass. "It was nice to meet you."

"You too, Liam." Darlene sighed.

"Let us know if you want to go to a pub or dinner," the younger sister added.

"Thanks." That wouldn't happen.

He headed out of the library with his plate.

Dolley sat in the parlor talking on the phone. For the first time in a week, her sparkle was back. Her curls danced as she gave a little bounce on the sofa.

He stopped, memorizing the sight. Maybe he'd done something right.

She might put the pieces together and realize

he'd done this for her. Not that he was looking for thanks. But he wanted her to understand he knew her dream.

He just wished he could be part of her life.

"I'M INTERESTED. VERY INTERESTED." Dolley could barely catch her breath. "How did you get my name?"

"One of the staff was checking out Savannah sights and found your blog. They brought it to my attention. Your pictures are excellent, and your writing style is engaging."

"Mr. Bennett, I love your magazine." She'd admired their articles and photographs both online and in print.

"Please, call me Evan."

"Evan. Of course."

"Would you be interested in doing an article on Bonaventure Cemetery for the magazine? It would be a trial." He gave her the word count.

"For *The Relaxed Traveler*? Absolutely." She couldn't keep from bouncing on the sofa. This was…unreal. To think her blog had gotten the attention of an editor.

"We'd need the article and photos by the twentieth of March." He named a price.

"That's no problem." The money wasn't fantastic, but she was just starting out. And she had so many cemetery and statue pictures already. Her biggest problem would be deciding on the focus of the article.

"I'll send a contract and sample articles."

"Thank you for this opportunity." She gave him her email address.

After Evan hung up, she closed her eyes. She had a photojournalism gig. Was she dreaming?

Wrapping her arms around her stomach, she pinched herself. *I have to tell Liam.* Rushing out the door, she pulled up short. Her shoulders sagged. She and Liam weren't talking. The excitement leeched out of her like a deflating balloon.

At least she could tell Abby.

She dug deep for her joy. This was what she wanted. She was going to live the dream. Become a professional photographer.

But because she couldn't share the news with Liam, the bounce had left her step.

CHAPTER SEVENTEEN

A camera is a tool for learning how to see without a camera.

Dorothea Lange

LIAM SHOWED HIS arm band and press pass to security at the barriers to River Street.

"Come on." The woman waved the crew through the line. "Good luck."

People pushed past him. The crowd was an undulating ocean of green, ebbing and flowing through the street. The yeasty scent of beer saturated the air. Drunk raucous voices rolled like faraway thunder. Were all the quarter of a million people trying to walk through River Street?

"We'll never hear you if we try and tape," Jerry yelled in his ear.

"Get crowd shots. I'll—" Liam threw up a hand "—do voice-overs."

Jerry nodded and set the camera on his shoulder, panning the crowd.

Tom was at Forsythe Park, shooting the greening of the fountain. Sonjia had another camera set up on a Carleton House balcony filming the parade. Dolley shot stills.

Everyone worked but him.

Dolley wiggled through the crowd, her camera aimed at Jerry. Then she swept over and took a series of Liam. She even pointed the camera at the pavement littered with beer cups and confetti.

She hadn't said a word about Evan's offer. If that didn't tell him how far into the loo their relationship had fallen, he didn't know what else would.

But Evan had raved about the work she'd turned in—four days early.

He couldn't stand here feeling sorry for himself. He tugged out a camera, setting up his own shots.

A drunk grabbed Dolley's shoulders and kissed her on the cheeks. Liam's camera caught the surprise on her face.

"Luck of the Irish," the drunk called, weaving through the crowd.

She shook her head.

The street was dangerous. He pushed his way to her side. "Maybe you should head back to the B and B," he shouted.

"I'm okay." Someone bumped into her, and she stumbled.

He wrapped his arms around her, and she curled into his chest. He took a deep breath, memorizing her warm scent.

This was right. Not being in Savannah. Not being with the Fitzgeralds. Holding Dolley was his sanctuary.

"Stop." With a small whimper, she pushed out of his embrace. "I want to get above the street. I'm going to the hotel."

"Not worth fighting your way through the crowd." And he didn't want to lose sight of her.

"Oh, come on, Delaney, where's you sense of adventure?" Her smile almost reached her eyes. "It's St. Patrick's Day. Live a little."

Live a little? His chest ached. He couldn't imagine life without her. "I'll come with you."

She took in a sharp breath.

He made hand signals to Jerry. Then he mouthed, "Meet you back at the B and B."

Nodding, Jerry was swept away by a group of half-snookered visitors. How could anyone think this was fun?

Somehow he and Dolley fought their way to the hotel. She talked her way up to the rooftop restaurant. River Street stretched below them, a teeming green snake. They both took pictures, but his heart wasn't in it. His pictures would be mediocre at best.

"I usually stay away from River Street on the holiday," she murmured as they headed to the elevator.

"I figured you'd love the noise and celebrating."

"Oh. I do like that." But her face scrunched into a frown. "Or I did." She shook her head. "When I was in college, we would come down here, but now—" she waved her hand "—it's too much for even me, the party girl."

They crowded into the small elevator with other guests. He faced her, waiting to hear more. "Party girl? Is that how you see yourself?"

"Sometimes." Her shoulders rose and fell. "I think that's how my friends see me."

He leaned down and whispered, "Why do you beat yourself up?"

"What are you talking about?" She really looked puzzled.

The elevator disgorged, and they were swept out with the crowd.

He pulled her away from the mass of people. "You think of yourself as the non-talented Fitzgerald sister and a party girl. Why can't you see that you're incredible? Why can't you see what I see?"

Her mouth dropped open. Her eyes were big green saucers. "What do you see?"

Someone bounced into Dolley's back, shoving her into him. He wrapped his arms around her, protecting her.

Tipping her head, he said, "I see the most amazing woman I've ever met. I wish you understood that."

Her hands rested on his waist. Her face had a deer-in-headlights look. She opened her mouth to say something, then snapped it shut.

"You shine like…like the brightest star in the heavens. Like Polaris."

"No. It's Sirius."

"See. You're amazing." He tightened his arms around her. It might be the last time he held her. "You don't need accolades and awards and recognition. You just need to *be* to shine."

"Liam." She buried her head in his shoulder.

"I..." He took a deep breath. "I love you."

Her head shook against his chest. "Don't. I know this is about my family."

"This isn't about your family. This is about you. Me loving you," he whispered. "It's not your family. I love you."

She pushed away. Tears shimmered in her eyes. "It's too late."

"I'm so sorry I hurt you." The hollow ache in his chest might never fade. He had to make her understand. They didn't have many days left. When he left, he wanted to believe the hurt that filled her eyes would disappear with him. "I'm so sorry."

"I know." She turned away but glanced back, her eyes brimming with tears. "It doesn't change anything."

DOLLEY'S HANDS SHOOK, making the Guinness bottles she was nesting into the ice chest clank together. Liam said he loved her.

It's not your family, I love you.

How could someone who hurt her so badly make her feel so comforted? When it came to men, she was a fool. She should have pushed away from him as soon as he'd hugged her.

Placing the last bottle in the chest, she grabbed the empty box and headed to the kitchen, her feet so heavy she had to force them to move.

Abby looked up as she pushed through the swinging door. "Hey."

"Hey." She broke down the box and put it with the recycling.

Bess came in the courtyard kitchen door. "Smells great in here."

Dolley sniffed. The earthy, warm scent of Abby's Irish stew and the buttery smell of biscuits filled the room. She hadn't noticed.

"Why are you chewing your poor lip?" Abby asked her. "It's swollen. Stop."

Liam was the cause. She couldn't confess that to her sisters. "I'm waiting for the editor to get back to me on the article I submitted. I'm afraid he'll think it's garbage."

She wished she'd told Liam about her article. She'd wanted him to review everything, but he wasn't going to be around every day to check her work. She had to have confidence in her own abilities.

Maybe the editor hated it. Maybe it had been so amateur, he wouldn't respond.

"The editor will love it," Abby insisted. "I never realized how much you doubt yourself. Why do you do that? You're amazing."

"He's lucky to have you putting together an article." Bess poured a mug of tea and warmed her hands.

Dolley blinked. "Have you both been talking to Liam?" He was her biggest advocate.

Abby frowned. "I haven't seen him in a couple of days."

"Neither have I." Bess scooted over to her. "Anything interesting happening between you and your dreamy Irishman?"

"Stop." It was strange that both Liam and her sisters would be so complimentary—all on the same day. She wasn't amazing. "I'm just…ordinary."

Liam made her feel like she was extraordinary. Her sigh blew a curl out of her eyes.

Abby planted her hands on her hips. "You are no such thing."

"You're my sister." Dolley headed to the coffee station and poured a cup of decaf. "You have to say things like that."

"I wouldn't say them if they weren't true." Abby put her arm around Dolley's shoulders. "What's up? You've been quiet for the last two weeks."

Dolley sighed again. "Why are men…so… obtuse?"

"Obtuse?" Bess asked. "They're dumber than a pile of dirt. Well, not Daniel. He's a lot smarter now we're engaged."

Abby squeezed Dolley's shoulders and headed to the stove. "What did Liam do?"

Dolley shook her head, walking over to stare out the courtyard windows.

"You're working all the time. Is he taking advantage of you?" Bess slipped into one of the armchairs in the sitting area.

She shook her head. "Liam said he was in love with me."

Both Abby and Bess converged on her.

"What?" Bess pulled her away from the window.

"In love?" Abby took her hands.

"The first time he told me, I was third behind our family and Savannah. And at that point he *thought* he was falling for me." Dolley sank on to the ottoman. "I was a distant third to the first two mentions."

"Dolley, not everyone is as literal as you are." Abby rubbed a hand on her back. "You've watched him fade into the background and observe. Why would you think expressing how he feels would be any different?"

"Because…because it should be!"

"And how did you react to his confession?" Bess sat in the chair and touched Dolley's knee.

"I broke up with him. The only reason he cares is because he wants a family—he wants to be part of the *Fitzgeralds*. He's thirty years old and still describes himself as an orphan."

"That's so sad," Bess said. "He needs a family."

"That's not the point." Dolley pushed off the ottoman and paced between the back door and the sitting area. "I don't want to be someone's afterthought. I'm not the means for Liam to acquire a family."

"You said that was the first time?" Abby asked.

Dolley rubbed her forehead. "He told me again today."

"How do you feel about him?" Bess asked.

"Confused. Like none of this was real." She sighed. "He only wanted a family."

"Then he doesn't deserve you." Abby hugged her.

Dolley took a deep breath. "Is it too much to hope someone will love me like Gray and Daniel love you two?"

"No." Abby squeezed her shoulders. "There's someone special out there for you."

Dolley had said the same thing to Bess when Daniel had broken her sister's heart. But she knew there was no happy ending waiting for her.

"No one treats our sister this way." Bess made it a group hug. "Do you want us to kick him out of the B and B?"

"I'll do it. And give him a piece of my mind." Abby's arms tightened around them.

"No." Dolley sniffed. "That would be bad for business. But I love you guys for thinking it."

"And we love you." Both Abby and Bess hugged her again.

"Family is more important than money," Bess said.

Family. She had the best.

Family is more important than money. Was it more important than fame and recognition? If she took the job in New York, who would be there for her?

LIAM HAD ONE more day of taping. Even though he'd booked the B and B for another week, he didn't need the time. And he couldn't spend seven more days around Dolley. He'd head to Ireland and take the final shots in Kilkee cemetery, rather than torture himself by watching Dolley's life from the sidelines.

This place was the closest he'd come to a home since his parents died. He'd let himself believe all the dreams and fantasies that went with being with Dolley. That they could overcome anything if only they were together.

"After we tape these scenes at Fitzgerald House, we're done?" Sonjia took a seat at the Carleton House dining room table.

"Yes," he said. "Unless you've come up with anything more?"

Sonjia checked her list. "We've got everything needed to take to editing."

"I want to wrap." Liam tapped the table. "I'm leaving tomorrow."

Jerry's head popped up from reviewing tape. "I thought we had another week?"

"Unless you find a reason you need me, I'm gone." He couldn't do this anymore. Couldn't be around Dolley and feel the knives cutting him to pieces. "You haven't found anything that needs re-taping, have you?"

Jerry shook his head. "None of the interviews. I want more River Street footage, but just for background."

"Good. Then there's nothing holding me here."

Nothing but a fiery redhead who'd made her way

into his heart and had him longing for things he didn't deserve.

The door swung open.

Dolley. She wore a jumper the color of her wounded eyes and jeans that hugged her in all the places he'd touched not so long ago. She made her way into the room and leaned against the table.

He wanted to erase the pain in her eyes. Wanted her to smile.

"The schedule says you're filming outside of Fitzgerald House today." She looked at Sonjia, not him.

The knife poked another hole in his heart.

"Yes," Sonjia replied.

"It would be quieter to film in the courtyard. We could keep the guests out for a while."

Liam headed to the coffee carafe on the opposite side of the room. He poured a mug, so his hands had something to do besides reach for her.

Nodding, he said, "I like that idea. But I'll still film on the entry porch."

She glanced at him. The sorrow in her eyes had him freezing.

Both Jerry's and Sonjia's gazes bounced between him and Dolley.

"I'll confirm with Abby and Marion so they can warn our guests." She started to text but looked up again. "Courtyard first?"

"We'll start at eleven." By that time, most of the guests would be off touring.

He sipped his coffee, watching Dolley. He wished for his camera to take some last pictures of her, but the camera never captured her sparkle. And she wouldn't sparkle now. He'd dimmed her light. He sighed.

She looked over at him.

Her phone pinged, and she read the message. "Marion will put up a sign so you're not interrupted."

"Thanks," he said.

"I'll meet you in the courtyard." She tapped her lip. Lips he wanted to kiss just one more time. "No, I'll start from the upstairs parlor and shoot down at you while you're setting up."

His feet were moving toward her, before his mind could stop them. "That's a great idea. My balcony has better sight lines. Why don't you start there?"

He knew because he sat out there night after night staring at Dolley's apartment.

He handed her his key card. Their fingers brushed, energy arcing between them with a sizzle.

Her gaze leaped to his. Neither of them moved.

"Dolley," he whispered. He wasn't sure what he could say. He hated the idea that this might be the last time they touched.

Her cell phone buzzed. She jerked and looked at the readout. "I need to take this."

She couldn't run out of the room fast enough.

There was his answer.

He would make it easy. He would leave tomorrow.

DOLLEY EXHALED, forcing out a shaky breath. Staring into the pain in Liam's eyes had ripped her heart out. She swiped her phone to answer. "Dolley Fitzgerald."

"Evan Bennett."

She hurried down the hall and sank into a parlor chair. "How are you?"

"Pleased, very, very pleased. Fantastic work."

"Thank you." Her heart should be doing back handsprings. She couldn't dredge up the energy.

"My assistant will send you information so we can get you paid."

"Thank you." She couldn't think of anything else to say.

"I'd like to give you another assignment, a little farther afield than your own backyard. I want to see what you can do with both research and photos."

"I'd like that."

"Good. Sorry to say, it's still probationary. I want to see more work before we send you out of the country."

Out of the country. Her body swayed even though she was sitting down.

"I'll give you a choice of assignments this time. What would you prefer? Charleston or St. Augustine?"

"I'd love to explore the oldest city in Florida. St. Augustine, please." This was really happening. "How long do I have to research and write the article?"

"This time I can give you three weeks. And my assistant will explain the reimbursement policy to you."

"I can't thank you enough for giving me this chance."

"You should be thanking Liam. He said you had talent. Even threatened to show your work to one of my competitors."

"Liam called you?" She choked out the words.

"Oh, shoot." There was a slap on wood on Evan's side of the conversation. "I wasn't supposed to tell you."

"No. That's...no." Liam? "Thank you."

"Don't be blabbing that I told you."

"Of course not." Liam had done this?

"He called, but your work won you the assignment. Don't forget that."

Somehow she closed out the conversation. Probably said *thank you* another half dozen times before hanging up.

She stared at her phone. Liam. He'd made the call to help her.

Why? What was in it for him?

Helping her with a job in the photography field wouldn't get him what he wanted—her family.

Her mouth dropped open.

What if he had been telling the truth and he did love her? What if it wasn't because he wanted to be part of the Fitzgerald family?

Her stomach twisted like she might be sick. She might have thrown away the only man she'd ever loved.

She had to talk to him. Thank him. And find out why he'd done this.

She ran to their meeting room. Empty. A glance at her phone showed it was a little after eleven.

He was setting up in the courtyard. She took the stairs two at a time, smiling at a new member of the cleaning crew as she flew down the hallway to Liam's room.

Sitting on the end table was one of the pictures he'd taken when they'd made love. Just a close up of her eyes. Her heart pounded a little harder.

She had a job to do. For Liam.

On the balcony she pulled out her camera.

He stood at the edge of one of the flagstone paths Bess had created. Even from here, she could tell that the rock carving of her and her sisters' faces would be in the camera's frame.

Dolley took a series of pictures as Liam and the crew set up.

With a zoom, she focused on Liam's face. Were new lines forming between his eyebrows? He looked as miserable as she felt. What had they done to each other?

She took his picture. *Don't be afraid to show the flaws.* He was flawed. So was she, but she loved him.

She rushed to the courtyard door. She may have made a mess of things, but she had to talk to him.

Bursting out the door, she hurried to where they'd set up. Sonjia turned around, a finger to her lips.

Dolley slowed down, even though she wanted to run.

They'd found that the click of her camera wouldn't be caught if she stood back far enough. She slipped to the side and followed Jerry as he moved with Liam along the paths.

Liam's blue shirt matched his eyes. She loved that shirt. The color mimicked Tybee Bay when the sky was clear and the ocean bright blue. His black hair gleamed in the sunlight.

"This is the house that James and Fiona built," Liam said.

He told the history of the house, what they'd learned in their research, what they'd pieced together in all their hours together in the attic. Even though she knew what he was saying, had written some of it up for the B and B's website, Liam made it sound fresh and interesting.

He stopped. "I want to run that again."

She started to move closer, but Liam had already begun to talk.

And it was like that for the next two hours. She tried to catch him. He would dash away or talk to one of the crew. Even when they ate lunch, as soon as she walked toward him, he pulled out his phone.

"I've got to take this," he said.

His phone hadn't rung.

She walked away, light-headed. He was avoiding her.

"Ready to move to the front porch?" Jerry asked Liam.

He slipped his phone back into his pocket. "Let's finish this."

Shivers ran down her spine at the finality in his voice.

She stumbled after the crew.

Sonjia bumped her shoulder. "Has documentary making been as exciting as you thought it would be?"

"Exciting?" Dolley thought back over the last three months. "Interesting, maybe. There's an awful lot of waiting around."

"And Liam works faster than most people." Sonjia smiled. "Will it be strange when he leaves tomorrow?"

Her heart stopped beating. "But his reservation is through next week."

"Like I said, he works fast."

He heart jolted. Liam was leaving?

THIS WAS MISERY. Liam avoided Dolley, but she kept trying to talk to him. Being around her was torture.

One more take. If he could do this in one take, he would be free.

Free to be miserable away from Dolley.

"You haven't given me this script to review." Sonjia came around the corner with Dolley.

"I know what I want," he said.

He'd planned to stand at the foot of the B and B's stairs, but he couldn't. Pain radiated from the cracks in his heart.

He lowered himself to the top step. He would do this sitting down.

"That looks good," Jerry called out.

Sonjia dusted him with a little powder. "You look perfect except for the circles under your eyes."

"Not much I can do about that now." He shot a glance at Dolley, but she was taking the lens cover off her camera.

"You sure you don't want me to review the script?"

"I'm good."

Tom shifted the mic into place. Sonjia stepped out of the frame. Jerry counted down.

"…Three, two and go," Jerry mouthed.

"Why did I start this project?" Liam looked into the lens of the camera. "It started with the death of my godfather, Seamus FitzGerald. He'd found the Savannah branch of the Fitzgerald family. I was instructed to bring letters from the 1830s between James and Michael FitzGerald to his Savannah relatives."

He smiled. "I wasn't thrilled doing my godfather's bidding. They weren't my relatives.

"But I looked up the family and discovered their

B and B. And found them—engaging. Intriguing. And the idea of doing a documentary on Savannah's Irish was born."

He walked down the sidewalk and pointed to the Irish flags hanging from the pillars. "The family still celebrates their Irish roots. And if you were lucky enough to be a guest in their B and B for the holiday, you were treated to magnificent Irish food, a glorious surrounding, hospitality and comfort."

He tucked a hand in his pocket, moving back up to the steps. "I thought this would be a story of the haves and have-nots. James and Fiona FitzGerald came here with money and built a successful shipping business. Most immigrants escaping the potato famine had to scrape together the coin for their trip to America. And with the mass exodus from Ireland, they were not welcomed with open arms.

"But that wasn't the case with James and Fiona." He waved his hand at the mansion. "They built this beautiful home, and when their countrymen and women filled the town, they hired them. Gave them meaningful jobs. Fiona's entire staff were immigrants. James hired his countrymen to work in his warehouses, man his ships and care for his properties."

He sat again. "Their descendants welcomed me, even invited me to share their Christmas holidays with them. Their kindness was unexpected and appreciated.

"The three sisters who run Fitzgerald House have

done so with generosity and grace. They've shown me what it is to be a family." His gaze homed in on Dolley. "And in the three months I've stayed here, they made me feel at home.

"That is how I came to be here at Fitzgerald House. And it was the best thing that has ever happened to me." He touched his heart. "I will never forget."

His sight wavered, tears filling his eyes. He signaled *cut*, unable to choke out any more words.

He was done.

DOLLEY ZOOMED IN on the tears on Liam's face. How could he say such nice things about her when she'd been so cruel? Dolley sank onto a bench on the front lawn, wiping away her own tears.

Fitzgerald House had always been a golden shackle around her ankles, keeping her here against her will. But seeing the B and B and her sisters through his eyes was a wake-up call.

It wasn't a weakness to have lived in the same town all her life. Traveling didn't mean she would be a better person. It was the way you treated others that brought happiness.

She brushed at another stream of tears.

"Are you all right?" Sonjia asked, touching her shoulder.

"Liam just…he made me see my family and the B and B in a different light."

"He can do that, can't he? Must be his photographer's insight, sees right through to the truth." Sonjia handed her a tissue. "Here."

"Thanks." Dolley wiped her face and stood. She had to talk to Liam. Had to…

He wasn't on the porch.

Jerry packed up the camera. Tom, the cords and microphone.

"Where's Liam?" she asked.

Jerry looked up. "He wanted a few more pictures before he left."

He was gone? "Where?"

Tom looked over. "Probably that cemetery. Bona—" He waved his hand.

"Bonaventure?"

"That's it." Tom nodded. "I sure don't understand his fascination with the place. It's creepy."

"Thanks." She dashed to her car, pulling out her keys. Tossing her camera and bag on the passenger seat, she raced to find him.

And ran into streets clogged with holiday visitors. "Let me through."

Every person acted like they had all the time in the world. She rapped her fingers against the steering wheel, inching her car into the crosswalk. Finally there was a break in the crowd. She hit the gas, her tires squealing.

At Bonaventure, his rental car was in the lot. "Thank goodness."

In the cemetery, visitors strolled through the

avenues. Guides led their tours through the plots. Where would Liam go?

Corrine's statue. She ran down the avenue. A stitch drilled into her side.

He wasn't in front of the Lawton family plot. She took in deep gasps of breath. Where now?

She fought her way through the crowds crammed in front of Johnny Mercer's plot. "Excuse me."

Not here. What if she missed him?

Gracie's plot.

Pushing through the tourists was like swimming downstream against migrating salmon. "I can't miss him," she muttered.

An elderly couple gave her a look like she might be talking to the spirits.

"I'm trying to find someone," she explained. "It's important. He's important."

The couple clasped each other's hands and gave her as wide a berth as possible.

Black hair bobbed in the distance. She skirted a tour group ambling down the path. "Liam!"

The man disappeared.

She dodged between people. Why did he have to come here when it was so crowded? "Liam!"

Someone shot her a dirty look for yelling. "Show some respect."

"I'm sorry," she gasped.

Respect. She slowed to a walk. The Fitzgerald plot. He might have gone to pay his respects to James and Fiona.

She cut down a small path, free from the crowds. The crunch of shell under her shoes filled the tree-lined space. She headed deeper into the cemetery.

One more corner and there he was. He knelt next to James's headstone, eyes closed, hand resting on the granite.

She left the shell path and walked on the fringe of grass. Now that she'd found him, what should she say?

At the black wrought iron fence she stopped, gasping for air.

His head snapped up. A smile started across his face, his eyes filling with joy. Then a mask of sorrow smothered his happiness.

"Liam," she whispered.

He stood. "Why are you here?" His voice was harsh.

"Why did you do it?" She stepped closer.

"Do what? Come here to Savannah?" He shook his head. "To bring you the letters and tell the story of the Irish influence on Savannah."

She shook her head. "Not that."

"Then what? Fall in love with you?" His laugh filled with pain. "It was inevitable."

"No." She stopped on the opposite side of the plot fence. "Why did you call Evan about me?"

"I…" He rubbed the back of his neck. "Because I wanted to help you with your career. I wanted to make you…happy."

"Happy?"

He closed the distance between them. Only the fence separated them. "Because it's your dream."

Her dream. Was that what she really wanted? She didn't know anymore. Before Liam, everything had been so clear. Now…

"What's your dream, Liam?" She had to ask.

His eyes closed. "My dreams don't matter."

Oh, but they did. "What makes you happy?" she asked, taking his hand.

"I can't do this again." His fingers squeezed her hand so hard, she winced.

"Please, answer my question."

His blue gaze caught hers and held. "You. You make me happy. I…I thought it was this place—" he waved his hand toward the historic district "—or your family. But it wasn't. It was you. It was always you. And I didn't understand until I'd ruined everything."

Her heart fluttered like a camera on auto shutter, clicking away.

She set her free hand on his chest.

He shivered under her fingers.

She pressed harder, so amazed she could touch him again. Touch him and not be afraid that his affections were just an act. "What if I told you I'm not happy?"

"*A ghrá.*" He brushed a curl off her face. "What can I do to make you happy? Is it that you can't stand me being near? I'm leaving tomorrow."

"*A ghrá*, what does that mean?" she asked.

"My heart." The words were like feathers on her face, stroking and calming her heartbeat.

He still loved her. She hoped.

"And if I said losing you makes me unhappy—" she reached up and cupped his face "—what would you do then?"

So much light filled his eyes they sparkled like sapphires. He stepped over the short fence, wrapping his arms around her waist. "I would have to stay."

The pieces of her life fell into place with a click as loud as her camera. "I love you."

His arms tightened so hard, she worried he would break a rib. But she didn't want him to let go. The world spun as he swung her around.

Their laughter exploded.

When her feet touched the ground, his mouth was there, joining with hers. Tongues chased each other. She wanted to be closer.

"Why?" he breathed. His lips brushed the shell of her ear and sent tingles through her.

"Because I was wrong." She arched her neck, inviting him to explore.

"Wrong?" He took her invitation, his lips trailing from her ear to her collarbone.

Her legs wobbled. "I should never have pushed you away."

Liam carried her to a bench. He cradled her in his arms, and her world righted.

There hadn't been a bench here when they'd cleaned up the plot. "Where did this come from?"

"I bought it." He buried his head in her hair. "I thought…it's nice to sit and think."

She cupped his head between her hands and tipped his face up. "That's why I love you. You're so thoughtful."

"If I'm so thoughtful, why did I treat you so thoughtlessly?"

"Because we both had to grow up to deserve each other."

"You? You're perfect."

She stroked her thumb across his lip, laughing. "Far from it. If I were perfect, I would have realized a long time ago that I am as important to my family's B and B as both Abby and Bess. I don't need to travel to have my talent recognized. And I don't want to. I belong here with my sisters."

"You can't give up your photography!" His face screwed up in anxiety, on her behalf.

She loved that. Joy shimmered inside her. She loved him.

"I'm not giving up my photography, but I can compromise. I don't have to be gone all the time. Plus—" she smoothed the wrinkles in his forehead "—Savannah is the most beautiful city in the country. Then there's the low country and the islands. And I can freelance for Evan and see the world. I just have to prove to him I'm worth the risk."

"You're worth the risk." He hugged her, hard. "What about your B and B?"

"I want it all. You. My photography. Working with my family. Maybe even some website work. But I'm not taking Barb's offer. No way. I'm a photographer."

She kissed him, drawing his tongue into her mouth.

His hands tugged her closer, binding them together like a vine and a tree. She was his tree. Could he, the wanderer, adapt to life in Savannah? She broke the kiss. "What do you need to make you happy?"

His arms tightened one more wonderful notch. "This. You."

"And if I make Savannah my home base?"

"My home is wherever you are. But I would love you to come to Ireland with me to see Michael's grave." His eyes twinkled. "Just a visit, mind you."

Her heart burst open like a time-lapse film of a flower blossoming. This was what she wanted. This was where she wanted to be.

Because she'd thought all she'd needed to be happy was to escape her sisters' shadows. But now she knew, all she needed was Liam's love to be happy.

"I love you," she whispered.

He brushed a kiss on her nose. "I love you more."

They walked hand in hand back through the avenues of moss-laden oaks. She let her head rest on his shoulder. "I've never felt so much...peace."

"Nor I." He brushed a kiss on her knuckles. "You're my family now. Will you come to Ireland with me?"

"How much time do I have to get my passport?" she asked.

"My love, I'll wait for you forever."

EPILOGUE

Which of my photographs is my favorite? The one I'm going to take tomorrow.

Imogene Cunningham

October

DOLLEY EDITED HER picture of an old man asleep in a hammock in Costa Rica, changing from color to black and white. She wanted to emphasize the deep creases in his face, the road map of his life.

Liam peered over her shoulder. "The black and white highlights his wrinkles."

"But the colors in the hammock give the photo life." She toggled back and forth.

"Both are wonderful."

She grinned and spun her chair to face him. "Are you done with your edits?"

"Almost. I got distracted by what came in the post."

"I hope it's a check." She ran her finger up and down Liam's cheek. "I like checks."

"Not a check." He nuzzled her neck.

She and Liam had bought one of Gray's River Street warehouse condos. She was close to the B and B and Liam loved watching the boat traffic. They'd even built a darkroom in the Carleton House basement.

She was on assignment a week or two each month for Evan. And Liam worked part-time in New York, editing the documentary, and the rest of the time in Savannah on a new exhibit.

He pulled her out of the chair.

She wrapped her arms around his neck and kissed him, letting the joy of her love fill the room. By the time the kiss ended, they were gasping. Reluctantly, she pulled out of his embrace. "I need to stop or I won't finish my work."

He pushed a box closer to her desk. "You might want to open that."

His nonchalance was suspicious. "What is it?"

He handed her scissors. "Only one way to find out."

She cut through the tape and pulled away the packaging. *Planting Roots in Savannah: The Fitzgeralds' Influence on Irish Immigration.*

"It's your book!" She bounced up and threw her arms around his neck. "It's here!"

"I thought you were observant. Look a little closer at the title."

She read the title and then the rest of the cover. *By Liam Delaney and Dolley Fitzgerald*

"But I sold the rights to those pictures to your publisher. I signed a contract."

"It wasn't right. I will never take credit for your pictures again."

She hugged the book to her chest. "Maybe I should have negotiated for a higher royalty percentage."

"That's the woman I love."

"Oh." It didn't matter how many times he told her he loved her, it always made her sigh. "I love you, too."

He grinned.

She no longer counted his smiles. He smiled all the time. So did she.

He pulled her into a hug. "I think we should do more collaborations."

"I like that idea."

They walked into the great room and stared down at River Street.

He tapped on his jeans. "I'm thinking of a more permanent collaboration this time."

"I may have to get an agent to negotiate with you. I have a hard time saying *no*."

"That's a grand opening for this negotiation." He pointed a finger at her. "Stick with that answer."

She frowned. "What answer?"

He pulled a jewelry box out of his pocket and flipped it open.

"Oh. Oh, my." An emerald surrounded by diamonds stared up at her. "Oh, oh, my."

Liam shifted. "I was looking for the answer *yes*."

Did he think she wouldn't agree to a marriage proposal? "I…I haven't heard a question."

Liam took her hands. "Will you marry me? Be my family and, most important, my friend?"

"Yes." She twirled, surprised when rainbows and glitter didn't fly off her. "Absolutely!"

He caught her in his arms, his grin splitting his face. "Thank you."

He kissed her. Took her on a whirlwind tour of paradise, right there on Savannah's River Street.

She didn't need travel or fame. With Liam by her side, she had the world.

* * * * *

Read more in the FITZGERALD HOUSE
*miniseries to find out how Abby and Gray
found their happily-ever-after,
in* SOUTHERN COMFORTS—
Harlequin Superromance, December 2014.

*Bess and Daniel's story is
A* SAVANNAH CHRISTMAS WISH—
Harlequin Superromance, December 2015.

*And keep an eye out for the next
Fitzgerald House book, coming in 2017!*